# THOUGHTS OF AN EATEN SUN

# THOUGHTS OF AN EATEN SUN

KYLE TOLLE

Edited by
MEREDITH TENNANT

BURNISHED LETTERS PRESS LTD.

This book is a work of fiction. Names, characters, places, and incidents either are the product of the author's imagination or are used fictitiously. Any resemblance to actual persons, living or dead, or locales is entirely coincidental.

Copyright © 2018 by Kyle Tolle

Published by Burnished Letters Press Ltd.

Edited by Meredith Tennant

Cover design by Caleb Jacob

Created with Vellum

All rights reserved. Thank you for supporting the author's rights and complying with copyright laws by not reproducing, scanning, or distributing any part of this book in any form without permission.

ISBN: 978-1-7325249-0-3 (paperback)

ISBN: 978-1-7325249-1-0 (epub)

ISBN: 978-1-7325249-2-7 (mobi)

Library of Congress Control Number: 2018908019

Printed in the United States of America.

First Edition

*For Karla,*
*without your encouragement and support,*
*this book would never have come to be.*

# CHAPTER ONE

FROM THE SHORELINE, Hantle raised a hand to the crew aboard the three-masted ship departing Founsel's small port. The captain returned the gesture as the vessel—laden with its cargo of logs—unfurled its sails and moved into the deeper waters of Trasach Cove. Hantle lowered his arm to wipe away the sweat on his forehead. As the sunset faded in color, the heat of the day began to abate.

His coworker and friend, Rounfil, shut a barn door close by. "I'll lock up the crane tower, Hantle. You can head on home."

"Thank you, sir. I'll see you in the morning." He walked around a pile of freshly hewn logs and made for the village. Shipping days were exhausting: he coordinated the ship's arrival, loading, and departure, while still being expected to fell trees for a majority of the day. When he factored in the temperature, the sweltering humidity had taken as much energy from him as had loading the ship. He exhaled—glad the day was done—and passed by a simple bronze post capped with an oil lamp; a finger brushed over the metal along a burnished line that recorded his habit.

When he approached a group of children playing in a meadow that bordered the street, he called out, "Hultier, Dolcium, come on.

Dinner time." Beyond the meadow, the forest rustled and groaned. His sons sprinted to him and each tossed a handful of grass when within range. He feigned surprise and recoiled. "Ahh, please don't hurt me."

The boys laughed and ran past, shouting, "We'll beat you home, Dad." How were they full of energy after playing the entire day? He had no inclination to give chase. Instead, he gave a resigned wave and trudged after them.

He stepped through the house's front door and the smell of potatoes wafted to him from the small table. The boys clambered into their chairs, but his wife called over her shoulder to them. "Hey now, you have not washed up. Don't sit down until you do."

They slithered down from their seats and to the corner where a washbasin stood. Lorenca emptied a kettleful of warm water into the bowl and the boys worked at the dirt on their hands. Hantle removed his boots and, when the basin was free, contributed his own muck. It was a relief to be rid of the salt from his face and neck. He ran a damp hand through his loosely curled brown hair and looked to his wife. Beside the boiled potatoes, she placed an iron pan, the fish within it still sizzling. Hantle joined the table and served portions to each plate.

He took a bite and savored the fish's seasoning before addressing the boys. "Did you see the ship today?"

Hultier, the oldest, rolled his eyes and stabbed at his potatoes. "Of course, Dad."

"Where do you think it was headed?"

"Back to the Fist?"

"That's right. Long way from here. Did you see the captain?"

His youngest, Dolcium, asked, "What did he look like?"

"She, you mean. She wore a white hat trimmed with yellow thread. She was the one giving orders onboard."

"Hmm," Hultier said. He chewed loudly for a moment, then nodded. "Yes, I think I did see her."

Hantle took a pinch from the salt dish and sprinkled his potatoes. He said, "I spoke to her while we worked to load the ship. Know what she asked me?"

"What?" Both boys spoke in unison.

"If I could load up some sunshine for their trip back. She said the weather here on the Far Finger was much nicer than that on the Fist. They've had heavy rain for a week or two now."

Dolcium's eyes widened as he looked up from the handful of fish he was about to bite. "You couldn't really do that, could you? Put sunshine on the ship?"

"No, sir, unfortunately not." Hantle exaggerated his disappointed look for the boy. "But that would be nice, wouldn't it?" Dolcium turned his attention to the fish.

Lorenca reached out and gently lowered Dolcium's hand to his plate. She pointed at his fork and smiled at him before reaching for the salt. "Maybe," she said, "they will get a break from the rain soon." She placed a pinch of salt on the boys' plates and then her own. "I'm glad we've had heat instead of that kind of rain."

Hultier's face squinched up with thought. "I like a rainy day, sometimes. Frogs are much easier to find."

"That's true," Lorenca said. "You're very good at catching frogs."

A smile filled his face. "Rounfil said he has caught *a lot* of frogs. He told us the best time to catch them is at night."

The mention of amphibians piqued Dolcium's attention. "I like catching frogs too. Can we go find some tonight?"

Hantle picked up his glass of water. "Not tonight, I'm afraid. You've got to get ready for bed soon."

"Catching frogs at night," Lorenca said, "is dangerous work. It's only for when you're older."

"Okay," the littlest conceded. "When I'm older, I'm going to catch three frogs and teach them to hop *fast*."

Once the boys had cleaned the dishes and been put to bed, Hantle moved to the living space adjoining the kitchen and sat in his upholstered chair. He reached for a box under the chair and pulled out his knife and a block of wood. Shavings hit the floor as he began whittling a small figure from a tree branch.

## CHAPTER TWO

HANTLE SAT ON THE GROUND, right at the base of a tree. He settled into a spot where the roots wrapped around him and supported his back nicely. A breeze carried through the area. It wicked away his sweat and he sighed at the relief. Could the humidity get any worse than this? That was a terrible thought. He unfurled the cloth bundle that held his lunch and spread it over his lap. Rounfil reclined in a nook to his side and tore off a piece of bread. Hantle picked up his favorite item of the meal and began peeling the hardboiled egg. Pieces of shell skittered across the pine needles as he flicked them off. After a moment, he broke the silence. "The boys last night mentioned how great you are at catching frogs."

Rounfil chuckled and replied through his mouthful. "Probably haven't caught a frog in a decade or more, but they don't need to know that." He winked and popped another morsel in.

"What exactly did you tell them? Do you even remember?" Hantle bit into the egg and a piece of yolk crumbled into his lap.

Rounfil shrugged. "Might've been something about catching a basketful of them during the last drought, owing to my keen eye and superior bait."

"Ha. Now you're spinning larger tales than a fisherman. Thanks to you, Dolcium has plans of teaching frogs to race."

"Boys got to have something to keep them out of trouble. I'm *helping* you, you see."

"Not sure I'll be so grateful, sir, when I'm the one cleaning frog slime off his squirmy hands before dinner."

"Fair point." Rounfil nodded his head. "Glad I'm not you, then." He leaned over to pull something from his waist and made a point of carefully checking whether anyone was near. His voice dropped low and he gave a mischievous smile. "Care for a sip?" In his hands was a small leather flask. He popped off the cork and took a pull before passing it over.

"Eh." Hantle pulled away.

"We're not getting drunk, Hantle. That's best done proper, at night. Just a small afternoon treat." The flask waggled between his fingers.

Hantle's eyebrows rose and his face softened. "All right. Give it here." A smoky burn flowed into his mouth, and he grimaced until the draught cleared his throat.

"Good, eh?" Rounfil plucked the flask from his hand, downed another gulp, and replaced the cork.

"Not bad. Not bad."

---

The wagon stopped and the horses stamped in place. Rounfil dropped the reins as he looked to the pile of equipment under a nearby shelter. "Ropes and blades, right?" Waves lapped at the cove's shoreline a few yards away.

"Right." Hantle stepped down from the seat. "Do you mind," he said, "if I go check on Wellif before we load up?"

"Not at all. I'll pass, though, and wait here."

"Still holding the grudge?" Hantle had been at the table during the poker game when Rounfil came to blows with Wellif.

"Bastard's a cheat, Hantle."

"Man losing a leg's a matter altogether different."

"A gimp can still cheat you."

"Uh-huh." Hantle waved off the insult. "I'll be back."

Wellif's house was on the south end of the village and Hantle arrived in a few minutes. He peeked in the window and saw Wellif lying on the bed, facing away from the front door, so he knocked. Wellif shouted, "Come in."

Hantle entered and extended a hand. "How's it, sir?" The young woodcutter had accidentally swung an axe into his shin the day following his birthday, the one on which he had become a man.

Wellif took the hand and shrugged. "Pain's down, for now."

"Your color is a lot better. The infection come back?"

"Doc thinks he got it with the amputation." The surgery took the lower leg to just below the knee. Bandages, still looking clean, wrapped the wound.

"That's a relief. You've had a bad turn, but we're all hoping you're on the mend now."

"Staying still's the worst part." The house was tiny. His bed occupied most of the space, and the remainder contained a table, short stool, and a battered trunk for clothes.

"I can imagine. He say how much longer you're laid up?"

"Till he says otherwise, I guess."

"Yeah, that's rough. Anything I can do for you?"

"Mind opening the door so I can watch the birds or something?"

Hantle obliged him and propped the back door open with the stool. He was sure having the woods for a view would only be nice for so long. "You eating okay?"

"Yeah, Liova's been bringing by meals. She's been great."

"Good to see you're doing okay, Wellif. I've got to get back, but I'll stop by again soon."

"That'll be good. See ya, Hantle." The young man settled back into his pillow and stared out the open door.

Hantle stepped into the street just as the children, finished with their lessons for the day, came out of the teacher's house. Hultier saw him, grabbed Dolcium, and they both ran his way.

"How was school, boys?"

"Dad!" Hultier completely ignored the question. "We were digging holes over by the creek. You know why?"

"No, what are the holes for?"

"For crawdads," Dolcium said, a wide grin on his face.

Hultier shouted, "Hey," and smacked his brother on the back. "I wanted to tell him."

"Ow," Dolcium growled and moved a step out of reach.

"We plan," Hultier continued, "to catch crawdads in the holes."

Hantle tried to keep a laugh off his face. "In a hole? How do you figure that?"

"The ones that are tired and weak are going to find the holes and think they look like a real nice place to rest. That's when we'll get them."

"Sounds like an interesting plan. What will you catch them with?"

From his back pocket, Dolcium pulled a contraption that lay flat until he expanded it. "We're making cages."

"His won't be as good as mine," Hultier said smugly.

"It will too," Dolcium shouted. Hantle knew this was a capital offense in Dolcium's eyes: he hated being reminded he was younger than Hultier. The boy lunged at his brother, fists swinging. "Stop saying that. Stop saying that!"

Hultier initially ducked out of the way, but Dolcium grabbed hold of his shirt and pulled him in. The two tussled and punched, swerving one way only to overcorrect and list the other. Hultier's height gave him an advantage, but Dolcium was scrappy. Hantle waited to intervene. He preferred they settle the argument themselves, even if there was a bit of blood and bruising. Dolcium spun around and used his momentum to drag Hultier with him before flinging him away. The older brother rammed into a wooden fence, broke a few of the slats, and fell through it, where his landing squashed several flowers. Dolcium huffed and clenched his hands. Hultier extricated himself from the fence fragments, grumbling, "You're dead. You're dead."

Property damage was where Hantle drew the line and he placed a hand on Dolcium. "No, you're done, boys." He looked to the porch and saw Liova, the village elder, sitting there with her arms crossed. "You've gone and broken Liova's fence."

"I didn't break it," Hultier objected. He stood and wiped dirt from his hands. "*He* threw me into it." He jabbed a finger at Dolcium.

"Well," Dolcium shrugged, pretending to care little, "you shouldn't be so—"

Hantle interrupted. "I said, you're done. That's it." He looked to Liova. "I'm sorry, ma'am. And so are they, even though they're too angry to say it. I know they'd be happy to help you fix the fence and plant new flowers." Both boys knew best to keep quiet.

"I should say," she replied. She shook her head and pushed herself out of her chair. "I won't stand for people breaking my things, especially not my flowers." Her lips pursed with unspoken annoyance and she walked to the flowerbed to inspect the damage. "Oh dear." She gave a long sigh, in which Hantle felt her disappointment. "These balsams were my favorite."

Hantle felt Dolcium shift under his palm; Hultier glared off to the side. He spoke for them. "I'm awfully sorry, Liova, but I know these boys will make it right." He patted Dolcium's shoulder. "Isn't that so?"

Both boys answered a quiet "Yes."

Hantle stepped back. "They're yours for as long as you need them." He made eye contact with both sons to make sure they understood. In no way would he tolerate shirking a duty. "And please, Liova, put any supplies from the Mercantile on my tab."

Liova plucked a petal from a fold in Hultier's shirt. "Either of you boys planted a flower before? Or do you only specialize in killing them?"

A peal of thunder rolled overhead and Hantle ducked out of the rain onto his porch. The storm halted their work that afternoon and he had come straight home. He ran a hand through his hair and flung the water from his fingertips. Inside, Lorenca sat at the table with the boys, playing a card game. Hantle removed his mud-caked boots and left them by the door. "Did Liova send you home?"

"Yes," Hultier answered. "She said it was dangerous to be outside in the lightning."

Hantle joined them at the table. "She's right. No one wants to get struck. I wanted to be sure you only left after she gave you permission." He turned his attention to Dolcium. "Did you tell your mother what you did?"

Dolcium laid a few cards down on the table and took one from the deck. "Yup. Said we got in a fight and broke Liova's things."

"And I told them," Lorenca said, rubbing Dolcium's hair, "that's what a respectful person does: makes up for their mistakes."

Hultier drew a card off the deck. "We aren't even done." He frowned and put his chin in his palm. "We have to go back tomorrow."

Thunder rattled the entire house. Hantle glanced out the window. "The storm cut my work short today too. We'll have to make do."

Lorenca took her turn. "Remember how just last night I was saying I preferred the heat to the rain? Doesn't it just figure that it'd rain today? Wonder how long this storm will stay."

Hantle leaned back in his chair and crossed his arms. "I doubt it'll keep up this ferocity for long."

Dolcium inhaled excitedly and set his cards down. "If it stops lightning, can we go look for frogs?" He bounced in his seat.

"I happen to remember your mother saying, also just last night, that was something only for when you're older."

Dolcium's face turned into a pitiful plea and Hultier chimed in with him. "This is the perfect weather though." "Rounfil said so." "It's not even got dark yet." "Please, can we, please?" "We're both very grown up now."

He found it difficult to keep from giving in but knew Lorenca would have none of it. "What about," he proposed, "if we go in the early morning? That will still be good conditions."

"Ugh." Dolcium lolled his head and his arms went limp. "No."

Hultier slapped a leg with frustration. "Frogs are nocturnal, Dad. Do you even know what that means?"

"Excuse me"—Lorenca wagged a finger—"that is not how you speak to your father."

The boy was smart but so often did his knowledge warp into condescension. It's hard being six, Hantle reminded himself. "If we go before dawn, that will still be nighttime."

Hultier only responded with "Hmpfh." Compromises were not his strong suit.

Dolcium sat up straight, looking as big and as tall as he could, and picked up in his brother's stead. "We wanted to go just the two of us, to prove we can do it."

"Unfortunately for you, you'll either go with your father or not at all. You can think about it until after dinner."

Hantle embraced the change of topic. "Speaking of, did you have anything in mind? If not, I'll make a stew."

"No, but that sounds good to me. We have plenty of vegetables."

Hantle moved to the kitchen. While Lorenca and the boys finished their game, he put together the stew and set it over the fire. Through the rest of the afternoon, rain thrummed on the roof and thunder occasionally roared. Inside, the boys' moods soured and they became increasingly surly. It was not often they were cooped up inside for so many hours. Repeated episodes of roughhousing and back talk resulted in them being sent to their room without dinner. Hantle and Lorenca, however, not having had dinner to themselves in some number of years, enjoyed the peaceful meal. Once the lightning had ceased, they moved to the porch, chatting and joking, with the rainfall a pleasant backdrop. Some time after nightfall, the couple retired to the intimacy of the bedroom.

# CHAPTER THREE

HANTLE'S MIND whiplashed to wakefulness and his eyes crept open but he did not register the sound that had woken him. Lorenca shouted again from the hallway. "Hantle?"

"Hmm?" he muttered through a dry throat. The sheets fell to his lap as he pushed himself to a seated position.

Lorenca stopped at the bedroom door, gripping the frame with such pressure that her fingers turned white. "Hantle, where are the boys?" The tension in her voice surprised him, but his brain was too slow to process anything more.

He cleared his throat and said, "Sleeping?" What was she getting at?

"No, they *aren't*." Her eyebrows bunched with annoyance. "Their bedroom window is open, though. I think they snuck out last night."

Hantle shook his head. "Why would they?" He tossed the covers back, stood, and moved to the chamber pot in the corner. The minute of quiet allowed his mind to stir and recall their discussion at dinner last night. He shook off at the pot, chuckled, and said, "Looking for frogs, I bet, after they scrambled down the trellis." He looked to Lorenca.

"It's not funny, Hantle." Her frown deepened. "They haven't come back and I'm worried mad."

He beckoned her with his arms. Lorenca plodded over, speechless, and walked straight into his chest. He wrapped his arms around her. She fretted easily, as mothers will, but he had a way of calming her. "Remember, Lorenca, the boys are older now." One of his hands made its way through her long, rust-colored hair. "They're likely playing with whatever little creatures they caught, congratulating one another for how grown up they've become."

Her arms hung at her side, trembling now with anger. "They won't think it smart once they're grounded."

"Boys have no foresight. I can't tell you how many times I did something like this in my childhood." He tightened his hug and ended the embrace with a kiss on her forehead. "I'll go. Try not to worry." His gaze lingered as he took a step toward the door. Her green eyes were most gorgeous in the morning. When he could delay no more, his eyebrows raised in a look that said, "Here we go," and he was out of the room. He tramped down the stairs, put on his boots (leather creaking as he pulled the laces tight), and left the house. The morning sun just above the eastern trees gave their home a shadow that stretched to the street. Turning south, he shielded his eyes against the daylight. Hantle continued on to Rounfil's house and landed three heavy knocks on the door.

It creaked open to reveal the man wearing a ragged robe. "What is it, Hantle?"

"Our boys snuck out in the night. Probably to catch frogs. Will you help look for them?"

"Yeah, yeah. Lemme get my boots." Rounfil laced up on the porch in the cool air. His robe matched the dirty yellow of his hair. With boots on, he stood up. "Ready."

Hantle led Rounfil to the meadow. "Figure we can start here," he said. "They play here every day. Plus the lamppost would have given them some light to see by." Rounfil nodded. Their work routine also led them past this meadow on a daily basis. The area looked no different from any other day but for the puddles scattered about, formed during last night's storm. "Shall we comb the area? I know your eyes are likely to catch something."

Rounfil swayed as he stood. "Too much beer last night, and this sun ain't helping." Hantle knew well his queasy look. "But we'll get to looking."

Dew fell from the grass as they made a pass through the field. Except for wildflowers standing brightly in the sun, the meadow contained nothing. "River would be my next guess," Rounfil suggested. The two then ventured into the woods, spreading out to cover more ground. Branches cracked under their boots and birdcalls came from far off.

Near the stream that flowed through the trees down to the cove, Rounfil found a boot. His shout drew over Hantle, who picked it up, softly. The knot had come undone and the laces loosed. A footprint in the mud next to it was the only other sign. Hantle recognized the boot as belonging to Dolcium and felt both relief and anxiety. Here was a trace of them, but it felt wrong. Boys their age should have left prints all over the place. He followed the watercourse to the cove, head jerking from side to side, looking for additional tracks, but he found none aside from a few belonging to raccoon and deer. The men spread their search farther afield.

---

Several miles and hours later, the pair crossed the meadow once more as they returned to the village. Here they split up, to weave through the houses and check the yards.

Hantle had just stepped over a low hedge when a call cut through the air, followed by a loud whistle. He jogged toward the sound and caught sight of Rounfil waving his hand from a house nearby. Hantle's own home stood beside it. He broke into a run. When he neared, he saw that Rounfil stood several paces away from a coop. The front mesh was ripped out and chicken carcasses lay scattered within it and around the lawn. A lone escaped chicken was near the house, pecking along the fence.

Blood lay thick on the grass, and the warm air suddenly stifled Hantle's breath. Stained feathers drifted in a breeze while others stuck in the ripped wire mesh. A drop of liquid, dark in color, caught Hantle's eye as it fell through the air. Maroon and thick, it joined a puddle on the ground. Was a chicken carcass dripping blood? His gaze drew upward. There they were, finally, hiding atop the roof. Except . . . Hantle's jaw set and he stared, disbelieving. On one side of the roof ridge lay his sons' faces, recognizable though ashen. Down the other side trailed their spines, long and grotesque. He followed rivulets of gore down from the shingles and noticed intestines spilled on the ground. His body tightened and his ears filled with the sound of his pulse. This was not real, he told himself. Not fucking real. Another drop glistened with sunlight before he screamed.

# CHAPTER FOUR

HANTLE'S CHEST heaved with thick sobs. He clambered up the broken boards of the coop and froze, crouching on the small roof. Tears welled in his grey eyes as his hands trembled, just inches away from Hultier's face. Rounfil backed up into the fence and turned to vomit over it. Another cry escaped Hantle, and this second wail drew neighbors to their porches.

Lorenca stepped outside, anxiously wringing a dishcloth. She looked at her neighbors and around for the source of the sound. As she turned, she saw Rounfil's figure next door. When she noticed her husband on the chicken coop, a puzzled look crossed her face. Then a possibility hit her.

The dishcloth dropped to the porch floorboards as she ran the short distance between houses. Without stopping, she swept her legs and dress over the fence, leaving fibers behind as she sprinted to the broken coop. One of her husband's feet had slipped off the roof and hung in mid-air but his grip held him in place. Hantle took up the entirety of the roof, so Lorenca was only able to climb part way up. She came to a rest with her hand gripping Hantle's belt, along his back.

"What, Hantle? What?" She peeked around her husband and saw Hultier and Dolcium, both with eyes closed. Their faces lay at an odd angle. Realization of their doom struck and she staggered back, but Hantle's arm reached out and steadied her. She went limp for a moment before a burst of energy brought her up to the roof. Forcing her husband to the side, she gathered up her boys—their heads lolling and spines viscid—and clutched them to her chest.

Both mother and father rocked with shock and grief until Rounfil had the sense to pull them down. He took the remains from Lorenca and laid them on the grass. She collapsed to the ground a few yards away. Hantle, though, stepped forward, gripped Rounfil's shoulders, and shouted, "Who did this to them? Who murdered my boys?" The horror on his face morphed into a plea. "You've got to find something, please. A clue as to who killed my children. Something."

Rounfil nodded and extricated himself from Hantle's grasp. He turned his eyes to the wreckage. Hantle huddled next to Lorenca and watched Rounfil scour the scene, speaking as he moved around. "I don't see any boot marks. I can't imagine someone not leaving a single one in the damp earth last—Here's something." He crouched down. "A print. Dog maybe? Too large, I think." He moved toward the coop. "Hmm." From a splintered end of a board, he pulled a tuft of damp fur and sniffed it. He turned over portions of the structure that had broken off. "And claw marks here." Scratches crisscrossed a section of the wall. "Ah." He straightened a section of crumpled wire. "We've a tooth." It was caught in a tight pinch of the mesh. "Definitely a canine, and freshly extracted." Standing, he searched the yard, meandering a bit until he spotted something of note near the fence, where he stooped again. "More prints. Yes, I believe these are wolf, not dog or coyote."

Hantle recoiled. "How did a wolf do *this*?" he shouted.

Rounfil didn't answer. When he had climbed over the fence, he followed the blood trail and prints into the woods. Upon his return several minutes later, he inspected the wounds around the boys' necks and, gravely certain, looked to Hantle. "Many signs point to this having been carried out by a wolf: prints, marks, fur, and tooth. More than I believe could be due to coincidence."

Hantle hung his head, dumbstruck, and leaned against Lorenca. His body suddenly felt weak and useless. The idea the boys had not been murdered by a villager—someone close to them who had exploited their trust—was small compensation. It was still gruesome, brutal, unbelievable. How, how, how could this have happened? His mind withdrew to spin on these thoughts, while Lorenca curled beside him, shuddering and keening.

Rounfil led the parents away, toward their home, and picked up the dishcloth on the porch. Once inside, he sat them both on the couch. Hantle's head rested in his hands and Lorenca stared blankly at the wooden panels of their floor, unaware of the tears and blood staining her top. Hantle's closest friend swallowed the knot in his throat and spoke. "I'll call Yilrouth to prepare the . . . boys. In a few hours, we'll gather the village for a service." Hantle and Lorenca broke down, each clutching the other. Rounfil set the dishcloth on the table, looked at them, decided no further words would suffice, and walked out.

---

Hantle watched through blurry eyes as his friend left the house. He squeezed Lorenca's hand in his before moving to the window. Rounfil walked to the doctor's house, where Yilrouth motioned for his family to head inside. The two men had a brief conversation before Yilrouth nodded, collected his bag of instruments, and followed Rounfil to the coop. Hantle saw little eyes peeking around curtained windows. It was fortunate they did not understand what they saw.

As the two passed his house, Hantle stepped onto the porch and addressed them. "I want to help, please." With the back of his wrist, he wiped his nose. "We need to be careful with them."

Yilrouth lifted a gentle hand to halt Hantle. "I think it best you stay with Lorenca. I promise I will be as delicate with them as possible."

Hantle furrowed his brow as he considered it, eventually nodding his consent. He did not agree, exactly, because he wanted to be there for his boys, but he was not sure he could see them again in that state without collapsing. Rounfil and Yilrouth moved past as Hantle pinched his eyes shut, swallowed his pain, and turned to rejoin Lorenca.

On the couch, Hantle's gaze oscillated between his wife and the window. He both consoled Lorenca—the act of which kept his own emotions at bay—and watched through the glass pane for the doctor to reappear on his way home. How much time elapsed before it happened, Hantle could not be certain, but Yilrouth and Rounfil did go by, carrying white cloth bundles, which he knew contained his boys from the deferential way the men handled them. Afterward, he witnessed villagers volunteer assistance with various tasks. A group with spades thrown over shoulders walked to the cemetery on the edge of the village to dig graves. Some, instead, prepared the central square for the funeral. Sounds of sawing spread on the air and cut to Hantle's core. He knew that would be the carpenter, Pirram, making coffins. Rounfil and others still moved through the area, but Hantle could not tell what chores they undertook. A wail wracked Lorenca and Hantle rushed to her side. Tears overwhelmed him once again.

Through her weeping and the hair that fell over her face, she said, "I should have heard them leaving last night."

Hantle shook his head in a wide arc. "No," he managed. "Don't you say that. No, you couldn't have known." He lifted his hand and pushed the stray hair behind her ear. "I'm the one who should have gone out with them, to watch over them." A vision gripped him and his stomach clenched him into silence. From a vantage point twenty feet above the grass, Hantle saw himself standing in the meadow. His aerial view allowed him to glimpse Hultier, just inside the forest's edge, stretch out a quaking hand toward him. The boy disappeared into the underbrush as the wolf dragged him off by the throat, which prevented him crying out. The vision of the night dissolved into daylight, and Hantle leaned over to embrace Lorenca.

―――

The afternoon drew on, and, as people completed their chores, they idled along the street and spoke in muted voices. Hantle—unable to sit still anymore—wandered out of the house and approached one of the groups. The individuals were immersed in a discussion and Hantle surprised them, but they opened the circle and he slotted in, quietly accepting the condolences offered to him.

A woman, Shec, brought him into their conversation. "We were just saying that none of us remember sighting a wolf this year. It's as if it came from nowhere."

Hantle read the fear on each face. He shook his head. "I've not seen one either. Rounfil saw its trail, though. We ought to follow it and see where it leads."

Crahul folded his arms and toed a cobblestone. "There'll be a time for that, Hantle, but I'm thinking it's not now."

The sound of hammer strokes rose out of Pirram's shop and reverberated along the street. Hantle cleared his throat. "I can't see a better way to help Lorenca than to make the beast pay for who it stole from her . . . from us."

Another woman, Eayol, added, "Aye, he has a point. We have a village to think of."

Hantle's face tensed. He had not heard what she said, but instead thought of his boys. "I owe them that much."

Shec clasped his shoulder. "*We* owe it to you and to Lorenca. After the mourning meal, we'll gather a party to follow the canine's trail."

A rumbling attracted Hantle's attention and he turned to see Pirram driving his wagon. It drew close and continued off, heading toward Yilrouth's. Hantle stared—his eyes glued to the uncovered bed and the two coffins lying there.

Rounfil walked past the wagon and approached Hantle and his small circle of people. He addressed the group. "We'll begin soon." Hantle noticed he already wore his black. Rounfil said, "Shall we get you changed?" Hantle yielded to Rounfil's guidance and was led home as those standing in the street dispersed.

---

Clad in the color of their grief, Hantle and Lorenca held hands and walked to the village square. Rounfil trailed several steps behind. The villagers sat upon an eclectic mix of chairs borrowed from various households. Rounfil directed the couple to the front of the seating area, where they sat in plush armchairs that belonged to Crahul, proprietor of Trasach Mercantile.

Hantle sat in silence, waiting for the proceedings to begin. Initially, he felt far removed from his physical body, but the sound of footsteps coming down the aisle grounded him. He noticed, for the first time, the arrangements. The coffins sat side-by-side atop bales of hay. Flowers and ribbons of several colors lay around and across them, yet no amount of decoration could lessen their dreadfulness. Both were full-sized, even though the remains would only fill a small portion. That normality helped Hantle focus on memories of his boys as he knew them: laughing and energetic.

The footsteps belonged to Liova, accompanied by her son and grandson, each of whom held an arm. Liova's progeny took their seats and she crossed the final distance alone. She spread additional flowers over the coffins before sitting on a bale in between. With a sigh, she closed her eyes and folded her hands. For a moment, only the buzzing of insects broke the silence. When she rose, she motioned for the assembly to do likewise. She took up two golden lilies. "I have the unfortunate duty to announce the passing of the Doolsun's boys,

Dolcium and Hultier. They were taken last night by a wolf. This morning, their father, Hantle, found them. That is something no parent should ever have to endure." Her voice wavered and she paused to collect herself before going on. "I wish to express condolences, from all of us, to Hantle and Lorenca during this tragic time. We are united, in triumph and in despair.

"In times such as these, we must remember the Mechanisms, which tell us how the world of Iomesel—this beautiful and wondrous home we inhabit—was created through the Cataclysm. The undoing of things past is not the end of all things. We find solace in that truth. All of Founsel will show Mister and Missus Doolsun support. We will recognize the grief they hold and do all we can to show them inclusion and understanding and love in our small community." She blinked away tears and turned to set a lily first on Dolcium's coffin then on Hultier's. Liova walked to the parents, took Hantle and Lorenca by the arms, and led them forward.

Hantle's composure deteriorated with each step toward the coffins. As long as he had remained seated in his chair, he was convinced the surreality of the day would eventually give way, whereupon he would jerk out of the nightmare. The act of standing led his mind to question that expectation. He was able to recall comforting Lorenca in their home, finding the boys just hours ago, sending the boys to their rooms, and, still earlier, the storm that sent him home early. Dreams were always based on a presupposition that, upon later inspection, one recognized as laughably contrived. His recollection, however, had a chain of events that clearly led from now to then and, crucially, maintained consistency with prior memories. Yes, this was undeniably real: the humidity, the villagers behind him, the names of his sons chiseled into the wood. By the time they stood beside the coffins, Hantle's breath came in ragged gasps and he held on to his wife for balance.

Lorenca's eyes were red and puffy, but no tears ran down her face now. She gripped Hantle, one arm on his side, another bracing his chest, and Hantle did not like how their roles had reversed. He closed his eyes and noticed that when she laid her head against his shoulder the contact helped soothe his quivering nerves. Once he was able to maintain his own weight, Lorenca stepped to the coffins. She twice bent and kissed the names carved therein. Hantle followed her lead, then rested his hands on both lids, feeling the loss more than the wood grain.

At Liova's instruction, a group of four came and shouldered the first casket: the one chiseled with "Dolcium." Hantle and Lorenca walked behind the bearers, while the elder and her boys followed them; after came the rest of the villagers. The procession continued beyond the cobblestone road and followed a footpath toward the eastern edge of Founsel. A long, forested hill sloped upward, and they walked to its top. Amid the trees, a clearing served as the cemetery. Two piles of dirt at one end indicated their destination. The freshly dug graves sat next to granite pillars that marked the resting place of Hantle's parents. Lorenca lowered a veil over her solemn features as the bearers lowered Dolcium to rest atop the grave. A pair of ropes ran across the grave opening and were staked into the ground to support the coffin. At Hantle's side, his hand sought out that of his wife. The bearers returned to the square and, momentarily, Hultier alighted beside his brother.

---

The wolf sat in a thicket a few yards outside the cemetery. From his shadowy position, he watched the cortege—the prospective meat. He licked his snout and bared his fangs. Where the tooth had been ripped out, he felt the stub of a new one poking through the gum line. The boys and hens had filled his belly, fueling his repair and growth. He idly considered attacking now, while the unsuspecting creatures were distracted. A wind stirred the trees and stabs of sunlight fell onto him, burning his face and blinding his sight. He growled reflexively. The bright orb was the sole reason he did not attack. The pain it brought spurred him to slink away instead. He would rest in deeper, darker corners of the woods until nightfall. Then, he would prowl again.

---

When Liova signaled, the four bearers, two on either side of the neighboring graves, removed the stake at their feet and took the rope in hand. They simultaneously let out lengths of it and both boys descended into the ground. Dolcium was the youngest the village had buried in years. Liova produced two mourning wreaths and gave them to Hantle and Lorenca. Each wreath would serve as a marker, along with the fresh soil, until headstones could be carved. The village elder stepped away from the two; her role was finished.

Using a palm, Hantle drove the wreath into the soil at the head of Hultier's grave. The ringing of the small bell at its center stopped him after the first strike. He let out a deep exhalation. The sound felt too cheerful to accompany a moment such as this. Though . . . maybe the boys would have liked it: the little metallic send-off. Yes, they would have liked it. He struck the wreath twice more and it supported itself. He made eye contact with his wife and dropped a handful of dirt into the pit. A sudden flare of malice licked at his mind, propelling him to pick up one of the spades nearby. He cast soil in the open grave as a growl built in his throat. Finally, he had a means to expel a portion of the energy that had accumulated in his body. His urge to *do* something instead of curl up and grieve had asserted itself. The individuals who had dug the holes stepped up to help but Hantle waved them off. This was a task he wanted to himself.

When the graves were filled, Hantle, drenched in sweat, followed the procession to the square. Cooks topped long wooden tables with a selection of meats, fruits, and early-harvest vegetables. Loaves of bread and baked dishes were brought out warm. A round table contained a selection of cordials and sweet wines. Hantle had no stomach for food, and Lorenca only ate a morsel or two; he watched the rest of the villagers, however, put away the spread. Heat bore down out of the cloudless sky and sank deep into Hantle's black. The discomfort boiled within him until the meal was concluded and he could steal away home with Lorenca while the others cleared the square.

Once inside, Lorenca said, "I feel drained—empty." She removed her veil and placed it on the kitchen table. "I'm going to lie down in their room."

She moved for the stairs, but Hantle intercepted her and brought her into an embrace. He whispered, "I love you." Her voice was thick enough to be incoherent; regardless, he knew what she had said. "I'm heading back out with some others to follow the wolf's trail. I will find this beast," he promised.

She looked up at him, the whites of her eyes run through with blood vessels. "I know you will." Her confidence filled him with hope.

In the square, Hantle joined Rounfil and waited for others to gather. Shortly, they were a group of ten, armed with long muskets, bows and arrows, and axes.

Rounfil wiped dirt and sweat from his forehead. "Hantle. As Liova said, we are all united, in triumph and despair. We'll do what we can to avenge your pain."

Hantle said, "I am fortunate to have the help." He shifted the musket on his shoulder. "Begin near the coop?"

The yard that had contained the coop sat empty. A group must have earlier dismantled it and dragged off the debris. Rounfil returned to the prints he had spotted that morning and tracked them beyond the fence. As they continued into the forest, Hantle loaded and primed his musket, chest thudding with anticipation.

A few dozen yards on, the trail curved to a small pond. "Took a drink," Rounfil said. Soon thereafter, the tracks disappeared amid brambles and rocky ground. Rounfil turned, face despondent, to Hantle. "I've lost it, I'm sorry. This ground won't hold a trail."

"Here," Hantle said. "Let me have a go." He pushed back the thorns with an arm, stepped in, and scoured the ground for any sign of the wolf's passage. Rounfil was right of course, but Hantle, reluctant to admit losing the tracks, waded into a denser stand of bushes. His motions became frantic, desperate; barbs snagged his skin and clothing. Eventually, he was forced to concede defeat. The trail was gone. He let out a savage shout and fired his musket at a nearby tree. He spun in circles, mind working to find a plan of action.

He nodded to the pond. "We can poison it," he said. "Its next drink will be its last."

"Other animals take water here," Rounfil countered. "Would you kill them all?"

"Yes, if it meant . . ." His shoulders hunched forward as he realized the consequences of this idea. "No, you're right. We'd just as likely poison a child."

Rounfil stomped off some of the muck on his boot. "Let's search elsewhere. There's a chance it wandered around a bit."

---

The hunting party returned in the early dusk, just after the sun set beyond a fiery horizon. Their search had yielded nothing fruitful, but Hantle was anyway glad to have spent the rest of the day working toward a goal. It was preferable to sitting in despair. His grief had kept a distance, though when he heard the sounds of children playing, it rushed back in and constricted his chest. How fortunate they were to be oblivious of grief or danger.

Back in the square, Rounfil put his arm across Hantle's shoulders and said, "We covered a lot of ground today. And we'll keep an eye out for the wolf."

Eayol added, "Aye, Hantle, we're beside you in this."

"Thank you all," he said. "Lie low tonight and, if it comes prowling, we can take up its tracks in the morning. G'night."

He left them and brushed a finger against the streetlamp as he passed through the pool of light leaking from its soot-darkened glass shade. His stomach grumbled and, for the first time today, he had an appetite. At their front door, he found a food dish left by one of the neighbors. Without paying much attention to what the dish contained, he scoffed a portion of it down. His thoughts replayed the coffins lowering into the ground. Lorenca was asleep in Hultier's bed when he entered the bedroom. He pulled back the sheets and curled his body to match hers. Through the window and over Lorenca's shoulder, he watched the sky's color fade until he did so himself.

## CHAPTER FIVE

WHEN THE NIGHT HAD DEEPENED, the wolf left his day hide and returned to the forests surrounding Founsel. He prowled through the trees and underbrush and, while pausing here or there for a time, watched the homes for signs of activity. Eventually the moon rose, bringing with it, to his frustration, a bright moonlight—waxing full. Not even nighttime was a refuge from the pain that light brought. Certainly the burn of it was less than at midday, but it was the sort of sensation that drew his entire focus. For some hours more, he circled the village, moving from one spot of moon-shade to the next, which helped assuage the pain but did nothing for the resentment and hatred that grew beside it. His stomach contracted with hunger, the pang of which added to his irritation. The boys devoured last night were the most satisfying meal he had yet had. The terror they exuded, as much as their meat, had satisfied in a way the hens had not. Over the course of the day, he had grown to twice his size, and he was now as large as a fully-grown male. In order to grow further, though, he would need more than a child.

Nearby, the wolf spotted movement and weaved through the forest's edge toward it: a teenage boy exited his house and walked across the backyard. The wolf did not attack quite yet. The boy held his lantern high and peered into the gloom beyond the light, liable to skitter the moment a leaf stirred. No, it was best to wait. As the wolf crept closer, he flicked his tongue and noticed his tooth had regrown entirely. That would be advantageous to the hunt. When his prey approached the outhouse, he set into motion. His tail wagged with excitement, and he hardly noticed the burn of the moonlight. In there, the boy would have no retreat: his quarry would be cornered.

His snout was in the jamb, which prevented the door from shutting. When the boy turned to see why, he snarled and pushed in. This forced the boy into the back panel of the outhouse. The lantern slipped out of his hands and crashed to the seat where its base shattered, releasing all its oil, and the wick toppled over into the fuel. A ball of flame gasped and leapt up. The wolf braced himself, keeping the boy pinned as he flailed at the flames spreading to his robe and searing his skin. His prey cried out with surprise that rose to a frantic, primal scream. Yes! He reveled in the sound—enraptured by the boy's struggle. An instant later, his instincts took over and his jaws clamped, collapsing the boy's throat and eating his cry. He backed away from the outhouse, jerking his prey toward the black woods.

―――

Sleep sloughed off Hantle so quickly it left him disoriented. A girl's wail, carrying from somewhere nearby, pierced the room, going on and on. It brought his heart to pounding. The wolf. He scrambled from the bed, leaving Lorenca there, and dashed to the living room. Here was his chance to confront the beast that had stolen his boys. Would its face still wear their blood? The wail trailed off. In the darkness, he found a boot near the door, balanced to slip it on, but instead fell to the floor. Snippets flashed by of the creature howling, clawing, tearing. What would he do if he came across it? He didn't bother to search for the boot that had tumbled off; instead, he reached for the second one. His hands quaked and fingers trembled, useless for the task. A man's shout came next. "The wolf has my boy. To me, all! Help me save my boy!" The voice sounded like Couveim, who lived opposite them and a few houses down. Hantle abandoned the boots, grabbed his musket, which hung above on the transom, and raced outside.

Hantle rounded Couveim's house and saw the outhouse completely engulfed in flames. No people though. Couveim must have gone into the woods after Trissol. When he approached, a layer of clouds obscured the moon, leaving only flickering flames to illuminate gouges in the yard where the boy had clawed against his captor. Rounfil joined his side a moment later, musket in hand and threadbare robe tied at the waist.

"You see them?" Hantle asked.

Rounfil shook his head. "Not yet."

Another call from Couveim emanated from the woods, and Hantle drove after it. Rocks and thorns jabbed into his bare feet. Commotion behind told him reinforcements were following. A branch whipped into his eye. Fuck. Hopefully one of them had a lantern. Why hadn't he grabbed one? Too eager to fight the damn thing and not thinking, that's why.

Listening for sound from man or beast, he stiffened his grip on the musket. An anxious heart pulsed in his chest. It was impossible to bring his boys back, but killing this wolf would ease the terror that gripped Lorenca and give him a degree of control over things. The moon reappeared and cast a chill dappled light whereby he and Rounfil could see enough to scour the ground for some indication of where they had gone, though it was difficult to make anything out.

A musket reported, followed by a scuffle and scream, quickly silenced. Hantle forged ahead toward its source. Presently, he came across a trail of crushed undergrowth and overturned litter. It led on a dozen yards before fanning out to a wide circle of trampled brush. Dark patches spattered the leaves and soil. He crouched to the largest patch and touched it, noting its warmth and the tack between his fingers—fresh-spilt blood. The moonlight winked out and he was suddenly aware of the silence. He whispered, "Rounfil?"

"Just over here." A branch broke beneath his boot, seeming louder than a musket shot.

"Did you see a trail leading off from here?"

"No, but I got a piece of cloth. Probably from one of their shirts. Can't see anything else without the moon."

"Come on, where are they with the light?" He threw a look behind. It was hard to tell how far off the others were. "If they don't hurry up we'll lose it. It's too damn fast."

"Right? I'm guessing it's carrying or dragging both of them along, but there's no sight of it now." Rounfil sounded in awe of the thing.

Hantle swallowed. "Unless it's waiting to ambush us." Would he even know if the thing lurked beside them, readying to pounce? The inky darkness gave way as a handful of people followed the trail to them. He shot a glance to his surroundings. No pupils glowing back, at least. Relieved to have his vision once more, he stood and spoke to the newcomers. "Watch the blood, there's a lot of it. We tracked the creature here so far, but we'll make better time now with the light."

Pirram, face still covered in sawdust, held aloft a torch. "Either of you get a look at it?"

Hantle frowned. "No, it was deep in the trees before I got out the house."

"And he beat me there, so . . ." Rounfil shook his head.

Hantle wasted no more time. He moved to the edge of the trampled circle where he discovered a few dribbles of blood leading away, but they ended abruptly. "All right, group up and spread out. Find the trail."

Several minutes later, a howl split the air. Hantle stopped in his tracks and spun his head around. Where was it? There! Its form scarcely lit by the moon. When the call stopped, the animal loped off and Hantle could have sworn something hung from its jaws. He called over his shoulder for Rounfil, pointing to the beast, but then his stomach dropped. It had disappeared again. "Follow me!" He sprinted forward, holding his musket with both hands. Rocks and sticks jabbing into his feet made him grimace, but he did not slow down. His eyes had not again left the location where he had spotted the wolf because he was afraid that blinking would cause the spot to meld into the indiscriminate woodland. Tears were streaming down his cheeks by the time he arrived. Others trailed behind him, leaving him without a light for the moment. He rubbed at his eyes and searched in what he thought was the same way the beast had gone. Everything looked like a clue. Had that branch been there before the wolf passed by? Was this pile of leaves scattered or not? What if the ground was too thick with litter to leave a print?

Rounfil joined him, apparently having taken a lantern from someone else. "Can you shine it over here?" Hantle could not stand still, even though he was sure there was a thorn in his foot. "There's bound to be a print where the leaves are thinner."

"Take it easy," Rounfil said. "You'll tromp on a print if you don't calm down."

"Then come over here and help. Come on!" He gestured wildly with a hand. "We're just seconds behind it, but we have to go *now*. The thing moves fast as hell." The light made the trail apparent. "Yes. We've got it now."

---

"I'm not sure it goes through," Rounfil said.

They had been searching for hours with nothing to show, but even the faintest of hints deserved to be followed. The rest of their party was spread out, similarly occupied.

"Oh well"—Hantle shrugged—"we need to be certain." He tossed his musket to Rounfil and waded into the undergrowth, ripping apart tangled branches and vines to clear a path. The ground below gave way to a hollow that Hantle did not see. He lost balance and, while planting a foot to catch himself, impaled it on a cluster of thorns. He hollered, frozen with the pain. Damn it all! Aided by a hand from

Rounfil, he extricated himself. When finally free of the mess, he tested the foot but found it too tender to bear weight.

"Here," Rounfil offered. "Steady yourself on me."

Hantle gripped his shoulder and leaned over to inspect the damage. Rivulets of blood ran from multiple points. "Just a few thorns," he said. Wincing, he extracted what pieces he could, tossed them aside, and wiped away the blood. A few other welts looked to contain splinters embedded too deeply to remove with only his nails. "This ground is harsh."

"You're barefoot, what do you expect?"

He was in no mood for jokes. "Shut up." Letting go of Rounfil, he put weight on the foot but hopped off it and sucked air through clenched teeth. "Ah, something's still shooting fire."

Rounfil shook the lantern and looked at the oil level. "Your foot's shot and the lantern doesn't have much time left in it." Hantle knew where he was going before he said it. "Maybe we should head back."

His eyebrows furrowed. "That would be giving up. We're *this* close to picking the trail back up."

Rounfil paused for a minute. Was that pity on his face? "We have been out here for hours, Hantle. We started with a trail, but now we're grasping at straws."

That was not true. They'd found plenty of leads. "Do you have something to suggest, or are you just going to complain?"

Rounfil huffed and opened his eyes wide. "I'm complaining? It's you who's not thinking. You'd be better off by getting your foot fixed up and waiting for daylight. Then we go back to the start, where we found all the blood. Start fresh there. We probably mistook the path somewheres back."

Fine. It was true. They were scrambling, and had been for a while.

"Plus," Rounfil continued, "I don't do my best work when I'm exhausted. Couple hours of sleep though, and it'd be a different story."

Yes, Hantle knew he was right, but something still felt wrong to him. But what? It took a minute, but he found the root of it. "Feels like we're leaving them for dead though."

Something clicked for Rounfil. "Oh." He nodded at first but changed it to a shake. "The difficult truth is they're likely already dead. Honestly, they'd be lucky to be, so many hours on."

Hantle conceded. "All right, you bastard, let's head back. But we'll be out shortly after sunrise." He shifted and a jolt of pain shot up his leg. "Eh. Help me out, will you?"

---

The search party returned to Founsel, grouped together but quiet. Coming out of the forest, Hantle saw the outhouse charred and smoldering, like a monument to his failure. He hung his head and the butt of the musket scraped across the ground.

Rounfil, on whose shoulders Hantle still leaned, said, "Someone's got to tell Olyul."

"Yeah," Pirram said. "I'll take care of it."

"Be delicate, sir," Hantle said, his recklessness subsiding. "We aren't yet certain what's happened to them."

"'Course, of course." Pirram gave a knowing nod and split off.

Without further discussion, the group disbanded and, as individuals returned home, Hantle, aided by Rounfil, hobbled to his door. He leaned against the doorframe. "Why didn't I shoot?"

Rounfil looked uncertain. "What?"

"When I saw the wolf, I gave chase instead of shooting it. I had a chance to kill it but wasted it. Why?"

"For all you knew, it had Trissol or Couveim." Rounfil retied the robe's sash at his waist. "Look, you weren't out there alone. The wolf escaped us all."

"I hate to tell Lorenca that, is all." The thought churned in his belly like spoilt milk.

"Not for lack of trying. We'll pick up the search in a few hours." As he backed off the porch, Rounfil tilted his head to Hantle's foot. "Get that fixed up."

The door creaked open and by candlelight Hantle saw the fury on

Lorenca's face. She wrung the dishcloth until her knuckles were salt-white. Then she launched it at him and stood, shouting, "I can't believe you just left me like that. Do you know how terrified I've been?"

The cloth struck him in the face, which he knew he deserved. He sat the musket aside and limped forward, holding his hands out in supplication. "I'm sorry," he said as she backed farther away. "I didn't mean to scare you. The beast took Trissol and Couveim." He was surprised to find hot tears streaking down his cheeks. "I wanted to save them, like I couldn't save—" He had to swallow down his own terror. "Like I couldn't save *our* boys."

Lorenca broke into a sob, took a step forward, and looked at his wounded foot. "Why're you limping? Where're your boots?"

He gave her a sheepish look and said, "Left them behind. Caught a thorn or two."

"Sit down, you idiot," she said, thickly. "Let me see."

He crumpled into his chair at the table. All energy was gone from his system, leaving him lethargic, sluggish. He heaved his foot up and Lorenca leaned close with the candle. She gave a disappointed sigh and moved to a trunk nearby. After rummaging for a moment, she pulled out a needle and held it in the flame. When the metal glowed red, she pulled it out and let the color dull. Then she fell to work on the splinters. He flinched and held his breath.

With a huff, she said, "You'll be lucky if it doesn't fester." She dug in with more force than he thought necessary, but he suspected he deserved that as well. "Well," she continued, "are you going to tell me what happened out there?"

# CHAPTER SIX

HANTLE YAWNED, raised his head to look past Lorenca, and saw it was light out. The bed creaked as he crept from under the covers, but Lorenca did not stir. In the kitchen, he flopped into his chair, which rocked with the impact, and inspected the bandage wrapping his foot. No blood, which boded well, but his body felt heavy. He was more tired than he had hoped he would be. It was dawn, though, and time for them to resume the search. After he pulled his boots on, he tested the foot, and, while not enough to render him immobile, it did hurt considerably.

The sun was still below the treetops, so when Hantle entered the street and saw a group of people standing near the cove, all he could make out was their silhouettes. On any other day the sight would have been innocuous, but today it was ominous. He uttered, "Oh no," and grimaced. Closing in, his hunch was confirmed. He plunked down to the street as hope rushed out and despair swept in to replace it. It was Couveim and Trissol, undoubtedly. Their two heads lay face down in the middle of the street, tilted toward him. Tongues—swollen and purple—hung out of the mouths, and spines trailed down from there, all surrounded by blood-drenched cobblestone. Worse than the scene itself was his mind reverting to the vivid, ghastly discovery of yesterday. Grief rose from somewhere deep and its swell broke upon frayed nerves. Couveim's face was replaced with a hellish projection of Lorenca's, and Hantle crept forward on hands and knees, transfixed. Flies walking across the waxen flesh finally brought him out of his reverie. He waved them away.

He looked to the group around him, noticing several of his coworkers and Pirram. Why were they standing here, staring at this gruesome scene? Were they stunned, or, more disgustingly, fascinated? He asked, "Has anyone told Olyul about them or gotten Yilrouth?" Blank faces turned to him, seemingly just realizing his presence. "Why has no one even taken the most basic of actions here?" He pushed himself to his feet and turned to Couveim and Olyul's house. "I'll talk to her." His gaze was drawn to a faint wisp of smoke rising from the outhouse wreckage. He locked up. Were he to take another step toward it, the outhouse would collapse, opening a hole that would widen and swallow him.

Thankfully, Pirram intervened. "Don't worry about Olyul, Hantle." He patted his back. "I'll go talk to her again. Why don't you get Yilrouth? Afterward, I'll start on the coffins."

It was only when Hantle turned that his bated breath escaped in a drawn-out sigh. Yes, he could manage that. He went to the southern part of Founsel, where the doctor and his family lived, to deliver news of the grim discovery. Yilrouth gathered his bag, left his half-eaten breakfast behind, and followed Hantle. Rounfil exited his house and Hantle told him of the finding as they returned to the cove. The rising sun brought out more people, who milled about and talked in hushed voices.

Before approaching the bodies, Yilrouth surveyed the scene. The sun beat hot already; he huffed and dragged his sleeve across his forehead. "Oy," he said. "One doesn't get used to this kind of carnage." He pulled two lengths of cloth from his bag, tiptoed through the surrounding mess, and crouched down to wrap the remains. Rounfil stepped in to help as he had yesterday, and Hantle averted his eyes. He could not stomach watching. His thoughts turned, instead, to what he should do next. What chance would he have of discovering a trail that led to the wolf itself? Surely, after having left behind the bodies of Couveim and Trissol, it would have roamed far and quickly. Tracking it had been difficult enough when the trail was fresh. Though perhaps it slept and rested rather close to Founsel; its proximity may have been a large factor in why it attacked the village. He knew little of the habits of wolves outside of the sort of general knowledge of them one picks up as a child.

"Hantle?" The sound of Shec calling his name brought him back from his rumination. She held out a brush. "Care to help scrub?"

He wordlessly took the brush and watched her empty a bucketful of water over the gore on the street, then return to the cove for another. Yilrouth had already started toward his house, white bundles in arm. He dropped to his knees and scraped the horsehair bristles over the stones. Beside him, Rounfil took up a brush and knelt. The water turned to crimson in the brush and snaked away through the cobblestones. Liova, her face creased in thought, walked from the village square, where others set out hay bales and chairs for the funeral.

"It's not normal, is it?" Hantle said to the group at large. "Not normal for a wolf to attack people like this, I mean."

"No," Rounfil replied, "it is not normal. They're fearsome predators, but around humans they get skittish."

"Unless provoked," Shec said. "They'll aggressively guard their young or food."

Rounfil nodded. "Sure, but I've not heard of them doing what this one has."

"This," Liova said, "goes beyond aggression. It's vicious, calculated." Her shoes scuffed as she looked about. "Something's strange about this creature." She paused, then pointed a bony finger. "This feels like a tableau. Meant to be found."

Hantle set the brush aside and stood. "You think it left them here on purpose? To make a point?"

"One cannot be certain of intent." Her shoulders rose with a shrug. "But I would guess that, yes."

"What kind of point?" Shec asked.

"Terror, for instance." A rasp in Liova's throat accented that first word.

Rounfil looked to Hantle. "It did have to bring them back after we chased it off. That took effort."

A shiver ran down Hantle's spine and he inspected the forest edge. "Would it be watching us? To see how we reacted?"

"Doubtful," Liova said. "Wolves cannot tolerate the daylight. Which, disconcertingly, means it knows how we'd react." She crossed her arms and started away. "I've a eulogy to prepare." Hantle heard her muttering, "Strange, very strange," until she was out of earshot.

He whispered to Rounfil, "Have you heard that about wolves not tolerating daylight?"

"Yes," he said, "from my father when we used to hunt together. She's more learned than he was, though. Went to the college in, where, Bansuth?"

"I think so." He ought to be certain: he had heard her mention those scholarly days many times while growing up, but, instead of listening, he had always tuned her out. "Maybe she's right then." But what he could do with that information, he was not sure.

---

"My friends," Liova said, "we come together to recognize and remember two more of our neighbors: Couveim, a father, known for his skill with snares and a musket. Trissol, a son, bright in his studies and eager to help others." She laid a lily on each of the coffins, across the chiseled names. Several feet away, Olyul clutched her daughter, Jiumsa.

"We know that life in the Far Finger is fraught with danger, but we still struggle to understand how something such as this can happen. Deep pain rends our hearts, much like how, during the Cataclysm, the

Void rent the All." Beads of sweat ran down the sides of her face to drop onto her blouse. Hantle felt the sunlight sink into his black, pressing him toward the ground. "Out of that turmoil, however, we have arisen. And we resonate with the music of the Song. I encourage us all to bear the memory of those we lay to rest, and honor that memory by focusing our love and compassion onto Olyul and Jiumsa, so that we might amplify one another, each a note to be heard."

He did not much go for the layers of meaning that people often put on top of the Mechanisms, but this time, the idea of amplifying one another struck him. After all, he was a member of Founsel—one part of the greater whole. Only with the support of the village did any of them make it through a day. He reached over and gripped Lorenca's hand. Without her, how—

"What will we *do* now?" someone shouted from the back. Hantle spun in his seat and watched Douth throw his hands up and continue. "We must prevent the beast from bringing hell for the third night running."

Muffled sobs escaped Olyul. She had slumped forward, head buried in her hands. Did this bastard not see her pain and heartache? Hantle's muscles tightened and his brain worked as he prepared to respond, but Liova beat him.

"You have cause to be upset," she said, "but this is not the place to voice it. Be seated." She pursed her lips and pointed to his chair, like he was a child.

After a breath, Douth nodded begrudgingly and resumed his seat. Hantle turned forward again. He swallowed and pinched his eyes shut to contain the energy loosed by Douth's desecration of the funeral. However much he felt them justified, a retaliatory yell and thrown punch would be equally profane. Liova more easily set the disruption aside and picked up the ceremony where she had left off. Hantle, though, kept replaying the scene in his mind, trying to come up with a satisfactory reply.

After the villagers cleared the mourning meal and led the grieving family back to their home, the day drew on to evening. Answering a call from Liova, Hantle assembled with a group in the now-empty square. Still offended by his prior outburst, he maintained a distance from Douth.

Liova approached from her house and spoke to them as she neared. "When I was a child, my family migrated to Bansuth. It was the first settlement on the Far Finger. People had just discovered the area's rich resources, and my parents thought they could better provide for us children there. We joined three other families and traveled from our home on the far eastern plains of the Fist." She stopped in the middle of the group and looked not at them but through the mountain range of the Knuckles and decades back.

Why had she called them there to share her childhood? He shot Rounfil a questioning look, only to receive an unknowing headshake in reply.

"During a night in the middle of our journey, a group of bandits raided our camp and raped a woman. My father caught and killed one of the men, while the others escaped. Before our trip, I'd heard people telling my parents that the road passed through dangerous lands, but, until that night, I had no idea what they meant. We were preyed upon by creatures of convenience.

"On the following nights, we avoided fires past dark and the adults took turns standing guard. I can remember just how exhausted my mother and father were. Thanks to their sacrifice, though, we traveled from there on without incident." Her look turned from the far-off to the group. "They showed me that when you take away the opportunity, you take away the threat. Maybe Founsel needs a night watch." She raised her hands and looked expectantly for their opinion.

"So she had a point," Rounfil whispered.

Hantle chuckled, then straightened his face as Liova looked to him. Douth's eyes flitted away instead when her gaze moved across the people gathered. No one spoke, and the quiet dismissal dismayed him. It was easy to be outraged, but was it easier yet to sidestep responsibility? "I'll do it." He stepped forward, resolved. "How could I say no to an opportunity to protect my wife and home?"

"Good." Liova gave him an approving nod. "Unafraid to take action, you're the perfect fit for this."

"All day," he said, "I've been uncertain of what I could *do*. Not knowing has been agonizing. This is it, though. Some way, at least, I can help Lorenca cope with our loss"—he sniffed and wiped a wrist at his damp eyes—"and, if the night watch needs a leader, I'll also volunteer for that role. But I will need help."

Rounfil clapped a hand to his back. "I'm with him."

Liova said, "You cried out for action first, Douth. Can we assume you're eager to help?"

"Uh, of course." He gave a strained smile. "Happy to." His tone belied his words, but Hantle was glad he did not make an excuse to avoid participating.

Liova spoke to the rest. "Who else is willing to join him?"

Shec drew up, saying, "Always respected Hantle's work. I'll help." Others volunteered and Hantle thanked each of them in turn.

"Eight for the watch? That should do," Liova said. "Can't expect Founsel to be here tomorrow unless our brave people fight for it."

"We'll have to figure out our approach," Hantle said. "I'm no strategist."

"During our travel," Liova said, "we stayed hidden in the darkness by avoiding campfires, but, knowing wolves have no love for light, such could be used here to advantage."

Crahul rested one hand on his portly stomach and tugged on his beard with the other. "I received a shipment of a dozen lanterns from Bansuth this week. I'm thinking I'd be happy to offer them for this."

"That's quite generous of you," Hantle said. "We could post them around the village. Anyone else have equipment to spare?"

Those who had not volunteered for the watch were more receptive to helping in other fashions: offering more lanterns, pledging weapons and ammunition, and spreading word that none other than the guards were allowed out after dark. Hantle discussed tactics with the guard volunteers for a time before they split up to tackle preparations.

---

The stairs creaked under Hantle's feet as he ascended to rouse Lorenca. She lay on her side, facing away from him, still in Hultier's bed. His soft knock fell on the door and he said, "Join me for supper?"

She rolled onto her back and stared at the ceiling. No reply. Grasped to her chest was Hultier's favorite toy.

"Our neighbors are kind," he continued. "Thanks to them we have a casserole and a few sides. Much better than what I would've made." She uttered a sound meant to dismiss him, but Hantle persevered and sat beside her. "You need to eat, Lorenca. Come on." Threading an arm between her back and the bed, he gained enough leverage to lift her to a seated position. Once raised, she became pliable and he led her to the kitchen table. He scooted her chair up to the table and spooned out helpings of the main dish for them both.

At his first bite, Hantle's taste buds lit up. "Hah!" His head bobbed and motioned with his fork to the plate. "That cream sauce is good." Only after savoring a few more bites did he go on. "You know, I haven't even tasted a meal in the last couple days. This is nice." He served the salad and seasoned potatoes. Lorenca ate a few bites but showed no real appetite. It was lucky enough to have her out of bed, eating a morsel or two, so he had no complaint.

A kettle whistled and his fork clattered to the plate. "Almost forgot." Lorenca's dull gaze trailed after him. He donned a rag and pulled the kettle from the fire. In his mug, the boiling water turned earthen the instant it mixed with the jursant leaves. Its bright scent roiled through the room.

She finally spoke. "Why jursant at this hour?"

"Just need a little pep for the night."

"What?" Her entire body turned to him. "What about the night?"

Walking back, he gave the full mug all the attention a scalding beverage deserved. "All day I've been wondering what to do next." With a loud sip taken off the top, he lowered the mug to the table. "Then Liova's got it: a night watch. Patrol the village. Keep the wolf away. Keep the village safe. *You* most of all, of course."

"You can't . . ." Her voice disappeared for a few seconds. "I need you with me. My heart will *stop* if I try to sleep another minute alone."

"Now, now, that isn't so." He used his most delicate tone. "Rounfil, myself, and two others are just part of the first shift. Halfway through the night, another group relieves us. So just think of it as me coming to bed a bit late."

"Wouldn't it be smarter to stay in with me?" She tiptoed to his side and whispered, "You and I will be safe in our own bed." The words draped as longingly around his neck as her arms.

He placed a hand on hers and a warm sigh left his chest. She was right. They would be safe there, and no one would question him changing his mind and staying with her. "I want to," he said. "I really want to. But I volunteered for this and they'll need me."

"I'm your wife, Hantle. *I* need you!"

"I'm doing this for you, most of all."

"I don't want you to." She stepped away, shoulders slumped forward. "What if you get killed?"

"I'll admit, I have been reckless before. Tonight, though, I won't take any undue risks." Her expression did not ease like he had hoped. "We have a chance here to be organized. To prevent someone else getting killed. We'll be there when it comes back, ready to kill it."

She gave a disgusted sigh and moved farther away, into the kitchen. Her head shook endlessly as she thought of a reply. The way she dealt with grief was to curl up. He understood why, yet he could not do that himself. How could he explain, in a way that she accepted, that he handled things differently? "I'm sorry," he said, "that you don't agree, but I have to do this. It's for you even though you don't think so. Because how could I live with myself if I let anything happen to you through my own inaction?" As a pathetic afterthought, he ended with, "Not to mention, if I didn't put myself to use, I'd go mad."

He stood and took a step forward, meaning to comfort her. Instead, the motion propelled her up the stairs. She shouted as she ran. "No, I won't hear it!" The door slam stopped him cold and reverberated in his chest. Well, shit.

After a long minute, he returned to the table and swallowed down the jursant. Doing what was necessary wasn't easy. He finished his plate in silence and had another helping before heading back out. Nightfall was nearly complete. Flames danced atop the wicks of the lanterns staked outside the village. His sluggishness faded away and, once he discounted Lorenca's anger with him, he felt ready for the night.

---

At last, the stifling, scorching day was over. The wolf had passed the hours huddled in what shade he could find, panting and cursing the day. In the short interim between sun and moon, he roamed the forest surrounding Founsel. Burning lanterns, staked out at regular intervals, cast wide circles of light between the homes and the trees. Squinting into the woods, he saw a pair of people walking the perimeter. The things they carried in their arms were meant to kill him, he knew. The father he had eaten last night nearly did so. Darkness had befriended and concealed him, though, inducing the man to aim too far to the side.

As the moon ascended, he stretched his body and moved to better cover. Several minutes later, another armed pair walked past in the same fashion. He was tempted to close in on them, to sink his teeth into their throats, to down their flesh and further spur his growth, but a qualm unsettled him. His new size and speed might have allowed for him to bring down both guards without taking injury from their weapons, were it only darker. As it stood, the combination of moon- and lantern-light would faze, disorient, and hinder him, throwing off his attack. He hated the odds and he hated them for it. A snarl built in his throat as he imagined darkness spreading from the trees to cover the village, absolute and endless. No, he would hold his position and wait for some other prey to reveal itself, unarmed and witless. The night had provided for him each time prior; shouldn't it do so again?

Hours on, he was hungrier, much hungrier, and tired of the waiting. None made an appearance beyond the watch-folk, who continued their circuit. When two of the guards made their next pass, the wolf crept nearer. The trees, the light, the night all fell away and he focused on them entirely. His tail whipped with excitement and drool rolled off his jaws. Oughtn't he savor the taste or would he—

A branch-snap smashed through his concentration and yanked his gaze from the guards to two others creeping and searching through the underbrush. He let out a startled bark.

Hantle jerked with surprise at the sound. Beside him, Rounfil swung around the lantern he carried. Two golden dots reflected the light, disappearing briefly as the wolf blinked. The wolf!

"The, uh," Hantle stammered. Yes, they had been scouring the wood's edge for it, but he had not truly expected to find it. Plus, it was enormous, similar to one of the coastal brown bears. Around its throat the fur was stained dark but elsewhere it was off-white. When the surprise lessened, he hefted the musket to his shoulder and shouted out the side of his mouth, "Here! We got it over here!" hoping to attract the guards patrolling in the village's clearing. There was just enough light to illuminate the creature as it looked from one pair of guards to the other. Just hold it. He cocked the hammer and took aim, but the canine came out of its stupor and bolted. Damnit. Swinging the barrel in an attempt to lead the wolf, he pulled the trigger. A cloud of smoke billowed forward and Hantle drove through it, eager to see the effect of his shot.

Initially, he could see nothing. Noises off to their side, however, drew his attention. The wolf popped into existence in a moonlit clearing before vanishing back into tree cover.

"Did the shot land?" he asked Rounfil, who slogged through a cluster of bushes.

"Eh, I think it struck a tree. Just up here."

Within a few minutes, they found the musket ball embedded in the trunk of an oak. Hantle shook his head and ran a finger around the hole. "Terrible aim, wasn't it?"

"Well"—Rounfil gave him a smile—"did you see how that thing took off?"

"Yeah." He shrugged. "We did that much at least."

Shec and Douth were to them, asking, "So what happened?"

"Ha," Rounfil said. "He scared away the wolf is what happened."

"Damn good job," Douth said. "No doubt about it."

Shec tipped her head toward the forest. "We heading after it then?"

It was not easy, but Hantle managed a "No." As promised, he would take no undue risks. "We stick to Founsel and the forest's edge. Goal tonight is that no one dies, us included." A small bit of relief set in as they resumed their rounds. They *had* done something.

# CHAPTER SEVEN

HANTLE HAD LITTLE MORE than drifted off when a knock came at the door. He hauled himself from his chair and opened the door to the midday sun. Crahul stood there, breathing heavily and tugging at a sideburn.

"I know, Hantle, you've searched twice for that wolf that's attacked us. Plus, last night, you and your group kept it away."

Something about his expression was off, but Hantle couldn't pinpoint what. "Yessir, we ran it off. What of it?"

"A shepherd," he said. "A shepherd is in my store saying *he's* had a run in with the wolf. You'll be wanting to hear his story, I think."

Hantle nodded and slipped his boots on, injured foot feeling nearly normal. "How did he escape alive?"

"Not sure." Crahul started toward the street. "I wanted to fetch a few others before he told the details. Who else should we round up?"

After the arrival of the quiet morning, most villagers had resumed their usual routines, meaning many were working out in the forest. "I see Rounfil sawing lumber. I can get him. Shec ought to be around. And someone else who is on hand, I guess?"

Shortly, they had gathered Shec from her smithy and Eayol from her nearby fields. The small crowd entered the Mercantile where the shepherd stood, holding an empty water glass.

"Here we all are." Crahul gestured to the villagers behind him. "Oh, let me get you some more." He took the shepherd's glass and pulled a pitcher from under the counter to refill it.

Shec, her face dark with soot, said, "So you've come across the wolf, eh?"

The shepherd nodded and in a faraway voice said, "Ruined by a damn wolf. A damn *huge* wolf."

Handing back the glass, Crahul said, "Now you'll be telling us your story in full, I hope. Mister . . ."

"Breenstul. I'm Weith Breenstul." He gulped half the glass, huffed a few times, and shook his head. "I can't believe it. I really am ruined, flat out." He did not seem to know how to continue.

To spur the man along, Hantle said, "You've been into Founsel before, haven't you? I recognize your face."

"Yes, I've come in before. My flock is in the Low Fields, just a few miles off." Weith leaned against the counter at the back of the shop and the words tumbled out. "Last night, well after dark, I heard the sheep moving around. They don't much stir after night's fell, and it seemed strange. I poked my head from my little shack and couldn't see much at first. Then the moon comes out from behind a cloud, right? I can see the pale fur of something. Then my sheep start running. I grab my musket and before I'm back out the sheep are bleating like mad. At first I thought it was a bear, but we've got no white bears here, right? I get a better glimpse and it's the shape of a wolf: lean and long. But this thing is larger than any damn wolf I've ever seen. I mistook it for a bear because it was honestly the size of one. Shoulders would be about chest height on me."

"I thought the same thing when I saw it," Hantle said.

Weith was taken by surprise. "Wait, when did you see it?"

"Didn't mean to interrupt," Hantle said. "You finish your story and then we'll share ours."

He nodded and went on. "Anyway, I got three sheepdogs. They do a fine job of herding. Quite protective, right? They hear the noises too and bolt straight out the shack. Ran up to that wolf, barking and growling and darting around. The wolf lets go of one of the sheep—mostly eaten now—and walks toward the dogs. Off to its side was another sheep it'd gotten its teeth into.

"That wolf lowers its head and steps closer to them. Teeth bared. I could see the moon shining off them. I raise my musket, but with the sheep running and the dogs, I couldn't get any shot, right? I've had my largest dog, Sep, for the longest too. She's ferocious when she wants, and she wasn't taking anything from this wolf. She starts barking more fiercely, and inching in as she swings around. Wanted to go for the flank, right? It's an instinct. The two other dogs aren't as aggressive, but they're barking their heads off too.

"Guess who sat right back on its haunches? That wolf. Lets up this deep, deep howl that scared me, all right. Sure gave the dogs a fright too. They got quiet for a minute and backed up some. I thought I'd have a shot, right, but then the wolf makes one swift motion and it's got poor Sep in its jaws, shaking her about as it jerks its head from side to side. Sep there got torn to shreds. The other two dogs were barking again, but then got scared and took off. The sheep ran off together into the forest south of the fields.

"I saw what it did to my faithful Sep and stepped back into the shack, closed the door, and snuffed out my lantern. A shot from my musket would've only served to anger it. I don't fancy being eaten like that either, right? Figured to lay low until it gets out.

"After waiting for however long, I end up falling asleep and woke up after the sun's up. Quiet as can be in the fields out there. I poke my head out of my shack again and make sure the wolf is long gone. I go out to see the damage. There's this huge tree standing naked in the field. Been dead as long as I had my flock there. Right up in the branches I see something. You're not going to believe this, but it's the heads and spines of eight of my sheep. Eight of them! Some of their wool is scattered about too, right, from the wolf's eating them.

"There's blood all over the ground, and then I see my two coward dogs slinking toward me from the forest. Granted, I'm glad they didn't get eaten too, but poor Sep was the best sheepdog I've ever seen. Come to think of it, I'm not sure I saw her body at all. After glimpsing all that mess, I made for the forest to look for my flock. I spent hours looking all over but they must have kept on running and running because I found none of them.

"Eventually, I decided to make my way to Founsel here, right? None of you owe me anything, I know that, but I am begging you to help me find my flock. Without them, I'm done for." The shepherd's eyes were wide with desperation, and he looked around the room.

Hantle stood quiet for a minute, processing the story.

Crahul was the first to move when he laid a hand on Weith's shoulder. "I'm sure we'll all do our best to help you. I'm thinking Founsel's a good place. Right, all?" He turned to the rest.

"Aye," Rounfil said, "we'll look for your flock."

"I'm astounded," Hantle said, "you went unharmed." He told of the wolf's attacks on the village, how his sons and two others were killed. "Last night, we posted lanterns around the forest's edge and kept a night watch. We came across the wolf lurking in the trees and chased it off."

"Must have gone," Rounfil said, "to the Low Fields afterward."

"It seems that way, doesn't it?" Weith nodded slowly.

Something else struck Hantle as odd. He said, "I first got a glimpse of the wolf two nights back. Decent size, sure, but nothing out of the ordinary. Nowhere near as large as it was last night."

Weith huffed and tapped the countertop. "You mean it grew that much in a single night?"

"Doesn't make sense"—Hantle shrugged—"but it must have. Liova was right, there's something strange about this creature. First, its blatant aggression. Now, its rapid growth."

"That mean we should expect it'll be even bigger tonight?" Rounfil asked.

Hantle exhaled, shook his head, and said, "I suppose so." This morning, he had been hopeful and excited because they had kept

Founsel safe. Now, all the validation fell away. "We will do what we can to help find your flock, Weith. Unwittingly, we pushed the danger away from ourselves and on to you."

Crahul motioned to the door. "We'll be heading toward the Low Fields now, I hope?"

The group funneled out of the store and walked down the road, past the threshold where the cobblestone ended and the packed dirt began. A mile later, it swung southeast toward distant settlements, the largest of which was Harsenth. Weith stepped off the road after some three odd miles and led them north to the Low Fields.

As Hantle stepped into the clearing, grass brushed his shins and a breeze turned his view into a shimmering green expanse. It was a beautiful sight but for the enormous barren tree, reaching out of the ground like some gnarled hand. The sheep heads hung in the crooks of the upper branches, which bowed with the weight. Trailing from each head was a spine. They all swayed in a gust of wind, but Hantle imagined them instead writhing in pain.

"How did the wolf," Shec asked, "climb so high?"

Weith said, "Tree must still be pretty strong, right? Though a few limbs did come down."

Hantle turned his attention to the rest of the field. "Which way had your flock run?"

Weith blew a short blast on his whistle and the dogs came to his side. "Over here." He led them to the area. The sheep had clearly trampled the grasses and underbrush as they fled south.

Rounfil and Eayol, the two most experienced with tracking, followed the trail until the ground turned hard and it disappeared. By spreading out and continuing in that same direction for several hundred feet, they came to a place where the trees thinned out and the ground became softer, putting a spring in Hantle's step. There, Rounfil located the prints once more, and the group kept on. They passed back over the dirt road as the tracks led into thicker forest. Again, rocky ground obscured the trail, but Eayol located a creek whose mud contained hoof tracks. Eyeing the spacing, she said, "They had slowed to a walking pace by this point."

As they crested a small escarpment, down which water tumbled, Hantle saw the first of the sheep. Others stood beyond, grazing on grasses that sprouted between thick tree roots.

"Oh, what a fantastic sight!" Weith clutched a hand to his chest. "But why did you all run so far?" With a chirp on the whistle, the dogs sat. Weith walked to one of the sheep and patted its head. "I'm sure glad to see you. Let's see how many of you stuck together."

Hantle gave a nod to Rounfil and Eayol. "Nice work, you two."

"Yes"—Weith clapped his hands together—"I cannot thank you enough."

"Just glad we found them," Rounfil said.

Eayol's cheeks blushed. "Well, you know how it's nice to put a skill to use, to help others."

Hantle looked about and spotted the source of the creek: a low-hung cave. The hindquarter of a lamb showed then disappeared. He approached the cave and found, just inside its mouth, several more of the flock. "There are more over here," he called as he crouched down to draw them out.

They ambled toward the others and Weith whistled for his dogs to round up the flock. After counting them, Weith's excitement dampened. "Thirteen? Oy, that's far less than half."

"How many did you start with?" Crahul frowned at the sheep.

"Thirty-seven. With the eight eaten, that leaves"—Weith did the calculation in his head—"sixteen missing, right?"

"Okay," Hantle said. "Still some work to do then."

Shec made a sweeping motion with her hands. "We can fan out to see if any are nearby."

The six of them scoured the surrounding area but found neither sheep nor indication of their whereabouts.

They were miles from the Low Fields. Miles over which those sheep could have splintered off. The thought of covering that amount of land was daunting, but Hantle felt a sense of duty toward the shepherd. Through the wolf, they had been brought together, and Hantle wanted to protect Weith just as he wanted to protect Founsel. "If we trace back," he said, "we might find where the group split."

Weith looked torn. "I appreciate the offer muchly, but we could be days looking for the remaining ones and still not find them. I'll count my luck we found this many." He turned the whistle over in his hand. "As much as I'm worried about the missing ones, I'm even more worried about staying here another night. It'd be worse to lose them all."

"We'll all be heading back to Founsel now, I hope," Crahul said.

Weith shook his head. "Staying in Founsel would draw the wolf in. The sheep are easy prey, right? I can't make you a target like that. Especially after you helped me like you did. I'll move farther east, at least until the menace has passed."

Hantle did not like the idea of Weith setting out on his own. "Our watch last night was effective. We lit up the entire village and patrolled the outskirts. I bet you'd be safest there with us." He noticed the sun riding low in the sky. "And the day's getting on."

Rounfil nodded. "We can put the flock in the village square, where they'd be best guarded."

"Honestly, I'll feel much better heading east. Got some family in the foothills near Bansuth. The flock'll do well in the rolling hills there." He put the whistle in his mouth. "We're all ready to move now, right?" It appeared he could not be persuaded otherwise. At his command, the dogs herded the flock north.

This was the first time Hantle had seen a shepherd at work. The dogs responded to Weith's whistles to sweep around the flank, approach from the rear, and nip at the heels of obstinate sheep. They made good time back to the dirt road, what with no trail to lose.

When they stepped out from the forest, Hantle made one last bid. "We're more than happy to have you in Founsel."

Weith looked to the ground. "You all have done enough for me already. Thank you for all your help, but I must be off." He gave a wave farewell and then started east with his flock.

## CHAPTER EIGHT

AS HANTLE and the search party reached Founsel, the sun dropped below the treetops. Tall clouds moved in on a wind from the north. From a distance, he saw Liova pouring oil into one of the lanterns staked around the village. She set the jar to the ground, lit the wick, and nodded as she saw the group.

She called out, "My, my, they did decide to come back. Who else is interested in hearing where they've been?"

As Hantle approached her, he joked, "Thanks, ma'am, for being discreet."

She gave a mischievous smile. "Don't sneak off if you don't want questions."

An eager crowd gathered and Shec asked, "What are you waiting for? Where did you all disappear to today?"

Crahul said, "I'm thinking you'll remember the shepherd that keeps his flock in the Low Fields?" He started the telling of Weith's story, then passed it to Hantle, who spoke and passed it on in turn, until everyone had told a portion of the search for the scattered sheep.

Liova looked past them, down the path. "Where is he now? Coming after you with the flock?"

Hantle shook his head. "No. He's heading toward Bansuth instead. Supposedly because he didn't want to make us a target tonight."

"Sounds strange," Douth said. "Not sure I buy that. Isn't he leaving himself right out in the open?"

"That's my thought," Hantle agreed. "I tried to tell him we would protect him and his flock, but he was insistent about moving away from the area. What can you do?"

"As much as you did, I guess," Shec said.

Hantle noticed most of the lanterns had been refueled and relit. "Liova, it's good to see you're already preparing for tonight's watch."

"Yes, yes, I'm happy to help. It was getting late, after all."

"Every bit of help against this creature is advantageous," Hantle said. "Rounfil and I were shocked last night to glimpse how the wolf had grown to the size of a bear, and Weith pointed out the very same thing."

Liova frowned and crossed her arms. "That is a worrisome development."

"Indeed." Hantle turned to the group. "We had two watches of four guards last night, though since we can expect the wolf will be larger tonight, we could use extra hands. Would anyone else consider joining us?"

"The more people out there," Rounfil said, "the better odds we'll all have of keeping it away."

Eayol stepped forward. "I certainly don't like the thought of that thing creeping around us each night. What do you think about me placing some snares where it has been lurking?"

"Proactive, yes." Liova's frown lessened. "That's what we need."

Rounfil patted Eayol on the back. "Let me help set them up, as a thanks for how much you contributed to the tracking today."

Hantle looked over the faces around him. "Anyone else?" The silence held until he was sure no one else would volunteer.

Then Crahul cleared his throat and bit his lip. "Last night, I was too nervous to consider it, but I'm thinking I'm ready tonight. Something about helping Weith today felt good. Felt right. I want to keep this demon away from our village."

"Good," Hantle said. "We're happy to have you, sir. That'll give us five for each watch." He couldn't help but yawn. "Been a long day, hasn't it?"

Rounfil rubbed a hand at his red eyes. "Sure has."

"Let's change the shifts up tonight," Shec offered. "I'll lead the first so you can get some rest."

"I'm happy to join the first shift too," Crahul said. "Got plenty of rest last night."

"I appreciate that," Rounfil said.

A knot formed in Hantle's stomach. He hadn't spent any time with Lorenca today, like he had hoped to. His face screwed up with worry. "Lorenca will appreciate that too, I expect."

Douth scratched his neck. "Any idea of how this wolf can eat as much as it does?"

Like the others in the group, Hantle shook his head. "Just as strange, to me," he said, "is how damn vicious it is."

"When Hantle and me caught it unawares last night, I got my closest glimpse of it yet. The look in that thing's eyes was . . ." Rounfil shrugged, looking for the right word.

Hantle knew what he meant. "Calculating?"

"Yes." Rounfil nodded several times. "Calculating. That's exactly it."

Liova folded her hands, sucked her teeth, and under her breath said, "My, my." She was deep in thought.

"What are you thinking, Liova?" Hantle asked.

"It's just—" Her faraway look persisted for several long heartbeats. "Reminds me of something I studied long ago." Her gaze returned to the present and she shook her head. She turned and without further explanation, walked away. As she trailed off, Hantle heard her muttering, "Strange, very strange."

Her unexpected departure left the group quiet for a moment, during which Hantle wondered what all she had seen and heard in her long years.

"So . . ." Douth finally spoke. "What else do we have to do?"

---

A peal of thunder followed Hantle through the door. Lorenca sat at the kitchen table. She looked up from the fork held halfway to her mouth, then pursed her lips. He froze, feeling the burn of the glare. When she focused back on her meal, Hantle could move once more. He shut the door, removed his boots, and slid into his chair at the table as gently as he could. The last thing he wanted was to provoke her ire. He spooned himself a serving from the dish that a neighbor must have brought over. At least she was eating of her own volition.

Outside, a patter of rain increased in severity to become a torrential downpour. Wind rattled the windows when Lorenca spoke. "Have a nice day?"

His nerves trembled like the glass panes. That question had no correct answer, he knew that with certainty. But still he had to answer something. He mumbled, keeping his eyes on his plate. "That, uh, wolf scattered a man's flock last night. He came in asking for help. The man did, not the wolf. So I joined the search party. Found the sheep, too, some of them, you know, and, uh, saved him from losing his livelihood." He finally looked at her with a small, conciliatory smile.

"Mmhmm," she said. When she stabbed the fork at the plate, he flinched. "Funny, though, since this morning you said we would have the whole day together."

"We're all in the same—" He paused and reconsidered his words. "Look, we've got tonight. We can fall asleep next to one another."

Her fork paused. "Really?" Disbelief and hope mixed in that single word.

She was softening, which encouraged him. "Yes, yes! I'm looking forward to holding your hand and talking with you and looking into your eyes." He took another bite and relaxed a bit. "And falling asleep beside you. I'm not going out until later. The second shift, tonight. So we have plenty of time."

Her hands slammed on the table. "Damnit, Hantle!" He immediately realized his stupidity. She took a deep breath and recovered her composure a degree. "Look, I'm proud of you for helping that man out. For joining the watch last night. I am." Her hands went to her lap. "But can't someone else do it tonight? There are plenty of good people in Founsel. Can't they function without you for one single night?"

He had expected that his success in keeping the wolf away would make her see just how much he had been right to join the watch—even though she did not like the idea—and how it would be right to do so again. Evidently, that was not what she felt.

"I am so alone, Hantle." Tears welled in her eyes. "I need you most of all, and I've hardly seen you. Can't a wife rely on her husband?"

"Of course she can. But I'm only one man. I'm trying to keep the peace with you *and* keep Founsel safe."

"Wow." She huffed. "Trying to keep the fucking peace with me? Is that all I'm worth?"

She was not hearing it how he meant it. "I'd give my life for you, Lorenca. That's what I'm out there doing. Last night. Today. And tonight. Risking my life for you."

She shoved the chair back and stood, shouting through her tears, "That's not what I want, Hantle! I don't need you dead. I need you here"—she jabbed a finger at the floor—"I need you with *me*."

His jaw opened but no words came out. This was impossible. Instead, he got up and moved to hug her.

She backed away until she hit the wall, and when he put his arms around her, she started slapping him. "Get off." He went for it anyway and she pushed him away, using the wall for leverage. "Get off!" Furious tears were streaking down her face. "I don't mean for one damn hour, which is exactly what you're thinking is perfectly fine."

He threw his hands up. "Okay," he conceded. "Okay. You've got me for the entire night. Not for an hour or two. For the entire night. It's no good going out there if it means losing you."

She sniffled and shifted her weight. "You promise?" He saw that mixture of disbelief and hope again. Another misspoken sentence risked snuffing out the hope completely.

"Yes." He took a small step forward, seeing what her reaction would be. "I promise." When she didn't recoil, he took another step, and another, until she was in his arms. "I'm here with you." He felt her tension lessen, slowly, until she returned the hug.

"You better not be lying," she said. It was a threat as much as a plea.

# CHAPTER NINE

THE SMELL of the flock carried for miles on the wind and lured the wolf from his shelter even before the storm began. He had ended the prior night full of flesh and sated but now felt as if he had not eaten in weeks. He tracked the sheep through the woodlands at a run and his shoulders scraped the lower boughs of many trees. When he neared the flock, he slowed to dampen the sound of his steps and to breathe deep of the scents thick in the air. The dogs he knew already; they had run off when he took the loudest one and shook her to silence. But who was the man with them? Had he been in the fields too? No matter, he would take them all tonight.

The downpour had tapered to a drizzle by the time he struck. He sprinted out of the trees bordering the road and had the man in his jaws before he could reach for his weapon. It clattered to the ground and his dogs barked while the sheep bleated and ran. The wolf enjoyed the man's screams, but after a second his greed could not be suppressed. On their own, his teeth sawed through the trunk and blood pooled on the ground, quickly followed by drool brought on by the taste of meat.

He zealously hunted down the dogs and sheep. Their death was immediate, unstoppable, but he did not swallow a one of them down just yet. Instead, he piled all the bodies on the road. Silence settled over the area when the last of them was stacked. Out of the corpses ran blood that he lapped up with a black-and-pink tongue. He backed away, wanting to appreciate the scene before devouring it. Yes, the night had provided. What a feeling of complete control and unadulterated ability, with sun gone and moon yet to come. None could withstand or outrun. He started into the pile, snapping bones and downing the tender muscle. The feast elated him. Nor would he be run off tonight. That village was not far away. Oughtn't he challenge them to use their weapons again? Of course, they could not do a thing to him in the darkness. It was his. And any of their lights could be put out. Why, he could swallow their lights as easily as he could swallow them. He would show them.

---

Sounds of gunfire woke Hantle from a fitful sleep and drew him to the bedroom window. Through the rain spots, he saw three guards retreat, shouting for Shec and Crahul to join them. Then the wolf appeared, dragging eddies of smoke behind it, and slid to a stop on the wet street. It clamped its jaws on the midriff of a woman. The wolf changed its bite to the neck, replacing her cry with a snap that resonated on the air. In a few more chomps and rips, she was devoured. Gore spread from the matted fur of its throat to mottle the rest of its pelt a blood-black.

"What is it?" Lorenca asked from the bed.

There was no way he could adequately describe it. "Come see for yourself," he said.

She scooted to the end of the bed and craned her neck, but came no further.

The guards jabbed the rods up and down the barrel a hundred times to pack shot and powder, and this provoked a deep growl from the wolf. The sound squeezed Hantle's gut and riveted his feet to the floorboards. The growl persisted as it stepped backward, and Hantle hoped the weapons would again be what kept the creature at bay. Shec and Crahul came into view, making it four to one. When it turned and ran, he laughed with relief. Instead of rushing back into the trees, the wolf continued along the forest's perimeter. The guards chased after it, two of them struggling to pour powder into the flashpans as they moved.

Hantle's excitement morphed into a groan when the wolf, without breaking its stride, swallowed one of the lanterns, whole and burning. How . . .? Within seconds, it had taken a second and third lantern. The grounds were significantly darkened, and Hantle temporarily lost view of the creature.

Shec slammed into the ground as the wolf bit at her shoulder. Her scream pulled Lorenca to the window just as the canine tore off a leg. The guards fell back several steps and Hantle realized the wolf's size: its raised hackles reached higher than any of them stood. Panic spread from Shec to the guards as her cry reached a new pitch; one dropped his weapon and fled. In an instant, the wolf drowned the sound, its punishing teeth ripping away her rib cage and extracting the lungs themselves.

When Crahul's musket failed to fire, he tossed it away, looking betrayed, and pulled a pistol from his waist. A yelp went up as his shot hit the beast's withers. The wolf reared and pounced on Crahul, whose body shattered under its impact. It clawed across the throat of the petrified guard standing beside, and before she hit the ground, had her in its jaws.

Lorenca sucked in air, trembling, and without looking away from the creature, said, "Why aren't you moving? Go. Help them!" Hantle sidestepped to the door, uncertain of whether she meant it. He was afraid of destroying their marriage by leaving the bedroom. She must have noticed his hesitation because she looked at him, eyes wide, and shouted, "Go!"

Hantle raced downstairs, grabbed his musket, and stepped out into the drizzle. In the brief interim, the creature had abandoned the bodies and ripped apart the last guard, who had tried to flee. Before Hantle could take aim, it moved off and blended into the gloom. Rounfil ran to his side, with Eayol just behind.

"Shit," Rounfil said.

Hantle moved to Crahul's side and felt for a pulse. "He got a shot in," he said.

"What?"

"Crahul," Hantle said. "He hit the wolf in the back, believe it or not. So the wolf is mortal, but only just." He closed his eyes and moved his fingers around, hoping to find the heartbeat. When certain there was none, he wiped a bloodied hand on his pants and stood.

Screams. Screams from the west edge of Founsel.

The three of them ran toward it. Who had it gotten now?

Hantle stopped and gasped for air, stunned to find that one of the homes had a hole where the front door ought to have been. The wolf had burst its way inside, and Hantle heard it clawing its way up to the sleeping loft. He saw two figures run at the window, but the canine dragged them away before they could undo the lock. Silence wrenched its way back into the village.

Hantle stumbled backward as the window exploded outward and glass clattered to the street. The creature dropped from the house to the street, stomach bulging. A group just down the street shouted and began to flee. He couldn't make out a single word, but the commotion drew the wolf's gaze. It would have to cross the village square to reach them. Just enough time to get a shot off. Hantle heaved up his musket and Rounfil did the same. The wolf sprinted and Hantle led it several feet. As flint struck frizzen, both muskets rang out in opposition. The demon's head jerked and it veered off course. Hantle's heart thumped. Please let them have hit.

Rounfil lowered his musket and pointed. "We got one of its ears."

Indeed, Hantle saw the remains of an ear hanging from the beast's head. Blood streamed from the wound and stained the fur on the side of its head. But the thing did not topple over. It closed in on the terrified souls. Eayol fired and a puff of dirt at the wolf's foot indicated the miss.

Others nearby poured out of their homes. Hantle dropped his firearm and drew a long knife. There was not enough time to reload before it attacked again. The sight of the villagers filled him with hope. He bellowed into the night and charged the wolf.

By the time Hantle reached it, the beast had swallowed two others and scooped up a third. It jerked its head side to side and pieces of the man came apart, hitting the ground like wet rags. Hantle raced in, blade raised high, and the wolf squared up. Aiming for the eyes, he brought the knife down. The canine read his move, backed out of the way, and lunged forward. Hantle missed, reeled his arm back, and arced the knife out wide, toward the wolf's flank. In mid-air, the animal lurched in an attempt to lessen the blow, but there was no avoiding it.

The knife sank into the matted fur near the shoulder just as the wolf's teeth sank into Hantle's arm. When its paws landed on the ground again, it sidestepped, drawing the blade along bone and muscle, and released its bite. With a yowl, it ducked away from the knife and retreated a few feet. Hantle saw the long, channeled tear in the flesh just below the destroyed ear. Pain flared through his mind and he crumpled to the ground, clutching his arm to his stomach. The bastard thing had bitten him!

A strange thunk sounded and the wolf staggered sideways. Rounfil gripped under Hantle's armpits and dragged him back. That's when Hantle saw the source of the sound: a hand axe stuck out of the wolf's ribcage. Eayol gripped a second axe in her hand and screamed, daring the fiend to approach.

With a final, sweeping look around the growing crowd, the creature thought twice. It contorted and, using its teeth, plucked the axe from its side. Then it scrambled back, turned, and sprinted off. They had scared it! Except . . . it was headed right for the guards they had left behind. Crahul and Shec! Hantle had scarcely finished the thought and already the creature loped toward the forest with three mangled bodies dangling from its maw.

Hantle staggered to his feet, grimacing at the agony stabbing up his arm, and watched the wolf dissolve into darkness. He reluctantly accepted that there was no way he could give chase. "Will someone get Yilrouth?" he said.

Without a word, Rounfil ran off.

Hantle's energy left him and he slumped down. How bad was it? He eased the arm out and saw a row of puncture wounds oozing blood. He had expected worse. Gore covered his shirt. Drenched it, really. They had gotten it pretty good too, but had it been enough? The pain swelled; he shut his eyes and focused on the sound of water dripping from rooftop to puddle.

## CHAPTER TEN

HANTLE SAT in Yilrouth's office, his right arm extended on the table. The bleeding of the wounds had slowed, but that was about to change. Yilrouth set a bowl of water on the table and adjusted the dial on a lantern for more light.

"I'm going to flush out and clean the bite wounds," Yilrouth said. "We want to avoid infection." He set a long, flat pan under Hantle's arm. "This will catch the runoff." He leaned over the arm, then looked at Hantle out of the corner of his eye. "Ready?"

Hantle turned away from the doctor's implements and focused on the lantern. "I guess." The initial wave of cold water wasn't bad. Sort of soothing. It was the prying, probing, and flushing Yilrouth did next that caused Hantle to clench his teeth. "Will it need stitches?" he asked.

Yilrouth set aside a bloody cloth and reached for a clean one. "I try not to with these sort of bites, but we'll see how deep they go."

Hantle watched the movement of the flame and lost track of the time until he heard a voice.

"Hantle?" Lorenca's face peeked into the doorway. "Hantle!" She hurried into the room.

Seeing her surprised him. "What's wrong?" he said. "Why are you here? Are you hurt?"

Lorenca's eyes grew wide. "Me?" Her tired laugh matched the circles under her eyes. "I was looking for you. You're the one who's hurt. I'm fine."

He shrugged with his free arm. "Yilrouth's taking care of it," he said. "The wolf bit my arm but I got it better."

Lorenca stepped forward, looked at his arm, then away again. She was strong in a lot of ways but not when it came to the sight of blood. "It looks horrible! How bad is it, Yilrouth? Is it horrible?"

"No." Yilrouth gave a small headshake. "It is not horrible." He stopped his work and took a breath. "Would you please wait outside so I can properly focus?"

"Sorry, sorry," Lorenca whispered and backed out of the room.

Within a few minutes, Yilrouth had moved on to swabbing the wounds with alcohol-dipped gauze. He became talkative. "Which house did the wolf get into?"

"The Gulfich's." Hantle flinched at the burn.

"Ah. They had two young ones. Has anyone looked in there yet?"

"I plan to do that next but don't expect to find anything."

Yilrouth nodded and pulled out a jar of ointment. "Shouldn't need stitches," he said. He spread the salve with a single finger. "I was surprised, but it doesn't look to have bitten you all that badly."

"That's a relief," Hantle said. "It let go after I got my blade in its shoulder."

"That said, it will still take some time to heal." Yilrouth unwound a roll of gauze and wrapped Hantle's forearm. "Try to be careful with it, especially the first few days." He finished off the bandage with a knot. "You're all set."

"Thank you, sir," Hantle said.

"You're welcome." Yilrouth moved to a bowl of clean water and scrubbed his hands. "I'll be out momentarily to gather the dead."

Hantle found Lorenca leaning against the side of the house and raised the bandaged arm for her to see. "All taken care of."

Her face eased as she inspected the doctor's handiwork. "Okay, good. That wasn't all too long."

"Didn't even need stitches."

"How's the pain?" She took his good hand into hers. "Can I do anything for you?"

"Pain's manageable. Why don't you head home, dear? The wolf attacked the Gulfich's house and I want to check that out."

"Okay," she replied, to his surprise. "You do what you have to do." Maybe seeing the wolf herself had caused the change in her attitude.

He kissed her forehead and said, "Thank you, Lorenca. I'll be home shortly."

---

Hantle and Rounfil approached the Gulfich's house. Rounfil lifted a lantern high, illuminating the fractured doorway and window above. Both holes in the dwelling were ragged with splinters and gaped black. Creaks from the floor followed Hantle into the building and a chill slid down his spine. The only light was from Rounfil's lantern, but it was enough for the small space. A mess of broken belongings lay scattered about.

"Hello?" Rounfil called. "Anyone here?"

Claw marks had gouged through the floorboards of the loft, allowing blood to drip through and pool on the ground. That seemed answer enough, but Hantle turned over the furniture, hoping that one of the children might have hidden and gone unnoticed. No one was hidden, though. They climbed the staircase, hardly recognizable now, and found the loft even worse off. Blood coated the floor and splattered the walls. Where the window and its wall had been broken through, the roof buckled and sagged. A jutting nail impaled a bit of fabric, which fluttered in a breeze. The bed and every other piece of furniture had been reduced to wreckage, and they found no person or any bodies. The family was a complete loss to the glutton.

Hantle staggered against a wall and felt the reality of the night settling over him. "The wolf took my sons, and every night since, it's killed more and more." He pointed to where the bed had been. "They were asleep, I'm sure, when it came in. Why does it—I mean, look at this. How does an animal do *this*?"

"I have no idea why this beast is after us"—Rounfil shook his head and set the lantern down—"I do know, however, we're giving it one hell of a time. One of us took off its ear, and there's a good chance our other shot landed." He became more animated with every word. "You sliced its side open, I know that for damn certain. Maybe got an artery. And Eayol landed a good blow with the axe. It was scared as shit when it turned tail and ran. I saw the fear in its eyes. You know what I think? I think it's bleeding out in the forest as we speak."

Rounfil made a lot of sense. "You might be right," Hantle said. Something still felt problematic, and it took him a moment to identify it. "But we wouldn't know for sure that it died. It could just as likely be off raiding some other group, like it did with Weith." Hantle pushed off the wall and moved to the hole on the other side of the room. The view looked out to the meadow in which his sons had played countless times. He imagined them there now, running and throwing handfuls of grass at each other. "The uncertainty would be terrible." His thoughts shifted and produced a broken coop in the air before him, topped with pale heads. "I'll only believe it dead when it's under my boot, with a shot in the head."

Rounfil put a hand on Hantle's good shoulder. "If it comes back tomorrow," he said, "I think we can manage that."

"Oh, it will be back tomorrow," Hantle said. "Larger and hungrier than before, which is what worries me most."

"We'll do what we can, Hantle." Rounfil took another look around. "Think anyone will live here again?"

Hantle shook his head. "The damage could be fixed but the horror won't wash out."

"Ready to get out of here?"

# CHAPTER ELEVEN

THE SUN HAD BARELY RISEN and already Hantle took a seat beside Lorenca in the village square. He placed a hand on her lap. She was not crying and looked stronger than she had on prior days; her eyes glowed green in the sun. Sure, he still had a pit inside, but it had not consumed him entirely. It was good to see hers had not swallowed her up either.

Liova shuffled down the aisle to the front of the square. Her shoulders slumped forward with exhaustion. There again sat bales of hay streaming ribbons. Since no remains had been found of the guards slain in duty or the family killed, there were no coffins. Pirram had instead constructed small boxes. "Would any friend or family," Liova said, "who has a memento to place, please step forward?"

Hantle reached under his seat and grabbed an item. He approached the box marked "Crahul" and laid it within: the pistol with which Crahul shot the wolf. The man was certainly braver than Hantle had given him credit for. Not only had he volunteered for the guard, he was the first to injure the wolf. He returned to his seat while others placed their trinkets and tributes.

Liova went down the line of boxes and closed their lids. Each sat at an angle to display the name carved thereon. She took a seat on a hay bale, cleared her throat, and spoke. "I feel today as if my heart has been plunged into the midst of a ravaging storm. Nine people were taken from us last night: Shec, Crahul, Feiss, Nolent, Beyoleth, and the four Gulfichs. Never before have we suffered so bitter a loss. We gather to remember each of them: beloved family, dear friends, and members of Founsel. The first five we owe a special debt for their service in the night watch. They sacrificed their lives. To protect us. To protect Founsel. They were a shelter against the storm and lessened its blows."

Hantle looked to his bandaged arm and felt a pang of guilt. It wasn't right. He deserved more than the bite, far more. He should have been out there with them. Instead, he had been in bed, resting while they faced the wolf. First, he failed to save his boys, and now he couldn't even be vigilant in their honor? Lorenca squeezed his hand and brought his thoughts back to the funeral.

"We must weather the tempest," Liova said, "just as the trees and mountains do. Even the winds do not last forever. They will spend themselves, and the branches will settle." She stood to lay lilies, a faint yellow, along the boxes. In nearby seats, the surviving family members clutched mourning wreaths whose tiny bells rang as they stood. "Let us lay these brave comrades to rest and take rest ourselves. This day is hard won. The Void is not everlasting, though it may seem so. We will cry and rage and be sick with grief. But at least we have that honor. This day is hard won." She invited up the bearers, who each took a box and led the procession.

Hantle fell in line and sweat raced down the back of his knees. Humid air seemed to buoy up the layer of clouds overhead. No gruesome findings today had been a respite, but it was marred by the fact that the wolf no longer needed those heads or spines to inspire fear. Anticipation of the coming night was dread enough. What hope did they have of preventing a recurrence tonight?

People milled about in the village square after the mourning meal and the lull brought out nervous chatter and speculation about Founsel's predicament. Rounfil ran a hand through his hair and huffed. "We had run it off two nights ago, but last night it killed every guard out there. What changed? Why weren't we able to run it off again?"

"It didn't just lurk on the fringe of the village, like before," Hantle said. "It came right in and attacked straight away. It's growing fearless."

"Eh," Douth grumbled. "If I had any sense, I would have packed up and left yesterday, like the shepherd had been smart to do."

The thought shocked Hantle. "Could you honestly leave Founsel?"

"Yes!" Douth said. "Why in the hell would anyone stay? That's what I want to know."

"Running would never come into my mind. Founsel's always been my home. Nothing—especially no animal—is going to change that."

"Suit yourself," Douth said, "but I don't want to die here."

"Dying in a strange land seems preferable, then?"

Douth opened his mouth to reply but Liova cut him off.

"Boys . . ." She tut-tutted. "We have better things to do than listen to your tiff." She yawned into her hand. "I was up all night poring over papers. Researching this." A few sheets of paper waggled in her hand. "I suspect this wolf is more than it appears." The papers disappeared into a pocket.

"What do you mean," Lorenca asked, "more than it appears? What're those papers?"

"My, my, it feels a lifetime ago, but in my younger years, I attended the College of Arcanum in Bansuth. My studies focused on the Three Mechanisms. Abstract, I know, but I've been taken by the stories ever since I heard them as a child. The chance to delve into the texts and all the essays and philosophizing related to them seemed a unique chance. I sought to understand how the Mechanisms relate to the wider world. In time, I did glimpse how *deeply* they influence everything."

Hantle was no scholar. He had no inkling of the essays and philosophizing she meant. "Influence in what way?" He feared sounding foolish, but wouldn't the rest of them be thinking the very same?

"Subtle ways," she said. "Ways that are dispersed both across the face of Iomesel and through time. Ways that stretch beyond normal human reckoning because the connection between them is faint—barely perceptible—even when you're looking for that thread of similarity."

"You're losing me," Rounfil said. "Can't you talk more simply?" Hantle felt relief that he was not alone.

"I'm getting ahead of myself, too. Before Iomesel existed, or any of the cosmos, there was the ethereal fabric, the All. A miniscule imperfection *in* the All spawned a tear, the Void, which started small but grew to consume the All, wreaking its havoc in the Cataclysm. That's the simplest description of the First Mechanism. There's more to it, but what's most important to us right now is how the Void arose with no warning and for no apparent reason. I see it as the original destructive force, later balanced by the constructive forces of the Song and, with it, life.

"As a flaw in the All spawned the Void, so it also seems that flaws in our world spawn calamities, however infrequently, such as hurricanes, quakes, or famines. Taking this a bit further, the wolf is, to my mind, rather like these disasters: striking with no warning and for no apparent reason." She paused, then added, "With me so far?"

"So," Eayol said, "you're saying this wolf is like a . . . a hurricane?"

"In a way, yes. But I'm establishing a groundwork that we can expand upon." Liova cleared her throat before going on. "The creature relates to my studies in another way. Several years in, after my mentor insisted I specialize, my focus gravitated toward the sudden disappearance of far-flung lands. Initially, it does not seem that there are many instances of this. Have you heard of any lost lands on the Fist?"

Hantle pondered this for a moment before shaking his head. Those around him did the same. She was really out in the weeds here. How was she going to bring this all together?

"That's because the Fist, and our beloved Far Finger, are relatively young lands—in terms of human exploration and settlement. Other lands—places we would have hardly heard of, let alone visited—are much older. Places where civilizations have been present for many centuries. Some of these places continue to thrive, having undergone changes along the way that ensured the survival of the city, kingdom, empire, what have you. Other locales are not so fortunate. You see, there are tales out there, if you ask the right people and listen at the right time. Tales of peoples and lands winking out." She snapped a finger. "Like so."

Lorenca leaned against Hantle. "Yes, okay," she said. "Where are you going with this?"

Liova held up her hands in supplication. "Bear with me, please. I have a point, and we'll be there presently.

"Each tale describes an event which results in the disappearance of a peopled land, but there are two other similarities between them: The doom was executed by a creature of immense power, and a celestial event followed shortly thereafter. I know, I know," she hurried on, waving off eye rolls, "this generality makes little sense. Let me give you specifics." She extracted the papers from her pocket, unfolded them, and handed them to the group. "I brought the three most detailed accounts I've gathered. Be sure to pass them around."

Hantle received one of these. He held it out so that Lorenca and Eayol could see. The text itself was written in an ornate script while the margins were stuffed with blocks of notes belonging to several different hands.

Liova went on. "The general theme is that, with no warning and for no apparent reason, a beast comes from the wild, devours everything it can, and wipes out an entire city or countryside. The destruction is followed by an upheaval in the firmament above. Take these three for example. In a mountainous country, a bear razed an entire kingdom, surrounding mountains and all. An archipelago in a major coastal trade route was bitten apart and gulped down by a shark, its location later marked by just flotsam. In the depths of a sweltering jungle, the whole of its capital city was scooped up and consumed by a jaguar, including several hundreds of feet of land beneath it, leaving only a gigantic hole in the ground. Each of these is correlated with a celestial event: the appearance of a guest star, a solar eclipse, and the arrival of a comet, respectively."

"You think the wolf is like one of these creatures?" Rounfil asked.

"I don't know so but I fear so."

Eayol grabbed the paper from Hantle and held it closer to her eyes. Squinting, she said, "How are the animals and eclipses and things related?"

"That's the question I've pondered most. Does the creature cause the cosmos to react? Or is the creature a portent of forthcoming cosmic upheaval? Unfortunately, this is another thing of which I cannot be certain. Though I hazard to guess that the creature is caused by the event, even though it comes before. Like the tingle before a lightning strike.

"The Void started as the tiniest of holes and spread from its origin to engulf everything. We may be witnessing something similar. The beginnings of a split in the cosmos that is growing larger, to culminate in the destruction of . . ." Her eyes focused to infinity beyond the crowd. "Well, again, it's hard to predict." Her gaze snapped back. "Founsel, at least. Perhaps more."

"I will be the first to recognize the wolf's danger," Hantle said, "but isn't it a leap to compare it to the creatures in these tales?"

Liova crossed her arms. "I am surprised to hear that doubt from you, Hantle. You have seen it several times." She motioned to his bandaged arm. "Even wrestled with it. Doesn't its size swell more each night? Instead of hunting, it embarks on a brutal rampage. Every aspect feels unnatural."

Hantle looked to clouds overhead and the few patches of blue sky between. "Why have we seen nothing happen in the sky?"

"This is still the tingle. The lightning strike comes ne—"

"Is there mention," Rounfil interrupted, "of whether the people ever fought back?"

"No, there is not."

"Well, shit." He tossed up his hands. "You're saying there's no way to defeat it?"

"We can't be certain they didn't fight it, of course"—Liova waggled a finger—"We can only be certain there's no record of it. These stories have survived through oral tradition long before they were ever placed in writing. It's only natural that some aspects have been lost to time. For the same reason, we do not know what happened to the beast after the ruin was wrought."

Eayol brushed a stray hair behind her ear. "Still, if it's a destructive force, as you've called it, operating on the scale of the cosmos, what hope do we have of resisting it?"

Clasping her hands before her, Liova smiled. "This is the part I find most encouraging. This is a force altogether different from storm or plague. This one has a body. Hantle can speak himself to harming it. And we have an opportunity that no other location has had: knowing what peril the wolf brings. Unlike the winds, there's a chance of stopping an animal. There are many brave people and loaded muskets in Founsel."

If Hantle understood things, there was no option of running it off, of resolving this without more death. They had not stopped the beast with five guards, but when the villagers spilled out of their homes and surrounded the thing, they stood a chance.

A chuckle started off quiet but grew louder and Douth's whole body moved as he shook his head. "She's out of her mind." He looked around the square, still laughing. "Telling us the world threatens to destroy us and expecting we'll wait for it to come down on our ears. Ha ha ha. Absolutely not. The sensible thing is getting far, far away."

Olyul spoke up from the back. "I'm no warrior and my daughter could not hope to outrun the demon. What about a middle ground? Board up our homes so the wolf has no way in and lie low overnight. Make the village look abandoned."

"That's an enticing thought," Hantle said, "but it took a large risk when it attacked last night. One that paid off. It'll grow more today, and I'm afraid that will make it more brazen yet. It would be folly to think it will pass through here peacefully."

"Now you can read the minds of beasts?" Douth seemed determined to mock Hantle.

Rounfil stepped forward and grabbed Douth's collar, twisting it in his fist. "Hantle here's got a lid he can put on his temper, but I ain't got one myself. If you're gonna scoot on out of here, you best get to it." He pulled his arm in so their faces nearly touched. "You hear me, coward? Scoot." Giving him a push, Rounfil let go of the shirt.

Hantle expected Douth would retaliate but saw uncertainty cross his face. Without another word, Douth backed away and stomped off.

Rounfil shook out his fists and turned to Olyul like nothing had happened. "That's a decent idea, but wolves operate on smell more than sight. It'd smell us all here, even if it couldn't see us. I have to agree with Hantle. I don't see it letting us be."

Hantle did a rough calculation. "We've got how many adults in Founsel? Fifty or so? What if every one of us were out tonight? We would have numbers on our side."

Rounfil smiled. "Fifty to one are odds I'd take."

"Fifty of us," Eayol said, "ought to give us no option but to bring it down."

Olyul shifted her feet, looking bashful. "Excuse me, but wouldn't that leave all the children alone?"

"I'll watch them." Lorenca squeezed Hantle's hand before stepping forward. "I thought Hantle foolish for wanting to join the night watch. But after seeing the wolf last night, I know how brave he's been to do so. He's out there not only for my sake, but for all our sakes. And any who join him are just as brave. Bring as many children over as needed. I'll keep watch over them, while you keep watch over Founsel."

Olyul gave her a hopeful smile. "Could you use some help?"

"Yes, of course. You know how rowdy children can be."

Liova patted Olyul's arm. "Really swells your heart, seeing how a village of close-knit people comes together."

"I've just remembered something else strange." Hantle said. "The wolf attacked the guard, but it also ate several of the lanterns we had hung out." Several eyebrows rose. "Ate them, yes. Burning and all."

Liova nodded, unsurprised. "That is further proof the canine is unnatural. I've said before, wolves have no love for light. It burns them, addles their minds, makes them fearful. Use that to your advantage. Set out every lantern we have. Then start bonfires. Founsel has no shortage of wood."

"Yes, we can light up the entire village." Hantle looked across all the faces standing in the square. "I know how daunting this might seem," he said, "but I hope every one of you will join us in the watch tonight. If you cannot, please consider another way to contribute. Liova said this day is hard won, and she is right. It is paid for in blood by those we lost. Let's make them proud of what we do tonight."

---

There was still a risk to having Lorenca, Olyul, and the children in a home. The wolf had broken into and out of the Gulfich's without issue. Pirram had the idea of driving nails through the flat side of wooden planks and affixing them to doors and windows. The spiked fortifications would deny the creature easy access. Hantle joined Pirram, Rounfil, and Eayol in the project and they had Hantle's house secured in short order. Others praised the fierce effect this gave the building and asked for the treatment to be applied to their homes. Since it did not require great precision or time, Hantle had no qualms about this. If protecting another home meant two more joining the night watch, then the effort was worthwhile.

It was when he and Rounfil hauled a set of nail boards to one of these other houses that Hantle noticed Douth talking to a handful of people. He could not make out their discussion, but they nodded and shook hands before splitting up. Each person returned to their respective home and, with their spouse and children, packed housewares and valuables into covered wagons. Douth had already pulled his wagon, overflowing with furniture and trunks, into the street.

Hantle nodded his head their way. "Do you see that?" he said. "Evidently, Douth recruited a few families to flee with him." He counted five wagons, including Douth's.

Rounfil frowned. "Didn't know yellow-belly spread so easy."

"That means, what, nearly ten fewer for the watch?"

"If they'll just skitter at the first sign of the wolf, then we're better off without them."

Hantle kept an eye on the wagons as he worked. Within an hour, a caravan formed on the southern end of the village. He thought of saying goodbye to them but couldn't bring himself to approach. He was afraid that listening to their excuses would give him the yellow-belly, no matter how much he despised it. Maybe some of the villages in Liova's tales knew about their creatures too, but fell apart when the fear took hold. He imagined her voice saying, "Perhaps, but we cannot be certain." Certain or not, he would join his fellow villagers in the night watch and attempt to avoid repeating their doom.

A tension left him when the clatter of wheels over cobblestone signaled the movement of the caravan. Dust from the procession rose above the treetops in the stagnant air. The haze was still visible after Hantle had finished supper and drained his second mug of jursant. He stepped inside, set the empty mug on the kitchen table, and watched as Lorenca spread out a blanket for one of the children who had just arrived. She smiled at the toddler, who blew a raspberry. Hantle envied how quickly the young forgot their fear. He gave Lorenca a hug and kiss and whispered in her ear, "I'm glad to see you smiling, love." He moved to take his musket from its spot on the transom and spoke so the kids could hear him, "Take good care of Miss Lorenca for me, okay?" The girl nodded in the enthusiastic way only possible for a little one.

Darkness rode the sky from east to west and filled the forest from the roots up. Hantle met the guards in the square and helped distribute the equipment: muskets and pistols, black powder and shot, knives and axes. In the glow of the lanterns and bonfires, the outfit looked grim and aggressive.

# CHAPTER TWELVE

THE WOLF CLAWED his way out of his day hide. He had searched long and far to Founsel's east for the cave to shelter from the day, but he had grown so large during his rest that he risked becoming stuck. The burn penetrating into his muscles reminded him each second that the sun was still in the sky. He whimpered. Several spots on his body seemed to concentrate the pain, with one of these being his right forepaw. He gnawed at it, the act repriving him momentarily, until he tasted blood. He stopped and cocked his head. An urge drove him to keep his teeth active, for this was the sole action capable of providing respite, but would he chew off his own leg to satisfy it? After licking the wound clean, he picked up a branch and set to stripping its bark instead. A glance to the sky told that darkness was still some ways off.

Once the branch was in splinters, he could no longer endure the agony. Dusk would be eons in the coming. He oriented his eyes away from the sun and moved off in search of a ravine or hill or cave larger yet—anything to provide shade from the lengthening rays. The wound where the axe had bitten into his side, which had initially bled fiercely then scabbed over when he lay curled up in the cave, pulled the musculature of his ribs taut, giving his gait a limp.

Miles later, he came upon a wide gulch formed by a creek. As far as he knew, it was the only meaningful depression in the landscape. Wide enough to contain him, certainly, but too shallow, even when laying flat. He excavated the mud, rocks, and vegetation until he was capable of escaping his entire form into shadow. Yet the misery did not dissipate. He panted and his tongue flicked out of his mouth, again and again, as if he were trying to be rid of some foul taste. Repetitious action and perseveration consumed him as the blazing orb lowered on the horizon. What could he do to avoid the light but wait for it to disappear? What could he do, what could he do, what could he do?

Eat it, he had eaten it. Yes, he had eaten them: the lanterns surrounding the village. The night was his and he could bring it to the lighted parts, eat his way through the lanterns until shrouded in black. Blackblackblackbloodblackbloodstained his legs and stomach; he brought that blood out by eating them and eating more each night. Under the shroud, he acted at his peak of ability and gorged on the terror and screams and flesh that yielded to his fangs.

Unable to identify why, he pushed himself up and sat on his haunches. Blindblindblindblazeblindstained his vision and mind; he sent up a howl, calling out to the orb that drove him to eating them and eating more each night. It was nothing but present and nothing but eternal. He leapt into the air, snapping his gore-stained jaws at the distant epicenter of his rage. Oughtn't he grow and eat it and become the present, the eternal? Yes! Yes, eat it! He had eaten them and he could eat the rest of them and the rest of it and find how the bloodblack presenteternal ends all his pain and starts all his life.

---

Twilight calmed the wolf's anxieties and he moved back toward Founsel. The travel took him longer than prior evenings because his size was such that now he had to pick a judicious path between trees or suffer a slog through the canopies of the lower-growing ones. Any hint of blue or purple was completely gone by the time he, still a small distance away, noticed the lights. Lanterns burned, shining beyond the edge of the forest. Fires popped, whirling sparks into the sky. An owl on a branch at eye level with the wolf hooted and took wing. Too small a specimen to bother with. There was better meat ahead.

The wolf lowered himself for a stealthier approach, but the noises the villagers emitted would have likely been enough to mask his movement, regardless. The trees thinned and eventually revealed guards circling the perimeter of the houses in various states of watchfulness. There were many more than any other night. He had provoked quite the reaction. His stomach gurgled. His quarry was right out in the open. In fact, he expected they would come to him when he howled. What ease. A drop of pus fell from his ravaged ear and a jolt flared through his withers. He was eager to bestow upon them some of the pain they had inflicted on him. Patrols covered each side of the village except for the north, which bordered the cove. There were only a few guards near the shore, all focused more on idle chatter than their surroundings. Instinct led him to strike the weakest first, and he stole through the woods toward the cove.

He entered the water, which lapped right at the forest's roots, and strands of saliva mixed with the waves that washed over his snout. Paddling to the middle of the cove was quick work but he shivered. Summer's heat had scarcely touched these depths. A wind out of the north rolled waves into the shoreline, where boats moored at the docks squeaked with each swell. He swam toward these. The cove's windblown surface concealed his position from those gathered at the bonfire closest to the docks.

His heart rate quickened, as much from the cold as from the excitement of his next attack. Fear-drenched flesh was most satisfying as it screamed in protest, ripped from the bone, and slid down the gullet. He left the water without shaking off and made for a pile of logs just beyond the boats. On the other side sat a man and woman more concerned with stoking the coals than watching their surroundings. Their slack was their ruin.

He leapt over the logs, which rose over twenty feet high, landed on the opposite side of the fire from the guards, then bounded through the flames. Water ran off his pelt, causing steam and ash to swell around him. The man's eyes found his an instant before his claws swiped. Pitched backward off his log seat, the guard wailed and bellowed. Such a glorious sound! Intestines bulged through slashes in his abdomen and waves of blood throbbed over his trembling hands. The wolf's tail wagged as he took the woman by the neck and dragged her, gurgling, to the ground. She flailed at the maw clamping her airway. No words left her, but guards nearby let up shouts of surprise in her stead. He bit, slightly slightly, until a snap ceased her struggles, and then released her. Her corpse crumpled at the end of the burn pit and the stench of singed hair marshaled his focus. Do not feed yet. End them all, stack them high; only then devour.

Already a wave of reinforcements rushed to the cove. He swallowed several nearby lanterns and darted for the forest once more, the ground shaking under his girth. None of the guards trailed him, however, and he, just yards past the forest edge, observed the whole of the night watch circle the one dying and the other dead. This stroke of luck was not lost upon him. He left the chaos behind and moved through the woodlands. Those brief seconds had taken the edge off the pain traveling through his spine in sickening waves, but relief was not yet his.

---

By the time Hantle reached the fire, Yilrouth had already removed his shirt and wrapped it around Doyen's stomach. He shouted for someone to retrieve his bag. Doyen squinted and huffed, intent on shoving the intestines back into his gut. Off to their left, the woman lay, and two others crouched beside her, but her missing throat made her fate clear. It wasn't like the wolf to leave them behind. Hantle dropped to his knees and offered his shirt to help staunch the blood. Yilrouth added it to his own, watched the fabric immediately soak through, and focused on talking to Doyen instead. "There, there. Don't fuss with it. Lie back and count to ten for me." It would have been better for the creature to finish him instead of leaving him to bleed out. Doyen's eyes slid back in their sockets and his head lolled about. Fluid leaked from his nose and mouth, running in thick strands to his hands, which ceaselessly clenched open and shut. His breath became more ragged and soon rattled a final time. Yilrouth sat back and wiped a wrist across his forehead, leaving a crimson streak in place of the sweat.

With the struggle ended, Hantle's attention shifted to the canine. Where was it now? Rounfil stood a few feet away, scanning the forest with his musket raised, but everyone else was gawking at the bodies. Hantle spoke to the nearest guards. "You two come with Rounfil and me. We'll check if it's sitting just inside the trees again." The muscles in his arm stung as he picked up his weapon—a reminder of its piercing fangs—and he changed his grip.

Screams. Screams, shouts, curses, and cries for help all went up at once from the south. Hantle's heart stammered. It was back. A realization broke upon him that nearly every guard was here at the cove. The wolf faced no opposition. Was it picking off another couple of guards? "Founsel's exposed," he yelled, "because we bunched up. Half of you come with me, but spread out. The rest of you, stay here and spread out. We must cover all of Founsel's sides, all night."

He led the guards through the street and rounded a building, bringing the wolf into view. Heat bubbled up Hantle's scalp and rivulets of sweat ran down. Wet fur lent the damn thing a gaunt look, but it was as large as the one-story home it stood beside. Mouth, neck, and chest were coated solid with carnage; portions of its back and sides were less contaminated. Thick scabs covered the gashes in the shoulder and ribs. It sniffed around a window's nailboards. Villagers fanned out to surround the wolf and it looked across at them, more curious than fierce. Around the fringes of the ear canal now in view, the skin was raw and inflamed; pus trailed down the side of its head. Hantle's stomach dropped. Not even these wounds seemed to slow the beast.

Its concern fell back to sniffing the house. Fearful calls rose again, but . . . Were they from inside? It should have been empty. Unless they had gotten cold feet, shirked the night watch, and holed up instead. Between the nailboards on the far end of the home from where the wolf prowled, he saw fingers jut out and grasp the wood. The planks did not budge at their pushes. "Fire," he ordered. "Kill it!" His musket and pistol joined the volley.

Undeterred, the wolf burst through the building's solid side wall, avoiding entirely the nailboards. It hunched down and clawed so its front half disappeared inside. The screams turned primal. It would take time before they could fire another round. Hantle dropped his musket and powder horn, charged the window, and heaved at the edges of the boards blocking the family's escape. Thrashing at the other end indicated the wolf's forward movement. Other hands joined his at prying and they loosed one of the boards enough to remove it.

The father inside shouted, "Please, get the children out!" Behind him, the wolf filled the whole space and inched closer.

Through the hole, Hantle locked eyes with the man and said, "Help lift them up." The opening was not large enough for either one of them, though. "One more board ought to do it."

Rounfil produced a fighting knife, slid the blade between the board and the home and hauled back on the handle for leverage. Splinters popped and the corner of the plank fell away, leaving too little to work against. "You fucking try," Rounfil said and handed Hantle the knife. Terrified eyes watched as he worked, but a shearing sound drew their gaze. The wolf's progress had buckled the front of the home, causing a load-bearing beam to slip and crush the father. Out of his hand fell a lantern that broke and its flame lapped up the oil, which trailed away and pooled about the kitchen table.

The children recoiled from the fire and retreated to a far corner. Hantle kept working at the board, but it would do no good if they were too afraid to come near. Flames licked up the legs of table and chairs. "Come on, come over here," he told them. "Once we get this board off, we'll pull you out. But you have to come here, so we can reach you." The nails affixing the board to the home squeaked as they slid out. "It's almost there, so you have to come here now."

They took a few hesitant steps toward him, their eyes locked on the spreading flames. The beast barked and the force of it resonated through the wood and blade into Hantle's hand. When the roof slumped into the space left by the fallen timber, the wolf snaked forward several feet and got its teeth on the unconscious father. The boy and girl staggered back into the corner and curled into balls. Crackling flames jumped from the chairs to a heap of burlap sacks and crates just below the window, and Hantle's stomach dropped. He had only a moment before the blaze would block this exit entirely. The beast tugged the father out from under the beam and its eyes reflected the fire. Its eyes! If he could blind one of its eyes, that would give them an immense advantage. Hantle shouted over his shoulder. "Someone give me a gun, now!"

The chill of pistol's barrel met his palm and he aimed it through the growing smoke and heat shimmers. Steady, steady, he commanded his arms, but they continued to tremble regardless. He squeezed the trigger until the flint drove headlong into the frizzen. The eruption echoed through the house and each bite mark in his arm seared with the recoil. He took a step back as the smoke from the barrel clouded his view, suddenly afraid teeth or claws would lash through the haze. A yelp joined the children's screams and the building lurched. The wolf stood, bursting the home open in the process. The fire enjoyed a breath of oxygen and smoke billowed through the collapsing roof. Hantle scrambled back from the sparks rushing out of the window. The children were trapped and helpless. Was there any other way in? Debris followed the creature as he stepped away from the house. In the fraction of a second between the wolf becoming visible and it running toward the guard, Hantle looked for indication of whether his shot had hit the eye, but the lighting was too poor to tell. Then it was moving again. The father hung from the beast's jaws, yet it was able to scoop up another three of the guards as it made for tree cover.

Hope welled in his chest. He had kept it from taking the children, or . . . did he have the flames to thank? Either way, there was a chance of rescuing the children. The wall here leaned at an awkward angle but was otherwise intact. He looked to Rounfil and said, "Can we go in through one of the other sides?"

"Let's try the hole it left behind." Rounfil moved toward the missing end of the house. "That's our best chance."

Hantle shouted to the guards nearby, "Be ready for when it returns," and followed Rounfil.

Lumber and housewares riddled the opening and Rounfil held his collar over his mouth in order to near the smoke-filled room. He looked back to Hantle, eyes saying there was no chance, but Hantle could not abandon them yet. If he crouched, he could find a path between the wreckage, get to the corner, grab the two, and follow the same route back. He drew in a large clean breath and stepped into the space.

Rounfil's hand gripped his shoulder, halting his advance. "Don't. You'll end up trapped with them," he shouted over the roar. "It's nearly engulfed."

Shingles from the fractured roof clattered to the floorboards before Hantle. It didn't matter. There was still a chance, however remote, he could save them, unlike with his own sons. Wasn't that their pleas he heard begging for him to grab them? He shrugged off Rounfil's hand and prepared to leap over the shingles.

Before he could jump, Rounfil wrapped his arms around Hantle's chest and lugged him back. "You'll kill yourself, you bastard." Off balance, Hantle struggled, but Rounfil had the weight advantage. "We need you alive more than dead." He kept pulling until they were on the street.

More framing drooped and the house coughed embers from its wounds. In the few seconds that had elapsed, the flames had embroiled every square inch of the room. He looked up to see others soaring dozens of feet above the roof timbers. The smoke itself glowed red. His legs gave out and Rounfil lowered him to the ground.

Rounfil took command. "Fetch water," he shouted. "Wet down anything wooden."

Hantle cleared the image of blistering, choking children from his mind and took in the scene before him. The structure's lean had only worsened, threatening to topple over and ignite the neighboring fences and houses. A line formed and extended to deliver bucketfuls of water from the farm's troughs. Hantle stood and joined them, to douse first the adjacent exterior of the home that would be reached when the leaning wall gave out.

They were focused on this task when a howl carried through the air. The hairs on Hantle's neck stood on end as the sound trailed off. He lowered the bucket to his side and walked toward the forest, aware that he had left his musket somewhere else. At the cove? Or the pistol, was it beside the window of the house? The ground seemed to quiver. He looked to Rounfil and then to the forest. "Do you feel that?"

"The tremor in the ground?" Rounfil nodded. "Yes."

The space between trees was colorless and featureless. As he stood there, Hantle noticed the shaking grow more pronounced. A faint popping noise registered with him, but it was not from the burning house. Then, the flapping of wings succeeded by shrieks, but the flock could not be seen. He stiffened with apprehension.

"Wolf's coming," he cried. "Ready your arms!" He dropped his bucket and looked about for a spare musket.

Quaking in the tree canopy caught his attention. Colossal boughs burst from trunks and fell to the ground; faint markings in the resulting gaps revealed the wolf's location. Muskets threw their voices into the night.

"Wait!" He threw his hands in the air and waved to his guards. "Don't waste your rounds. Wait until it comes out to shoot. Reload and wait!"

The woodlands quieted and the ground stilled.

Then the tree line exploded outward. Leaves, branches, and fur rushed toward the group. The demon closed its jaws over a woman's midriff and flung her skyward. Her arms and legs splayed and she tumbled two, three times before hitting the ground with a sickening staccato. It leapt toward a group of guards and Hantle dashed for the musket that had fallen from the woman's hands. He found the hammer still cocked, and, hoping it was loaded, pivoted around and sighted the beast's stomach. His musket roared with authority and others joined his.

Shaking with the impact of the rounds, the beast raised his hackles and howled. This deep call pierced Hantle's resolution; its wavering modulation mimicked an entire pack. Eayol let up a cry of her own and hurled a hand axe, which the wolf saw but did not attempt to avoid. The bit sank into the wasteland clotting its throat but could not reach sufficient purchase, retreating with each inhalation until, finally loose, it fell uselessly to the ground.

The remaining will of the night watch dissolved, and guards threw down their weapons and fled for the forest themselves. Hantle remembered the need to reload his musket and set to it, keeping an eye on the wolf. A curtain on a house's second story fell shut, and Hantle knew another family would be trapped in the very home they had imagined safer than standing guard. The wolf suffered no setback as it thrust its head through the window and Hantle closed in, tamping powder with the ramrod.

Rounfil was beside him, pointing to his stomach. "See how it reacted when we shot its belly?"

"Yessir. We'll aim for that again?"

"Damn right."

Hantle dropped the ramrod and opened the flash pan to receive a pinch of powder when the wolf, head inside the house, shook violently to and fro. The structure disintegrated. His snout caught the roof, flinging it up and away. Hantle could not move quickly enough—

Black.

# CHAPTER THIRTEEN

HANTLE WAS first aware of his breath, how the back of his throat burned with each intake, the wheeze on the exhale, and the shortness of it. His face lay in damp grass and, as he lifted it up, he noticed the wooden cover over him and the shingles strewn about. As if from a lifetime ago, a vague recollection surfaced of the roof dislocating from its house and blotting out the stars overhead. A dense layer of smoky fog floated just above the ground visible through a hole in the gable end ahead of him. Nearby flames, diffusing through the fog, were all that lit it up. So it was still night.

His left eye was swollen nearly shut; his forehead just above the eye throbbed. A tingle in his throat started him coughing and he could not get a full breath. There was pressure on his back. Looking and reaching toward his feet, he found the beam responsible for it. With weak arms, he tried crawling forward, only to find movement impossible. He was pinned. Turning his head to the other side, he saw Rounfil looking at him, face pale and hand outstretched in his direction. Hantle whispered to him, "Are you stuck too?" This single question brought him to coughing again and when it faded his eyes locked on the wooden beam protruding from Rounfil's chest. Hantle reached out a hand as far as he could, gripped the grass, and tried to pull himself a bit toward his friend, but his hand slipped, leaving his fingers tacky with blood. "Hey, Rounfil. Can you hear me?" He choked back a sob and shouted, "Hey, Rounfil! Damnit, man, say something." But no reply came. Tears welled in his eyes and he clawed at the ground. Now a little stronger, he slid forward an inch. He pulled again and heard the fabric of his pants rip on a splinter. With agonizing slowness, Hantle extracted himself from the wreckage of the roof.

Once free, he rested his head on his forearms, feeling relief at finally getting a deep breath, and waited for the pins and needles in his legs to settle. Then he got up, crouched under the rafters, and took Rounfil's hand. It was cold and limp. Hundreds of pounds of woodwork transferred their weight through the beam that drove through his friend's chest. He would not be able to move a thing without many others to help. How hadn't it killed them both? A dim light fell on the spot he had been stuck. As far as he could tell, a small depression in the ground was all that spared him. Another inch, he imagined, and the beam would have snapped his back and trapped him. "I'm sorry, Rounfil." He gently drew down his eyelids. "I'll see if I can get someone to help lift all this off. I'll just . . ." He lost the thought, hung his head, and made his way out from under the roof.

Hantle stood and, keeping a hand on the roof, tested his unsteady feet. The ripping sound earlier had been the waistline of his pants, which now threatened to fall off completely. To prevent that, he bunched up the material into his fist and held it tight at his belly button. Thusly secured, his attention shifted to the quiet night surrounding him. The fog was too thick to see farther than a few yards in any direction. It occurred to him that the wolf might still be in the area, so he listened. A few minutes passed before he presumed it clear; the beast would not have been so quiet.

He left the roof and said, "Hello?" A wind picked up and split the fog, allowing moonlight to pierce through. Murky puffs of smoke, shimmering with an odd quality, drifted up and away. He crept his way through the village, unconsciously wary of making much noise. Every home he passed was demolished, many burnt and aglow. All let off an acrid stench. Aside from the tongues of flames and drifting patches of fog, nothing moved. His thoughts violently wrenched to Lorenca. Where was she? What of the children she watched? Forgetting his caution, he sped to his house. Upon seeing smoldering rubble in its place, he dropped to his knees and a pitiful wail escaped him. A glint of hope: mightn't she be crouched and hiding under some debris like he had? In order to free up both hands, he stripped off his pants, then waded, completely naked, into the ash and charred remains. First, he flung back the largest fragments and called out, "Lorenca. Lorenca. Lorenca." There were no signs of her at all. The soot he kicked up triggered another coughing fit, but he continued to turn over bits of furniture and shards of housewares, desperate to find some sign of her. Using the leg of a chair, he dug through a patch of charcoals cooling to a deep red. A glint in their midst grew his eye. He fished out the object and let it cool before picking it up. A ring, one he had given to Lorenca on her last birthday. The heat and collapse of the house had warped the silver, but, after wiping it on his chest, its stone shone green. Was this all he had left of her? As for the children she had been so eager to protect, there was nothing to show they had ever been there. The wolf was thorough. Tears mixed with the grime on his face, and he wept. At the start of the night, he had worked with a village full of people to defend his wife and their home. All of it now gone.

He found himself talking to the ring, talking to her. "We shot it again, you know? Rounfil and me. And the other guards too. Shots to the belly hurt it the most. Where's it now though? I suspect it's gone on to find more people. In fact, I know it has. Harsenth is closest. Yet . . . they won't have any warning it's coming, unless I can get there. I . . . I let you down. And Hultier. And Dolcium. I let Founsel down. But I'll get to Harsenth to warn them and help save them. I'll see it through. I'll see *it* dead. Make up for not saving my own. It can't take you all from me without repercussion. No, it can't take you all and not pay."

Closing his fist about the ring, he stepped out of the remnants of his life and explored further. All the lanterns had been either eaten or cast to the ground, so he was glad for the moonlight to help see by. Periodically, he shouted for survivors but received no replies. Even the farm animals and horses had been taken. A shirt, pants, and shoes he found and put on, placing the ring in the breast pocket so he could feel its shape against him. Food spilled from a few of the unburnt houses. He ate some of the bread, jerky, and fruit before gathering more into a small sack. Many weapons lay strewn across the village, giving him his choice of musket, powder horn, and bullet bag. Slinging the musket over his good arm, he winced. The pain stuttering down his back outweighed that creeping along his arm. As a counterbalance, the food in his stomach lent him energy and, when the pain subsided, he set off down the road. It was sheer luck that kept him out of view and alive at all, and he felt determined to make good use of that fortune. Bloody paw prints carrying for a ways on the dirt road lent credibility to his hunch that the wolf had left Founsel and was making its way toward Harsenth. They deserved to know about the threat coming their way. The larger settlement should have better options for both defense and offense. He was not sure how long the walk there would take, but the entire day was before him. With a sprinkling of additional luck, he might arrive before dusk.

---

Birds chirped in the predawn light as Hantle came across the first pieces of the caravan wagons. The road and bordering grass were filled with debris, but the largest piles were humped up at the forest's edge a few yards away. He guessed that when the horses spooked, they trundled toward the trees, pulling their wagons along until the wheels lodged in the roots. He searched the woods and shouted out to the miracle he hoped hid somewhere nearby, but, again, found no one.

The most terrifying aspect of the wolf was its ability to devour completely. Hantle resumed his walk eastward. Ahead, the rising sun illuminated a sheet of clouds coming over the Knuckles. He took the ring from his shirt pocket and turned it over between his fingers. It was all he had left of family, home, or village.

## CHAPTER FOURTEEN

THE MOON PULSED and throbbed with light in the night sky. Hantle burped and his legs felt too small for his body. Suddenly, his hands dragged on the ground as he walked forward. But only for a moment, because he rocketed up on legs that dwarfed the trees in the surrounding forest. He saw for miles ahead of him, thanks to the moon's pulsations. He strode on—now a giant. His legs created tornadoes as he swung them forward for his next step. Ahead was the wolf and, even though it also rose out of the forest on tall legs, to Hantle it looked like a pewter figurine.

In just a few steps, Hantle approached the wolf and towered over it. It had destroyed a small settlement and the rising smoke diffused before reaching Hantle's ankles. His new perspective was surprising and Hantle laughed. The sound boomed and echoed off the Knuckles in the distance and the forest canopy below swayed with force of the sound.

The wolf looked up from his meal and locked eyes with Hantle. The tides had turned and Hantle capitalized on the moment. He raised his foot from the crater his shoe left in the ground and brought it down, swiftly, before the wolf could react. A little pop—like a pine needle in a blaze—was the last sound the wolf made. Hantle-giant bent over and picked up the decapitated carcass between thumb and index finger. The canine's head had shot off and he watched it roll to a stop. So much trouble caused by this beast. A sound behind him. His wife's call carrying on the air. She was still in Founsel.

Hantle came back to the world and the morning as his boot caught on a root. He regained his balance and shook off the vision of squashing the wolf. Conquering the creature would have to be done at his current size. The distance he had yet to cross would take more than a few steps. Birds chirped in the forest and the air was still cool. How far off was Harsenth?

---

The sun sat overhead and the atmosphere filled with the heat it brought. Hantle's back ached and a sharp pain in his hip forced him to change the way he carried his weight. He finished the last of his food as he came upon a home. Everything but the chimney was destroyed. Smoke still rose from the stone column and he saw the fire smoldering yet on the hearth. Toppled trees behind the house led deeper into the forest.

So the wolf had beaten him there. He knew there was no one left to find, but he looked anyway. Inside, he held the small hope that someone else would have the same luck he had. But no remains turned up in the wreckage he overturned. He was just a lucky bastard. No others would get his odds.

---

The dirt road continued flat for some time and a scene played before Hantle. The wolf chased a man along the way. And when the man looked over his shoulder, Hantle saw his own face. The figures evaporated. He laughed. It was he who chased the wolf, wasn't it?

The sun began its descent toward the west and Hantle felt a stabbing in his side that he could not address. Pain splintered up his torso every few steps. Furthermore, he had passed no villages whereby to procure food. Nor did he have time to hunt. Setting his stomach's grumbling aside, he appreciated the fact that the swelling in his eye had reduced.

The ring was cool and light to his touch as he withdrew it from his breast pocket. Sooted and mangled, but tactile. A testament to the family behind him. Totemic and sole reason he pressed onward, through pain and hunger and need for rest. He chased after the chance to right things. Whatever that meant now, with his family gone. But he would not focus on the guilt, because that would bring further failure. He would focus on stopping the wolf and preventing it from desecrating other families. He would somehow right things.

---

Farther along, a small grouping of homes lay some distance from the road. All leveled but for a single broken lantern that lay in the clearing between the homes.

Hantle's exhaustion had settled in but not overwhelmed him. A cursory look and a few shouts were all he gave. His hope of finding any survivor had evaporated, and it detracted from progress toward his real goal: Harsenth.

Another vision appeared before him. Nighttime fallen and the wolf howling outside homes that were still inhabited. Lorenca and their boys burst from the back door of one and made for the forest. Hantle felt an urge to move forward, but fear of the demon prevented him from taking a single step. The beast enjoyed the chase and played with his small, pitiful toys. The urge to vomit brought Hantle back to the present. He was afraid, yes, but he would not shirk his duty. He trekked onward.

---

If only he knew Harsenth's location, he could gauge how far or close he was. But as it stood, the sun sank beneath the horizon and he was an indeterminate distance away.

The day was spent, but there was still part of the night to beat the wolf there. Mindful of how much his pace had slowed due to weary legs, he resolved to speed up. He saw and felt his limitations spread over every step that lay before him. The wolf, seemingly, had no limitations. What made that so? What set them apart?

---

The final bits of sunlight left the sky and one tree root succeeded in bringing Hantle down. Pain shot up his injured arm—another limitation. His musket served to help him up, then he slung it back over his shoulder. To ignore the burdens threatening to halt him, he steered his mind to thoughts of what he would do in Harsenth. From an eagle's view a thousand feet in the sky, Hantle saw the wolf arriving at the town similarly late. It began its attack and the people crumpled under it only for sunlight to blast over the Knuckles and push the wolf, clawing in protest, back into the forest. He willed himself to focus on the road, but the wanderings of the mind were hard to keep at bay.

# CHAPTER FIFTEEN

A HEAVY LINING of trees fell away from the road and the midmorning revealed smoke drifting into the air from a few smoldering places. It was quiet in the small village. Every building razed, even those of stone. Their cornerstones lay far from the foundations.

A few minutes up the road, Hantle found another village's remains. He spent no time on a search. There were more settlements between Founsel and Harsenth than he realized. Columns of smoke in the distance could indicate life or death. The warmth of the sun did not match the coldness of the dead places. He shuddered.

---

Hantle reached the third village, which was also destroyed and filled with more rubble from larger buildings. Claw marks cut across the road, leaving cobblestones strewn about. He looked around and noticed the midday air felt obscenely empty without birdcalls. How many more ruins were there to discover?

As he rounded a pile of stones and wood, Hantle found himself looking at a man in uniform, shouted, "Hey whoa," and backed up several steps, fumbling for his musket.

"Well, shit." The other man startled as well and drew a holstered pistol.

They each pointed a weapon at the other, stunned, until the uniformed man's shock subsided and he called over his shoulder. "Lieutenant Vurm. I got someone here."

Hantle let out a bated breath, removed his finger from the trigger, and lowered the musket. "I was *not* expecting to see anyone here." A living being in all this wreckage? How sure could he be this was not another vision?

"Neither were we," the soldier replied. He kept his weapon up but used one hand to adjust the kepi he wore and scratch under its brim.

The lieutenant picked his way around piles of rubble. His legs covered great distances with every stride. He also wore a kepi atop his bald head, although a flourishing symbol made of red metallic thread set it apart. Precise creases ran down his tan pant legs, accentuated by flanking red stripes. Hantle noticed the lieutenant's eyes narrow and jaw tighten.

"I am Lieutenant Vurm. You are?"

Hantle straightened. Even so, he had to look up to meet the lieutenant's eyes. "Hantle Doolsun, sir."

Vurm continued on so quickly Hantle doubted the man even heard his name. "Where are the other survivors?"

Hantle shook his head and raised his hands to indicate uncertainty. "I've only just come into the area. Alone. What do you know of what happened?"

Vurm removed the kepi to reveal a pale bald crown shining with sweat. He tugged at the neck of his uniform jacket. "My squad and I were sent to investigate rumors of disaster. You're the first person we've encountered." Brass buttons ran in a single line down his front and the wool looked too warm for this weather.

To a woman off to his side, Vurm shouted, "Any survivors your way?"

"No, sir," she said. "None."

Hantle nodded and glanced around the village. Several other troopers walked through the area, scanning the debris. "May I ask," he said, "who sent you?"

"Gully Rhet, mayor of Harsenth."

Hantle felt a rush of excitement. He had stumbled upon an armed force. One he might coordinate over the coming night to stand against the wolf. The opportune encounter served as vindication for his slog through exhaustion and hunger and many miles to get here.

Vurm turned to Hantle as he replaced his hat. "I'll ask you a few questions now?"

"Okay," Hantle said.

"It's strange you're the only one here." He waved an arm to indicate the wasted village. "Say you've just come in, have you? Where from?"

Hantle looked directly into the man's eyes and cleared his throat. He wanted to properly frame his forthrightness. "I spent all of the last day and a half walking from Founsel, on the Trasach Cove."

"Why so far a distance in so short a time?"

Hantle told the lieutenant of the wolf destroying his family, home, and village. How it grew with every person it ate. As additional evidence, he raised his arm. He pulled back the bandaging to reveal the inflamed puncture wounds. The skin stretched taut around the injuries and Hantle winced. "I'm certain," he continued, "the wolf was here as well. Last night. Two villages just west of us have also been taken."

The other trooper, the soldier Hantle had first encountered, asked, "If the wolf can lay entire cities flat, how did you survive?"

"Pure luck. But I now chase it hoping to stop it from taking more lives."

Vurm huffed and shook his head. "You want us to believe a wolf is responsible for this?"

Hantle exhaled. "I'm telling you what I've seen. You're welcome to go on and witness the destruction for yourself. Same destruction as here."

Vurm's eyes focused on the distance. Hantle turned and saw plumes of smoke standing dark against the sky. He turned back with another query. "Is Harsenth just up the road? I'm eager to speak to the mayor."

The lieutenant said, "We must complete our investigation before we return to the mayor."

"I'm happy to leave you to it." Hantle gave a quick nod and started to move around him, but the lieutenant placed a hand on his chest.

"I'm sorry, but we must escort you back." Vurm motioned and the other soldier stepped forward with his chest thrust out.

The physical contact surprised Hantle and he did not like the implication. "Am I being held here?"

"Being held? No. We just ask that you give us a few minutes before we show you on to town."

Hantle knew the impression he made here would be pivotal to securing Harsenth's support. He yielded. "Of course. I would be grateful for your guidance."

Vurm rounded up a few more of his unit and addressed them. "We were tasked to bring back evidence, if we found anything had happened. What could carry more surety than the cornerstone of the village hall?" He pointed to the block in the middle of the road. One of its corners had fractured. "You two, make a stretcher to bear the stone back." Vurm ordered the rest of the soldiers to attention.

Hantle stood quietly as the soldiers found materials, prepared the stretcher, and loaded the stone on. It felt nice to stand still.

Within a few moments, the project was complete and those soldiers fell back in formation. The strongest trooper in the squad, a tall, brawny woman, took up the improvised stretcher and hauled it to the end of the line. The lieutenant indicated for Hantle to stand behind the stretcher-bearer and he himself took up the rear. Vurm called the march, and they began eastward to Harsenth.

Hantle looked about him as they walked. To his left sat the stable yard. The barn was in pieces, as was the fence, but Hantle noticed something in the mud. "Ah, Lieutenant?" he said. "Do you see the mark in the mud of the stable yard?"

Vurm called for the squad to halt. "What mark?"

"It's a large depression, just beyond the fence line. May I inspect it?"

He waved Hantle on.

Hantle stooped down as he neared it and was thankful for this sign. "It seems the wolf left a print." He made eye contact with the lieutenant and beckoned him over.

Vurm raised an eyebrow. "That's the size of my chest. It's no wolf print."

"Except this wolf is larger now than any other, with all the flesh it has consumed." Hantle pointed out the four pads and claws that sank a foot into the mud.

Lieutenant Vurm stood quietly and considered the print's shape and the size. "I wrote you off as demented, but there may be something to your story. If anything, it's a hell of a report." He called out again, "March." The stretcher left grooves in the dirt road reminiscent of claw marks.

## CHAPTER SIXTEEN

HANTLE and the rest of the squad walked through a gate in the ten-foot-high wooden walls of Harsenth. They were a new sight for Hantle. He had grown up, worked, and lived entirely in Founsel, which had never been large enough to warrant a wall. Would one have made a difference in Founsel's fate?

Within the town bounds, scores of people filled the streets. Half-timbered buildings lined the roads. Each was thin, front-gabled, and three to four stories tall. The top story extended out over the face of the structures, and a beam projected from the roof ridge and ended with flags whose colors varied between buildings, looking like birds with beaks hanging over the street, colorful worms in mouth. Nearly all of them had patches of moss growing under the eaves. People leaned out from the gable windows and looked to the west, from where the squad had come. He turned back and, through the gate, saw smoke trailing in the distance. That would strengthen the rumor.

A group thickened around the marching squad and a hundred questions filled the air. Lieutenant Vurm ignored the onslaught and raised his voice to be heard above the noise. "Stand back and stop asking. We have a report to take to the mayor." Yet the questions kept on and the group followed closely.

"But who's the man you found?"

"Is he the culprit?"

"Why isn't he in chains if he done it?"

Hantle knew to keep his mouth shut. He was content to observe and keep moving.

"What's she dragging there?"

The group turned its focus from Hantle to the stretcher.

"Some sort of stone. What's the big deal?"

The year and text on the cornerstone was best visible from those hanging out of the gable windows. Someone shouted as they read it, "'Village of Toupil.' Is that a cornerstone?"

The crowd's excitement hit a new high and they pressed in further.

"What could destroy a stone building like that?"

"Could it have been raiders?"

"Raiders that'd level a building? You'd need an army."

The lieutenant raised a pistol above his head and countered. "Fall back, I've said. Keep off the squad if you know what's good for you." Hantle watched a bead of sweat run down the back of his neck. The crowd obeyed his command and gave them space.

The squad passed by a group of children dressed in outfits two sizes too large. They rattled wooden swords and shields and shouted. The leader of the pack piped up, "Let us go over and we'll sort it out."

Hantle furrowed his brow as the crowd speculated about what happened. Rampant guesswork was common when the truth was unknown. Anything and everything seemed most likely then. Yet this time, reality was more far-fetched than what they imagined.

Hantle's group came to a low fieldstone wall that delineated a newer quarter of town, this section built of stone. The road passed through the wall and ran to the foot of a hill. Up the hill climbed a tall white staircase that gave rise to what Hantle guessed to be the town hall. No moss grew on its bright, pale facade. Around it and behind it sat other stone structures like homes and shops.

The squad marched to the foot of the staircase, where Vurm called a halt. He waved over a second soldier to help the woman lug the cornerstone up the steps. He and Hantle followed. They entered through a set of double doors into a large foyer. Desks sat about the space and each was occupied. Workers and townspeople scurried about. Vurm took the lead, and they filed into a hallway that cut farther into the building. At the hallway's end, it intersected with another that ran perpendicularly. A door stood before them, flanked by two guards. Vurm pointed to a spot beside the guard on the left. To Hantle he said, "Stand there and wait until summoned." He disappeared through the doorway and his two stretcher-bearers followed.

This hallway sat in quiet relief to the bustling foyer they had walked through: nothing moved. Hantle took in the scene as he waited. Hanging from the rafters of the ceiling were red tapestries embroidered with a bright silver thread. The thread formed an icon for Harsenth: a shield embossed with a tree flanked by axes.

The doorway to the room beyond was still open, and Hantle could hear sounds. He shut his eyes and focused to understand what was said. The first voice he recognized was the lieutenant's.

"Mayor Rhet, we come bearing proof of Toupil's destruction. This is the cornerstone of the town hall."

The next voice Hantle inferred to belong to the mayor. "Please tell me you covered it before you brought it through the streets."

"Well, uh"—Vurm cleared his throat—"no. I did not."

The mayor laughed. "Wonderful. Now everyone in town is sure to have seen it. Did you think of how the rumors would multiply?"

"I am deeply sorry, sir. I did not consider that."

"Of course not. You're only the lieutenant. Bet you figure that sort of thinking above your pay grade."

"Absolutely not, sir. I was merely in a hurry to bring news to you of what we found."

"And what did you find?"

"The village ruined. Every building destroyed. We found no people, living or dead. Anything of wood was smoldering."

"Fine. Fine. We know now the rumors were true. Something destroyed it. Yet the cornerstone itself does not indicate *what* befell the place."

"We did recover something else of interest."

"Which is?"

Vurm said, "Bring him in."

The two guards standing near Hantle motioned him through the doorway and escorted him down a carpeted aisle. The room was bright, the white stonework lit by torch and tall windows. Stone archways flanked them, containing wooden sculptures. The mayor sat on a stone dais. Behind him hung another tapestry embroidered with Harsenth's icon. When Hantle stood before the mayor, the guards returned to their posts in the hallway.

The mayor looked at Hantle and raised an eyebrow. "And who is this?"

Vurm replied, "We found him in the ruins, walking through from the west."

The mayor rolled his eyes and said, "Let *him* answer. Who are you?"

"Hantle Doolsun, sir. From the village of Founsel, on the Trasach Cove."

"Some timing to arrive in Toupil just as it's destroyed. What do you know of it?"

Hantle gave the mayor the same information he had earlier given to Lieutenant Vurm and added a summary of what Liova had shared of her studies.

When Hantle finished, the mayor nodded, a distant look on his face. Then he came to and shook his head. "A wolf, you say?" He gave a chuckle. "I'm supposed to buy that tale of yours? It's more like a story to tell children when they misbehave. 'Behave, or the wolf will eat you.' *You* are more likely to have been behind all this trouble. Where's the evidence of this wolf?"

Hantle stood straighter and replied, "Your soldiers themselves saw the print of a giant wolf."

The mayor turned to Vurm. "Is this true?"

Vurm stood speechless for a moment. "Sir. We *did* happen to see a print on the outskirts of the village. Had the form of a wolf print, only many times larger than normal."

"And you didn't mention this first off? Or bring back evidence of it?"

Vurm cocked an eyebrow. "I'm not sure how we could bring back that kind of evidence."

The mayor shrugged him off. "I ought to have gone with you to be sure of things. The only competent person is oneself." He resumed addressing Hantle. "Even still, how does that prove a wolf destroyed Toupil?"

Hantle wondered what else he could show to convince the mayor. A pain shot up his arm and reminded him of the evidence he bore on his body. He pulled back his sleeve and bandage to stick his arm out. "I have fang marks from that very beast."

The mayor leaned forward, motioned Hantle forward a few steps, and examined the wounds. Hantle was momentarily thankful for the inflammation and redness that surrounded each puncture mark. It looked much worse than it now felt.

But the mayor sat back and asked, "If the wolf attacked you, but you claim it's so dangerous, then how aren't you dead?"

Hantle replied, "I worked with a group of villagers and our numbers forced the wolf away after it bit me. Later, when it returned and destroyed the village, rubble fell on top of me. It knocked me out and hid me from sight."

The mayor waved a hand. "Pfah, you're nothing but a distraction. Looking for a moment of fame."

Hantle pressed back. "That a wolf could rend a town is an absurd notion, I will grant you that." He nodded in the direction of the stretcher. "But the cornerstone there didn't work itself loose. And this building's cornerstone won't just work itself loose either. A treacherous foe is set against us." Without quite realizing it, he added, "Don't you have a duty to those living under your authority? A duty to protect them?"

The mayor stood, towering above Hantle on his dais. "And who are *you* to walk into this room and spit in my face? I have been mayor of this town for fourteen years! The people here trust me. Love me. It is not the first time I've faced a threat to my town."

Hantle was glad to have struck a chord but took a step back, hoping to diffuse the tension. "Then return their love and save them once more. I urge you to deploy your army tonight against this creature. At worst, if I'm wrong, the morning will come calmly and you can put me behind bars."

The mayor sighed, shook his head again, and looked around in an attempt to find words.

The woman who bore the stretcher gave a cough to gain attention and interjected. "Sir?"

"What?"

"Earlier this morning I heard a man say he escaped from Toupil last night. Said he saw the destruction."

"Are we all just hiding everything of interest?"

"Of course not, no, sir. I didn't think anything of it until now because the man's a known drunk. I assumed he was running his mouth. But, after hearing *him*"—she nodded toward Hantle—"maybe there's something to the drunk's story?"

"It sounds that way. You didn't realize earlier I might care to know this? I would have known right away this was important."

Hantle wondered how the people of Harsenth could love such a leader, but he was curious to hear what the man had to say so he kept his mouth shut.

The mayor sat down and looked to the soldier. "Go and find him. Bring him back here."

She exited the room and an awkward silence fell over the group.

A few minutes passed and Hantle felt an exhaustion creeping in through his temples. He tried to shrug it off by adjusting his footing.

Most of all, he was tired of dawdling when they should be preparing for the night.

He lost track of the time until the soldier returned with the drunk in tow. Hantle caught a whiff of the man's stench as he passed. When he reached the feet of the dais, the mayor asked, "You saw Toupil destroyed last night?"

"Aye," the man replied. "I was drinking in Toupil since yesterday evening. Spent most of the night into the bar, eh, in the bar." He swayed as he stood. "Until I got kicked out for falling asleep. Coming home I fell into a ditch and fell asleep there. That musta been the first time that happened to me."

"Fine, fine"—the mayor moved his hand in forward circles—"keep on with it."

"Uh, okay. I fell asleep until I woke up for the ground shakin'. I sat right up and sees a wolf jumping at the buildings. Its head and shoulders was taller than the roofs." The drunk raised a hand as far above his head as he could. "And all the roofs was on fire. I pissed myself from fright—not the drink, you know. It was eating the village! Pssh, then I got up and ran on back to Harsenth. I tried tellin' people what I saw, but no one believed me. I tried tellin' 'em."

The mayor shifted in his seat. "And has the drink never given you strange thoughts before?"

The drunk caught himself leaning backward. "These wain't thoughts! They's visions. I saw it. No drink could make me see what I seen." He burped and nodded his certainty.

Hantle watched the mayor's features soften as he considered the statements. He spoke again, hoping to bring the point home. "Sir, this man has independently confirmed what I spoke of. There can be no doubt now."

The mayor turned to Hantle. "What did your village do when it attacked?"

Hantle spoke of the night watch and their attempts to first run it off and, later, kill it.

"Who led this group?"

"I helped organize things, but we had no professional soldiers like your fine town has." He hoped to appeal to the mayor's vanity. "With such a force, the wolf would be hard pressed to even enter Harsenth."

Mayor Rhet looked to the soldier who summoned the drunk and said, "Get him out of here. Through the back of the building, this time." The soldier took the unstable man by the arm and escorted him from the room.

Hantle spoke more loudly. "What are you plans for the coming night, Mayor, when the beast comes? For it will come. Something must be done, surely."

The mayor placed a hand to his chin and looked to the rafters. "Yes, we must do something."

Finally. "Say it so and begin preparation."

The mayor gave a knowing chuckle. "Were it only so simple." He stood and made for a chamber off the back of the room. "Vurm, call in my council."

Hantle exhaled and shook his head. Was this man incapable of making a decision without the approval of others? The door to the mayor's chamber shut and the sound echoed around the room. He glanced to the windows, wondering how much longer they had until nightfall.

## CHAPTER SEVENTEEN

HANTLE FOLLOWED Lieutenant Vurm back into the hall and took up his spot beside the guards. Vurm nodded toward Hantle and said, "Stay with him while I summon the Council members." The guards nodded and the lieutenant walked down the hallway through which they had originally come.

Hantle leaned against the wall and closed his eyes. He took a deep breath to hold back his frustration. In Founsel, they took action immediately. There were no lengthy meetings to endure. No decisions to defer to a committee. But if this waiting meant that come nightfall he had more people, real soldiers, to join him in the stand against the wolf, it would be time well spent.

Deep weariness seeped through him. He lowered himself to the ground, legs thankful for the rest. As he closed his eyes once more, he imagined the wolf's current size. How many people had it consumed in the last night alone? Easily more than all previous nights combined. It would be larger and fiercer tonight. The largest and fiercest yet. How many enlisted soldiers were in Harsenth? Enough to make any difference?

The first council member walked past Hantle. She was dressed in fine clothing and wore a pendant of Harsenth's icon. Three others, outfitted just as nicely, arrived in the span of a few minutes. The mayor re-entered his hall and made small talk with the group. Hantle noticed most their lack of urgency. The fifth and final council member strode by, accompanied by Lieutenant Vurm. Her arrival spurred the group to retire to the mayor's chamber for privacy and drinks. Vurm returned to the hallway to stand with his guards. Still sitting, Hantle brought his legs up to an angle so he could place his arms across the knees. Then he rested his head on his arms and, powerless, he waited.

---

At high noon, Rounfil and Hantle walked through a forest. They had just felled their one hundredth tree and set to using axes to remove all its branches. Once the tree was debranched, they hauled the log back to the village by means of a cart and oxen. The hundred logs lay in piles around Founsel. Both men set to shaving the tops of the trunks to points. The work passed in the blink of an eye. The sun was setting and they lifted the last of the pointed logs. Its blunt end the two buried in a hole. Now, the structure was encircled by enormous spikes. Hantle patted Rounfil on the back for a job well done. Each house in Founsel was like a porcupine. Hantle wanted to see the wolf contend with the spiked defenses.

A howl filled the air.

---

Hantle jerked awake to someone kicking his foot. The guard said, "Come on, get up. The mayor summoned you again."

He shook off the dream and stood. The guards escorted him to the mayor. Five council members flanked the stone dais in chairs of their own. The mayor rose and introduced each of the council, but Hantle paid no attention to the names. He clenched his jaw to stifle a yawn instead.

With introductions finished, the mayor sat and a council member took over. She recapped their discussion of Hantle's story. "We then discussed other options. Natural disaster. An attack by raiders. Plague. Hysteria. But none of them seem a realistic sequence of events."

Another council member interjected. "I still worry this man is on powerful drugs. Perhaps he's colluding in the fabrication with the drunkard. Check his pupils, at least!"

But the woman ignored the man's comments. "The complete destruction of the villages hints to something unusual. And an unusual cause is what you propose."

She stood from her chair, took a few steps, and planted herself before Hantle. He straightened up, returning her look. He dared not break the stare. To his relief, her eyes softened and she gave him a faint smile.

She glanced to her fellow council members. "The only thing I see in his eyes is weariness. His experience over the last week gives reason enough for that."

Next, she turned and walked an invisible line as she addressed him. "This council is comprised of Harsenth's most prominent business- and land-owners. Lieutenant Vurm commands the town's forces, but those forces belong to me. Any business owner is reluctant to put his or her livelihood at risk." She indicated the one who accused Hantle of drug use. "Galbien will tell you how farming is largely mitigating risks. And unnecessary combat is a risk for a mercenary force. Yet yielding to complete destruction is a greater threat. None of us wish to give up our lives or enterprises." She extended a hand, palm up, in Hantle's direction. "Mayor Rhet has mentioned your recognition of risk. You're willing to be put behind bars if you are incorrect?"

Hantle nodded. "Yes. I am certain of the threat to Harsenth." He recognized now what motivated the mayor and his council. "Of the danger to your names and fortunes."

The mayor pushed himself up and stepped to the edge of his dais.

"And of the risk to our denizens, of course. That, Eamel, is paramount."

"Yes." Eamel turned to him. "The townspeople are the lifeblood of Harsenth." She yielded, lowering her head and shrugging her shoulders. "Of course."

The mayor looked satisfied at having made his point and returned to his seat.

Hantle exhaled. "If I could not save my own town, I at least hope to save this one."

Eamel looked to Hantle again and beckoned him forward. "Please tell us what you would recommend."

"Set up a force, call for aid if any is near, and be ready to face the wolf head-on. If we cannot prevent the hammer fall, we can lessen the blow."

Galbien said, "We could send to Bansuth for aid?"

The mayor shook his head. "I would ask them for nothing before other options are exhausted."

"Why do you say that?" Hantle asked. Was the man solely driven by ego?

"Bansuthians consider us backward imbeciles. Yes, Bansuth is indeed many times larger, but we are just as hard-working, driven, and forward-thinking." Mayor Rhet slammed his fist onto the chair's arm and spoke more loudly. "The two thousand in Bansuth dwarf the few hundred farther out on the Far Finger, but they still rely on us. The harsh terrain of the Finger keeps most away, but the rugged and willing few provide food and lumber for the growing many."

Hantle said, "Surely then, their mayor would understand their reliance on Harsenth and recognize the utility of fighting alongside you, however begrudgingly."

The mayor's forehead wrinkled as he shook his head more defiantly. "Only after they laugh at us for not protecting our own. There must be another way."

Eamel walked to stand beside the mayor and placed a hand on his shoulder. "We must seriously consider this option. Bringing in

Bansuth would place fewer of Harsenth's resources at risk. Why should Harsenth weather this alone when Bansuth has as much to lose?"

Hantle breathed with relief. She worked toward the same end as he, even if it were for different reasons. "How far away is Bansuth?"

The mayor replied, "Two or three days ride, unless the rider was hell-bent on the journey and could get fresh horses."

The mayor, Galbien, Eamel, and the others discussed who should be sent, where fresh horses could be obtained, and what message would be most persuasive. The leadership was now animated and energetic. Hantle listened for a time, because the idea was attractive: bring in a larger power to help fight for the town. But a larger problem still remained.

Hantle spoke above the rest of the group. "We do not have multiple days to wait for reinforcements. The wolf will come tonight. The drunkard earlier described the wolf as tall as the buildings of Toupil. And I know from experience that as it feeds each night, it grows larger. Tonight, it will be bigger yet.

"We must prepare the town today, or Harsenth will be reduced to ruins like those towns your soldiers found this morning. Your life's work, names, and legacies laid low like this town hall's stones. Yet if you succeed, your names will be spoken in every home in Bansuth. You will enjoy the renown of the entire Fist."

"So we are alone in this fight," Mayor Rhet said.

"No," Hantle said. "We are far from alone. Out there are soldiers. Each one a force to be reckoned with."

The mayor looked to his council. "We are not left with much choice. To risk death or bow before it. The consolation being that, if we set our arms against the threat, we will persist and earn glory." Hantle noticed Rhet looked hesitant to give a "yes."

Eamel nodded. "You are correct. And without a town to safeguard, what good is a mercenary force?" All pretense of protecting the townsfolk first and foremost had vanished.

Galbien stood, saying, "Call a town emergency and order all indoors. That will show we are taking serious action."

They broke into further discussion about options, actions, and preparations. Tension in Hantle's shoulders lessened. It took appealing to their vanity, but he had brought this group to a decision. How many hours had they until the wolf appeared?

The mayor left the council's discussion and motioned to the lieutenant. "Lieutenant Vurm, add Hantle to your squad. He has experience we can leverage. We are trusting your word here, Hantle. If this night goes poorly, you are to blame. Not us."

Hantle nodded and accepted his fate.

———

Hantle exited the town hall with the lieutenant, who collected the members of his squad. The sun rode lower in the afternoon sky. Their first task was to call a meeting in the town square for the mayor to address the denizens. Cries went up to announce the imminent speech.

Hantle was eager to have well-equipped people to fight against the wolf. Numbers were still their best chance of killing the beast. He imagined landing the fatal shot to the wolf's heart while a hundred troopers stood behind him, all having fired and now reloading their weapons. Musket smoke would swirl in the air. And the sun would rise on a saved town. With the wolf dead, he could return to Founsel. There he would find Lorenca. Learn she had escaped the village when the wolf came, and that she hid in the deep forest. He would pull the ring from his pocket—the ring he saved for her—and place it in her hands. Once reunited, they would fix the ring and make it round and right again. Just like they could make the family right again. They might even try for more children. After all, he would have made the world safe at last.

Hantle realized his daydreaming and came back to the world as the mayor stepped into the daylight on the town hall's veranda, closely followed by his council, who took up seats just outside the door. Mayor Rhet continued forward and took his position at a podium while Lieutenant Vurm leaned over to whisper, "The mayor rarely makes public speeches. I can feel the town's curiosity as to the reason why."

The square was filled with people of all ages eager to hear the mayor speak. Bordering the square were the mercenary soldiers. Hantle leaned back and asked, "How many soldiers does Harsenth have?"

Vurm thought for a moment before answering. "Around fifty at the moment. With another twenty in reserve."

Hantle's eyes widened. "Large number for the town."

"Politics are powerful here, just like elsewhere."

The mayor cleared his throat and began. "Good afternoon, denizens of Harsenth. I have called this meeting to discuss the rumors that have sprung up in our beloved town. Investigations of our neighboring villages have revealed their demise. The cause I cannot speak to with certainty, but I have received intelligence that indicates our town is at risk. As a precaution, I am declaring a state of emergency for Harsenth. All soldiers, whether active or in reserve, are mustered and called to duty. Any individual not in the force is ordered to remain in their home until the threat is dealt with."

A murmur went through the crowd and the mayor shifted his footing. He spoke over the spreading conversation to end it and keep the focus on him. "Our forces shall be fully armed and posted throughout the town this evening. Lieutenant Vurm will lead the preparations. Our soldiers are well trained and disciplined. I have every confidence they will see the morning safely rise over our homes."

The mayor looked to Vurm and said, "Lieutenant, please see these people back to the safety of their homes."

Lieutenant Vurm saluted the mayor and turned to the crowd. "You heard Mayor Rhet. Please return to your homes now and remain there for the duration of the evening."

The mayor and council entered the town hall once more. Vurm, Hantle, and the rest of the platoon ushered people from the square. Most residents obeyed without fuss, which freed up a majority of the troopers to begin preparations. Those few who caused scuffles were quickly contained. The streets were cleared by just after sunset.

Hantle returned to the square, his hopes raised. The platoon's performance impressed him. They followed orders, handled their weapons well, and needed little oversight. The professionalism they embodied was apparent. Hantle's excitement stifled a yawn. Pushing through the distance between Founsel and Harsenth led him to this moment. He brought these forces to attention and the town would soon be arrayed against the beast. His success gave him the means to ignore the exhaustion in his muscles, push aside the pain in his arm, and keep working into the night.

Lieutenant Vurm approached Hantle's side and spoke in a hushed voice. "I know you're no soldier, but you have the most experience with our enemy. That's experience I want to tap into. What is your opinion on how to best counter the wolf?"

Hantle reflected on each of the nights in Founsel. Nothing had stopped the wolf, but what had worked best? "Each night we had patrols that encircled the village. One of those evenings, we were able to surround the creature. That was the night it bit me. With the guards around it, it gave up and fled. If we could encircle it again, with the numbers we have tonight, we may be able to bring it down. We found its stomach to be a weak spot."

The lieutenant nodded. "Yes, I can see that working. Surround it and shoot for the gut. Our troopers can patrol the town's edges, and close the circle if the wolf enters to attack homes."

"Can you remind me how many soldiers you have?"

"We have one platoon of ten squads for a total of seventy-four troopers." Vurm saw Hantle's yawn. "You look worn out. Do you need some rest before nightfall?"

"No. I am fine. Your force here is impressive. I will not miss my chance for revenge. All I need is some food. That will give me another wind. And perhaps some jursant."

"There's a hall nearby where you can eat. While you do so, I will coordinate with my sergeants. Mayor Rhet was intentionally vague with the townspeople, but my soldiers must know what they are up against."

---

Hantle left the mess hall and saw the activity in the streets. The soldiers were well geared and establishing their patrols. Groups carried equipment to stake alarm bells and lanterns, light fires, and gather additional fuel. Hantle had another idea while eating and sought out Vurm to share it. He found him building a scaffold for sharpshooters to gain elevation and have sights across rooftops.

Hantle climbed up the framework. "Do you have artillery units?" he asked. "The heavier weapons could play a major role in bringing down the wolf."

"Yes, we have two cannons. But they are largely ceremonial. A few troopers are trained in their use though." Vurm set down his tools and wiped his damp neck with a rag.

Hantle was glad to not be wearing a uniform in the heat that still had not abated. He turned and pointed to the west, toward Toupil. "I expect the wolf to come from beyond the villages it destroyed last night. If we could head it off, we would have more warning of its coming."

Vurm tucked the rag into his back pocket and looked over the rooftops. "And those cannons would catch it by surprise. With two squads, we would have ourselves an ambush."

---

The cannons rumbled over the stone streets, drawn by horses. The artillery led the squads Lieutenant Vurm had assembled for the mission. Hantle, carrying a torch, brought up the rear. He took in the town as they walked the roads. Soldiers had set up blockades and traps at various junctions. Fires burned in intersections and alarm bells hung on wooden poles, waiting to be rung. The squads exited the town walls and continued for a ways. They reached a location where other soldiers had assembled false hedges, which were used to hide the cannons and troopers. Once the artillery was in place and the troopers spread out, they extinguished the torches. Hantle felt formidable with the cannons and the soldiers by his side. Night deepened and all Harsenth lay quiet.

# CHAPTER EIGHTEEN

TO MAINTAIN their element of surprise, no fires or lights burned near the two squads on the western edge of Harsenth. All of the soldiers crouched behind the fake hedges along the roadside. In the darkness, Hantle opened his eyes. Had he just shut them for a second? Or had he nodded off? He was not sure. With a grunt, he shifted his weight, brought his legs out from under him, and sat on the ground. Shimmering specks appeared in his eyes and he felt light-headed. His thinking seemed cloudy. He reassured himself this was fine. It was not most important to be clear-headed. This was the time for pure action. The dots faded, to be replaced with an image of him swinging an axe as if to fell a tree, but he aimed instead at the wolf's neck. With a few strokes, he decapitated it and waved the head in the air to show the soldiers surrounding him. When the wolf was dead, and Harsenth saved, that was when he could seek rest.

The razed village ahead of them lay quiet, still, and empty, lit by nothing more than the faintest of starlight. He listened for anything to break the silence. The smallest whispering could be the fiend coming upon them. He had not spoken enough to the soldiers besides Lieutenant Vurm to know their quality; though even if he had a sense of that, there was no way to know how prepared each would be for the grim reality of the beast, its size, ferocity, and speed. How could one predict your reaction to such an outlandish event until it struck, catching you unawares and throwing your body and mind into some sort of instinctual reaction? Except . . . Wasn't that what he did with the recurring thoughts and imaginings? Perhaps there *was* a way to prepare for it, to condition your mind for what to expect. Playing out various scenarios so that, whichever of them happened, you might react more effectively and efficiently. Or was it a form of obsession or madness whereby the incessant thoughts would distract him, warp his focus, and leave him wildly hopeless when the moment came? It would be just as fitting, in a terrible sort of way, if his tired and drained mind spun on useless wonderings, leaving him confident but ill-equipped when action was needed. He yawned. What had even started him down this line of thought? Feeling unprepared . . . Ah, yes, how the soldiers would react. He turned his attention back to the pitch-dark, hoping to be the first to spot the thing so he could be an example to follow. Over the last day, he had pictured many ways of ending the beast. Which of those would tonight become reality?

The clanging of an alarm bell came from Harsenth. Hantle growled, said to Lieutenant Vurm, "Those are only for emergencies," and threw a look over his shoulder. He froze and gawked. In the distance, illuminated from beneath by some bonfire on the edge of the town, a form towered above Harsenth. The wolf had come. Even the tallest of the buildings fit between its legs without touching its underside. Blotches of black fur broke its lighter pelt into jagged shapes. Horror fell over Hantle as he realized their plan had been turned back on them: they were flanked and the beast enjoyed the element of surprise.

Vurm was the first to stand and issue orders. "Fall in, soldiers. We will return to Harsenth. Artillery, follow as can." With the soldiers gathering, he spoke to Hantle. "Stay with the artillery. Find me when they're close and we can deploy them." Before Hantle could even acknowledge him, Vurm moved to the head of the formation, calling out, "Double time, march."

The artillery soldiers lit torches, brought around the horses, and began attaching the cannon carts to the horses' harnesses. Hantle's stomach tightened. The opportunity to defeat the wolf was slipping from him already. His prediction of its attack was completely wrong. The fog in his mind grew thicker still. The cannons—the most crucial piece to taking down the wolf—were useless until they hauled them closer, a movement that would cost time. What had seemed a clever plan felt now to be a fiasco.

Moments later the artillery rumbled toward the town—albeit at a torturous speed—where Hantle hoped they could salvage the night. He was able to see the wolf from afar but unable to do anything to curb its destruction. It stepped over the walls, into Harsenth proper, and lowered its head to clear a swath of the tall, half-timbered homes. Screams filled the air as the behemoth sought blood and flesh. Reports of musket fire went up but made no noticeable impact on the creature for its paws and claws and teeth blurred, toppling structures a block at a time. A blaze grew in the wreckage left behind and jumped from one ruined building to the next.

Watching the beast move unimpeded was agonizing. By the time the artillery arrived, their window of opportunity could have passed, rendering useless the entire day Hantle had spent traveling to Harsenth. He could no longer bear to accompany the cannons, to walk when he should be fighting. He shouted to the artillery soldiers, "I have to move ahead, to scout out a location to deploy these, so we waste no time when you arrive. I will meet you ahead."

Hantle ran the remaining distance to Harsenth and stopped just inside its outer walls to take stock of his surroundings. The streets were filled with families fleeing or looters carrying armfuls of pilfered items. Other individuals hung out from gable windows to fire weapons at the wolf, but it paid them no mind. Hantle walked on, looking for a clearing. The streets of Harsenth wound and curved; some abruptly ended while others narrowed so as to be impassable by a cart. He doubted his ability to find a suitable location for the weaponry, but the lieutenant . . . Vurm knew the city well. Surely he would have an idea.

Hantle followed the largest streets until he identified the sound of dozens of muskets firing in unison. He followed on to find the lieutenant standing in a square, several squads of soldiers—as well as what looked to be a dozen civilians—with him. The wolf was some blocks away, its head lowered to root through the buildings at its feet, when another row of structures behind it erupted into flame. Vurm called out for a volley, and the soldiers harnessed eruptions of their own.

As he worked to reload his musket, Vurm spotted Hantle. "Are the cannons with you? They moved quickly."

"No, sir," Hantle replied. "I ran ahead to find you and decide on a place to deploy them, so as to waste no time when they are arrived."

"We've had difficulty even trailing it to this point," Vurm said, packing his shot. "It's quick. This is a fine location for the cannons, but if it moves off again, we'll have to reevaluate."

Hantle addressed the soldiers. "The wolf *can* be damaged. I've done it. See the ear? The gash along the shoulder? Those wounds are from prior nights. We can fell this beast, if we work together." The soldiers let up a war cry and, when their muskets were ready, fired another round.

The wolf raised its head and revealed a group of people clenched in its teeth. The sight of legs flailing and hands clenching initially struck Hantle as comical, but the sense of dread returned when the beast chomped and shook its entire body side to side. Limbs separated from the poor individuals arced away and tumbled through the air. When the wolf stopped shaking, it swallowed and licked the fresh coating of blood from its snout. It barked with excitement and surged a few blocks ahead.

"Damnit," Vurm said. "If it ever stops moving, we can spread out to surround it." He spoke to the soldiers, "Forward! Advance on it from the rear. We need to press in as close as we can and continue to fire at its stomach."

Hantle stayed at Vurm's side as he and the squads picked a way through the rubble-strewn roads. The cannons would be farther behind, but Hantle's preference was to move with the vanguard and join the battle until the artillery arrived. He passed through a haze of smoke that wafted from a cluster of stores and homes. Fire followed close on the wolf's heels, engulfing what the wolf did not trample. Hantle climbed over the fieldstone wall that demarcated the newer section of town and reached an intersection, where he stopped, for he had come upon the wolf as it drained water from an ornamental pool.

The blare of a horn sounded and Hantle traced it to Mayor Rhet, who stood with his council members on the town hall's veranda. The hall, with its position on the hill, rose higher than the wolf, but only just. Hantle could hear nothing the mayor shouted, but neither did those nearer give it any heed. The wolf, however, momentarily looked up from the pool, and a wave of pandemonium swept through the scores of fleeing civilians within its reach. It sparked fear into the council members too. They hurried into the town hall, with the mayor right behind. Was that all the leadership of Harsenth would do? Were they already giving up? Would they too flee?

When the wolf finished its drink, it set upon the stone buildings bordering the pool. Hantle, Vurm, and the soldiers formed a line just a block from its rear legs. With a hand signal from the lieutenant, they peppered the wolf with another volley. All except for Hantle. He had the wolf in his crosshairs but could not pull the trigger. The creature, along with the rest of the world, went out of focus. Two blurry beasts loomed before him, then three, then only one. He lowered his weapon and gripped the remains of a wall for support.

The force reloaded around him and, before his vision cleared, another barrage of musket balls sailed through the air. The wolf must have noticed these shots because it sidestepped its rear legs to one side while keeping its head lowered in a group of victims. Vurm and the soldiers fired a third time. With an aim finally sharp, Hantle contributed a shot of his own. The wolf kicked a large building, causing it to collapse to the street, but the structure managed to stay largely intact. In order to separate stone from mortar and search for people within, the wolf was forced to paw and bite at it. A small bit of hope crept into Hantle as he realized the creature could not raze the stone buildings as easily as the wooden ones. Neither did the flames spread as greedily. He caught Vurm's eye and pointed. "The stonework has slowed the wolf."

"Yes, it has." The lieutenant shouted to the force at large, "Keep firing as you can. It won't move as quickly through these buildings. That will give us the chance to encircle it."

Hantle counted heads. Between the troopers and the civilians that had joined along the way, there had to be nearly eighty in their group. It was by far the most sizeable force Hantle had seen yet. Behind him, he heard the distinct clattering of wagon wheels on cobblestone and looked to see the cannons rolling along, having just come through a break in the fieldstone wall a block away. At last, the cannons were near enough to turn the tide. "Lieutenant," Hantle said, "the cannons are near!" He shouted for the artillery soldiers, who acknowledged him and directed the horses toward the intersection. A vision before him played of the leviathan toppling onto the town hall, dead from the cannonball launched by the torch he would hold. Perhaps it was a blessing the thing paid them no attention. The fell stroke would soon fall, unseen.

"Spread out," Vurm cried. "Form a circle around the wolf and close it in. The cannons at the rear and the muskets all around will overwhelm it." A great clamor arose as the wolf dragged a claw through the town hall, crumbling a portion of it down the hillside. The musket fire paused as the soldiers stood and watched. "Go," Vurm ordered, and the force advanced.

The artillery soldiers arrived and set about deploying the cannons. It was then that the havoc around them really struck Hantle. Most wagons on the streets were unable to move because of the flood of people moving on foot. Cattle, chickens, and dogs made a racket as they too fled. A layer of clouds overhead wiped out the view of the stars and the wind shifted, carrying the wails of people trying to escape the choking smoke and raining ash as much as the fanged menace.

Hantle coughed on a passing plume and batted ash from his face. Focusing on the wolf once more, he noticed how the fires in the streets under it cast an eerie tinge on its coat of fur that, when combined with the blood from its feasting, made its snout and neck look like smoldering coals.

"Hantle." Hantle turned and saw the soldiers pour powder down the barrels and lug the cannon balls from the cart. "You have to move," Vurm said. "You're right in the way."

Hantle's daze broke and he moved to the side. "Sorry," he muttered. He had lost track of what they had been doing. "How . . . What can I do to help?"

"Just stay right there." The soldiers packed the shot with long rods and Vurm rotated a crank to adjust the aim.

The wolf, intent on digging through the town hall and its rubble, had not moved in some time. It would be the easiest shot they could have hoped for.

One of the artillery soldiers said, "Ready." Vurm nodded and extended his hand for the torch, which another worked to light.

A sergeant arrived at their side and slid to a halt, shouting, "Lieutenant, Lieutenant Vurm!" Her chest heaved as she caught her breath. Hantle turned toward the sergeant—

Hantle's forehead impacted the ground and rebounded. A stupor drove in through the bruise caused by the roof in Founsel. He let out a grunt and his leg muscles failed to move as instructed. A cacophony had washed over him, now followed by multiple, smaller boomings, perceptible more through his contact with the ground than through the great ringing in his ears. He turned his head and saw a ball of flame rise, slowly morphing into smoke.

Fragments of wood, metal, and stone rained to the ground around them. Hantle covered his head until the bombardment ended, then watched the black mushroom billow higher, fueled by something still burning, until it reached the clouds themselves. He looked to the wolf and pushed himself to his knees. The beast had paused to eye the source of the explosion. The final stones flung by the wolf's digging flew through the air to crash into buildings farther off or bury into the ground. Hair standing on its hackles was wild and frayed, like the wire of the coop in Founsel. Hantle could still see his boys' blood dripping from the rooftop, glinting in the sunlight.

A groan in the street to his side drew Hantle's gaze. A mother clutched an infant to her bosom and struggled to climb over a pile of timbers barricading her way. But the groan was not from the woman: a storefront wall listed and leaned farther and farther from the upright. As Hantle's feet were still unwilling to participate in moving him, he could only watch as the wall lost its balance and buried the woman and her bawling babe under several thousand pounds of granite block. Yet another two he failed to save.

Vurm crouched down, slung an arm around Hantle, and helped him to his feet. "You okay?" he asked.

"I think so," Hantle said. "Hit my head when I got thrown. Legs felt like they had gone numb."

"How about now? Can you stand on your own?"

Hantle tested his footing and, once sure of his steadiness, nodded. "Yes. What happened though?"

The sergeant, with her breath returned, wiped sweat from her brow and said, "A weapons cache. The building had caught flame and its roof must have finally collapsed and lit the ordnance within. I tried to find the lieutenant so that we might draw the wolf near it before it exploded, but ran out of time. Obviously."

A howl set Hantle's chest to reverberating. The canine looked to be reveling in the chaos; its monstrous tail wagged and buffeted the town hall. Terror gripped trooper and civilian alike. Hantle stepped toward the cannons. "We've still got the artillery."

"Yes." Vurm crouched beside one of them to double check its aim. "Quickly now. Before it moves off."

An artillery soldier picked the torch off the ground. Its flame had been extinguished by the shockwave, and he pulled steel and flint from his pocket to relight it.

"This one's ready," Vurm said. "I'll check the other. Hantle, set the torch to the fuse."

Hantle took the torch from the solider and approached. The ground shook and Hantle braced himself, expecting another explosion to wash over them, but it was the wolf, pouncing on the town hall. Just hold still, he thought. He lit the fuse and the cannon lurched back as its projectile sped off. Instead of impacting the wolf, however, the cannonball embedded itself into the hillside. He looked to the Lieutenant. "What the hell?"

Vurm's eyes went wide and he looked through the sight again. "The bastard thing's thrown off the aim with its pouncing." Metal scraped against metal as he cranked once more.

The wolf lunged away from Hantle to follow a street where it scooped up a line of evacuees. "No!" Hantle shouted and kicked at the cannon's wheel. "Vurm, can you re-aim to follow it?"

The lieutenant watched the canine for a moment, occasionally looking back through the sight. "I'm afraid it's out of range. We'll have to haul them closer."

"Shit." Hantle threw the torch to the ground. "That'll waste even more time." The roads were in such terrible condition and filled with so much wreckage that he was not sure whether they could follow it any farther. That became irrelevant, however, when the wolf drove along the road (devouring the entire line of people as it went), continued beyond the eastern fringes of town, and disappeared into the dark. The chance was lost.

The clouds overhead appeared to have thickened and a peal of thunder rolled in from the distance. A girl wandered toward the cannons, looking disoriented and wearing ragged clothes. Vurm knelt before her, wiped blood away from her ears, and inspected a head wound.

"That way lies Bansuth?" Hantle asked.

"Yes," the lieutenant nodded. "Though a far ways off." He took a kerchief from a pocket and dabbed dirt and ash from the child's injury.

Around Hantle, the bones of Harsenth were shattered and scattered, but some of the people had survived. He had not failed them entirely. Would the demon travel as far as Bansuth tonight? Or would he have an opportunity to beat it there?

Lieutenant Vurm lowered his voice and spoke to the girl. "Do you know where your parents are, dear?" She gave a squeak and began to cry. "Hey, hey." He pulled her into an embrace. "You stay with us, and we'll see if we can find them."

Hantle looked down at the lieutenant. "Will you pursue the wolf with me?"

Vurm looked shocked. "You *want* to chase it? After it left on its own? You could help us here instead. With all the injured and lost." He nodded to the girl. "Ones like her." The girl sniffled and picked at her tangled hair. "And," Vurm continued, "what if the thing comes back?"

"I doubt that will happen. There's only scraps left here."

Vurm gave a resigned shrug and stood. "Scraps we may be, but we survived. We have homes and families and friends to tend to. And I have my duties as lieutenant." He led the child away.

Hantle considered the options. The town was largely destroyed, but it was not devoid of life, like the other places he had left behind. Staying was an attractive notion, but he had still not slayed the wolf. It was out there. The ones alive in Harsenth were ones he had saved, okay, but how many in Bansuth were now in danger? His duty here was done. Bansuth ought to have an even larger army. Might they fare better if he did not make another colossal mistake? The clouds above let loose and rain poured down.

Decided, Hantle walked after Lieutenant Vurm. "I cannot stay," he said. "I am glad you have a chance to put the town back together. But there are thousands of lives ahead to rescue from the beast." The numerous fires nearby sputtered with raindrops. "What lies between here and Bansuth?"

Vurm stopped the girl and faced Hantle once more. "Small homesteads in a few places." He took a deep breath before going on. "I'm sorry you lost your family, Hantle, but saving others won't bring them back."

"No"—Hantle shook his head—"it won't. But it will keep others from needlessly dying like they did." Through the raindrops, he thought he saw a hint of understanding cross the lieutenant's face.

Hantle had forgotten the sergeant until she spoke. "You must have a death wish," she said, "if you're chasing after *that* thing. It was the definition of terror."

Hantle tensed up. What did she know of his struggles? And how could he even hope to express it? He was spared a response when Vurm said, "Death is not the only way to destroy a person."

It seemed that Vurm did understand. Hantle met his gaze and gave a small smile of gratitude. Perhaps the lieutenant would do Hantle a final favor. He asked, "Do you have a horse to spare?"

"Yes, you'll need one to get to Bansuth, won't you?" The lieutenant resumed his walk. "We can give you a horse and provisions."

Hantle soon had a pack, jacket, and torch. He placed his powder horn and ammunition in the pack and mounted his steed. Once in the saddle, he fastened his musket in a sling that ran under his leg. The horse stepped anxiously as lightning streaked the sky, and he checked the reins. "Thank you, sir."

Vurm tipped his kepi, water running off its brim, and said, "Good luck, Hantle."

With a kick, Hantle's horse trotted down the road. The sun would not rise for another hour or more. The muddied path would be his companion until he arrived at Bansuth. Thunder crashed overhead. To Hantle, it sounded like the wolf's jaws snapping shut.

# CHAPTER NINETEEN

HANTLE TUGGED on the reins and slowed the horse from a gallop to a trot. The press to Bansuth would be long and he could not afford to exhaust the animal. As morning had come, the rain let up. While his legs were drenched, the jacket had kept his torso warm and dry, a thing for which he was grateful, for the air had a chill to it. His arm ached as he slid the pack from his back. Inside, he found nuts and jerky, also dry. Both pack and jacket seemed to share the same coating. The road sloped upward and, bouncing with each step of his mount, he chewed on a strip of jerky. He rummaged through the rest of the contents to find a clay jar of oil for the torch and an herb sachet. A sniff told him it contained jursant. That would be helpful as he pushed through the night.

A few final booms of thunder brought to Hantle's mind the cannons in Harsenth. He could not stop thinking of how the night should have gone: one cannonball shattering the wolf's leg, another impacting the beast's neck. As it collapsed to the ground, Hantle would have run up to slit its throat, to let the demon bleed out onto the ground as reparation for all the blood it had taken.

In reality, though, he had been too slow, too late. He was the fool who led the lieutenant and two squads away from the city they were meant to protect. His mistakes had harmed Harsenth in the same way his family had been harmed: they fell prey to the wolf. And it was not just his family who had died. Indeed, Rounfil's corpse still lay pinned under the roof in Founsel. What animals now picked at his skin, tore into his abdomen, or bore into his eyes? He shook off the gruesome thought and stifled a yawn.

All of his travels since Founsel blurred into a single long day. The constant motion sapped him of energy and concentration. He rode for the death of the wolf and vengeance for his family, yet how could he expect the coming night to be any different than the last? He would be a drained man against a draining force. Even the cannonballs might not be much to its new size. It seemed pointless, but, in spite of that, he kept on. Why? What did he chase? There was *some* reason for him to push on to Bansuth. If he could shake the fog from his mind, he might have a chance to pinpoint it.

---

Hantle's head drooped, but he caught himself before sliding out of the saddle. When was the last time he had rested? Back when he had a family, a village, a future, wasn't it? It was near to midday, but not much warmer than it had been at dawn. Clouds above dispersed enough to reveal the Knuckles, separating the Far Finger from the Fist. He stared in awe at the dark craggy peaks. In spite of the countless miles from here to there, they towered over him.

Coming around a bend at the base of a hill temporarily put the mountains out of his view, so he looked to the ground. Thick brush bordered the road on his right, but through it led a small path that ended in a clearing. Farther back, he could make out the shape of a homestead, now in ruins. He had passed other homes earlier and took the time to look for any who might have survived. None had, of course, and he had since given up that specific hope. Something else drew Hantle to pull back on the reins: thirst. In his rush to set out from Harsenth, he had left without any water. Yet another way blind obsession left him unprepared. He dismounted and led the horse along the muddied path to the farmhouse.

The smell of pinesap filled Hantle's nostrils. Behind the structure, many trees were trampled down, others shattered to splinters. As he pictured the wolf chasing a person from the house into the trees, a trickling of water caught his ear. He followed the sound to a springhouse, which had remained undisturbed by the wolf. The horse was immediately drawn to the creek, and Hantle tied him off at its edge. Inside the low building were stores of carrots, turnips, and corned beef. Alongside the food was, to his great relief, an empty waterskin, which he filled from the spring, twice draining and refilling it before screwing closed its lid. It was a welcomed addition to his gear. Turning next to the food, he ate some of everything. He could not shake, however, a deep weariness. If he lost a battle with his body to exhaustion and his mind to fog, there was no chance against his foe. His family's revenge ended with him. He could not let them down by dying in the attempt. Forced to recognize his limits, Hantle lay down next to the springhouse. An hour or two of sleep would be a start.

---

A raven flew overhead and croaked, which woke Hantle. He stood, stretched, and looked toward the sky. Not more than a couple hours had passed. It was a small miracle he had not slept the entire day by accident. He collected the horse, which looked well rested, and left the homestead behind. Riding along, he glimpsed a wider view of his situation. He had heretofore considered himself a storybook hero. In surviving the attack on Founsel, he was chosen for a task. Through the sacrifice of sleep and food, he would reach Harsenth, rally the soldiers, and kill the wolf. Except he had blundered and let victory slip through his grasp. His goal was *not* appointed. Neither was his success guaranteed. Going forward, he would take short breaks. It felt paradoxical, stopping so he might get there sooner, but to be effective, he needed more than rage to drive him.

Mind clearer now, he recognized that when he set out from Founsel, it was with the sole intent of killing the wolf. This was not, however, the only way to avenge his family. Alerting Bansuth to the danger was a goal in and of itself. Warning was a privilege Founsel never had, but it helped spare a fair number of lives in Harsenth. If, through his push to Bansuth, Hantle—he being the only one capable of and willing to bring the message—could give thousands the opportunity to act in whatever way they chose, then they might escape complete annihilation. That was a worthy ambition.

―――――

Dusk spread its ink across the east and Hantle, coming to a tall rock wall, stopped his horse. The road led into the wall through a fissure. His heart sank at the sight of fresh mud, stones, and uprooted vegetation fanning out from the canyon's entrance. A thread of water trickled through the detritus. It looked to have been washed out by the storm earlier in the day. Hantle dismounted and looked for an indication of another way around or through the wall, but it rose a hundred-odd feet and ran otherwise unbroken as far to the north and the south as he could see in the fading light. The canyon it was.

He bent in half and stretched, feeling the stiffness in his back give way. He had decided to respect his limits by taking breaks, but what might the approach of night do to his resolution? Seeing the washout unnerved him, and he hoped that the canyon did not go on for too many miles. It was a shame, though, to have no idea of how far off Bansuth lay. If he knew it to be close, he could sprint there; if he knew it to be far off, he could pace himself accordingly. The worst possibility was to sprint now, exhausting the horse and himself such that one or the other collapsed along the road.

Had the wolf come this way? Hantle straightened up and looked for some sign of the wolf's passage: paw prints, strands of fur, or claw marks. The mud sucked at his horse's hooves as it stamped, but there was nothing obvious of a creature any larger.

A snapping to his side drew his gaze and he noticed a horse grazing in a thicket. He huffed with relief. A fresh mount. What fortune! Hantle approached the animal, which looked glad to meet another living being. A small camp hidden behind the thicket was abandoned. It was only after Hantle lit his torch that he noticed the blood spattering the ground, tents, and equipment. So it had been here. While there was no hope for the wolf to have fit into the canyon, what was not apparent was whether it chose to go over or around the wall. He hoped for the latter, as it would give him better odds of reaching Bansuth before it did.

Hantle stripped the saddle and musket from the horse that had carried him here. "You may rest," he told it, "even though I cannot. There should be plenty of food for you here." After he had saddled the new horse, Hantle mounted and steered it to the wall. With the lit torch, he confirmed this canyon was unlike any he had seen before. The gash at its top was just a few feet wide but the bottom widened a bit more. Farther in, the road's grade increased but it remained relatively clear of debris, thanks, he guessed, to floods that regularly washed through.

He cued the horse and they set off into the slot. The torch was invaluable in the deepening gloom. Overhead, the remaining sliver of sky held stars, until trees growing on the wall's top crowded together and blocked out the view completely. He had never before felt the fear of a confined space but did now. The path was so narrow that three horses would not have been able to walk abreast. If any water flooded down the slot, he would be swept away and battered to death against the walls. He was glad for the fresh horse, because it gave him no need to make any stop before they exited the canyon. True, he could not press the horse on the incline, but it would carry him steadily upward.

When the bandage on Hantle's arm had come loose several times over the day, as it did again, he had retied it without much difficulty. Holding the torch however, made that prospect more difficult, and he pried the cloth back to inspect the wounds. The scabs were thick and the surrounding skin still tender, but he felt comfortable enough with the state of the healing to leave it exposed instead of attempting to retie the bandage only to burn himself with the torch in the process. He removed the cloth and tossed it in his pack, in case he reopened one of the wounds later. Seeing as he had the pack opened already, he rummaged around for the sachet of jursant. Placing a pinch under his tongue immediately countered his mounting desire to sleep.

He plodded along for a few minutes, focusing on the horse's rhythmic gait, until his attention was drawn upward by a flash that briefly illuminated the stone walls that rose beyond the light of his torch. The canyon's tree cover had failed and revealed once more a tear of sky. He was not sure of the cause of the light until, some number of flashes later, he realized a meteor shower played out in the empyrean. For observers outside of the slot canyon, it must have been quite the sight. His breath ceased. Dread lashed through his mind, raising the hairs on the nape of his neck. Liova was right! This was the celestial event that she had predicted would accompany the wolf.

The story of Founsel might be told and passed on until memory of the village's name itself faded and all that remained was the vague hint of a lost land on the wooded coasts of the Balon-wrenth. All notion that real people lived lives and struggled and succeeded, individually as well as in a group, would be forgotten. Although, if the wolf beat Hantle to Bansuth and destroyed it as well, then the disappearance of the larger city would overshadow that of the smaller. The lost land rumored about would be Bansuth, not Founsel. Had the other creatures in Liova's stories started out feeding on and destroying camps, settlements, or villages, which, due to remote location and small size were never discovered to have been lost? It was as if these beasts could eradicate entire portions of the world's history. Hantle shuddered. At best, these animals replaced the tale of a people and their lives with idle speculation about their mysterious end. At worst, it was as if a people had never been at all. Hantle brought his horse to a trot; damn the idea of keeping a pace. The penalty for failure was worse than just having failed his family. His failure meant he, and they, had never existed.

# CHAPTER TWENTY

THE WALLS of the slot canyon shrank over the course of many miles and soon melted away completely. Hantle reentered the expansive night and towering forest. Meteors overhead drove through the sky and winked out. He had no sense of the time, and that worried him. Anxiety took the place of fatigue. He shook the reins and kicked his heels into the horse's side, and in an instant they were at a gallop.

As the horse bore him along, a fog filled the road and forest from the roots upward. It swirled behind his mount as they pushed through the final distance to Bansuth. Several miles in, the horse showed signs of weariness. Hantle slapped its flank to keep it at a gallop. The land here was fairly level and there could not be much farther to go. The mountains seemed right before him.

---

He broached a small crest in the road and detected a faint glow in the fog. Bansuth neared, but the mist was too thick to know anything more. A wind, cold and heavy, descended the mountains. It tore back the fog in strips and the glow of the city grew brighter. The wind resisted Hantle's approach and he squinted his watering eyes.

It had taken him more than a full day of riding to get here and his body felt every mile. His back ached and his legs were raw. Yet the wolf would not care. Had the beast come yet, or would Hantle arrive with a moment to spare?

Forest gave way to field. Above, the sky tinged purple and the outlines of mountains sharpened. The last shreds of fog dispersed and the city's walls were silhouetted by light behind. Hantle cocked an ear for sounds, but the wind dominated any other noise.

For a long moment, his mount seemed to inch closer. Then time jerked him forward in a frantic second. A gust of wind dissipated smoke from a structure just outside the open gate, but the flames coughed soot and grew taller. He discerned fire behind the city walls. A few yards before the gate, Hantle dismounted and left the horse behind as it gasped for air. He held his torch high and ran to the gate's stone archway, passing between enormous stone braziers. He stopped. His stomach dropped as he saw Bansuth for the first time. No, no, no. Rubble filled the streets and countless flames licked the sky. Panic flooded him and he sucked in ragged breaths. It had beaten him here. He was too late. No building appeared untouched. A silent desolation spread vast before him.

The main road was filled with timbers and stones and housewares and blood. How many of the thousands had any time to react? Hantle imagined them being taken in their sleep and the buildings falling aside as if made of nothing more than ash. Soon ashes would be the only remains. Until a gust scattered them and Bansuth was forgotten, Founsel erased.

A knot formed in his throat as he moved farther in. The city was nearly leveled and he staggered at its size. The network of streets was clumped with wreckage and he picked his way through as best he could. He felt the need to surround himself with the ruin and ash and smoke. To enmesh himself in destruction once more. The scale and completeness was surreal. The uncontested wolf had taken the entire city, leaving him like a tardy scribe to take stock of the losses.

He stepped over a timber and broken glass ground under his boot. Another sound then surprised him and he jerked his head in its direction. The dim shape of a woman moved between sources of flame. She called out a second time. For a moment, Hantle could do nothing, so taken aback was he that someone shouted *to him*. A lone soul in the waste stretching for miles. She started to run toward Hantle, across vague heaps of former city blocks. The mood that had settled over Hantle shifted and fell away. Finally, his legs moved and he rushed to her.

With half the distance between them left, she folded and retched. As Hantle closed in, her strength failed completely and she slumped to the ground. He knelt, set his torch aside, and raised her to a seated position. Her skin was so pale and the light so dim that she looked like a phantom. A cloud of smoke washed over them, she coughed, and the illusion was broken. She was flesh and blood, just as he.

Her light-green eyes parted and her mouth moved but no sound came. Hantle managed to sputter, "You. You survived. How?"

With an arm, she pushed herself up a little more and speech returned to her throat. "What do you mean, I survived? What happened here? To the city?"

"I only just arrived," Hantle said. "But I will help you as I can. What is your name?"

"Dalence."

"Okay, Dalence. I am Hantle. Can you tell me what you saw?"

She brushed black hair, matted and clumped, out of her face. "I was visiting with my parents. For the last two days I've been sick and they were taking care of me. I had sweats and was in their cellar to keep cool. I fell in and out of sleep. But, when awake, I had hallucinations."

"What do you remember of these hallucinations?"

"I finished vomiting and heard drums in the distance. My mother and father left to see what the commotion was. They walked up the stairs and I was alone in the cellar. Then I heard them scream." She became more animated now. "Our house was ripped from its foundations. In the sky above, an enormous paw swiped at other houses nearby. Then the face of a wolf breathed fire as it moved through my view. A moment later, it came back into sight. It moved quickly and bit at the ground. Oh, what good does it do to share my nightmares?"

"Please, do share everything you remember. It is all important." He scooted closer.

"Well, when it sat on its haunches, it let up a howl that shook the ground. I felt my chest reverberate with the sound and the mountains seemed to shake too. The night sky buzzed and fizzed and popped behind its glowing face. Axe marks spread across the sky, like someone was chopping at the firmament.

"Bricks and bones fell into the basement around me. I could hear so many people screaming, but I couldn't see any of them. There were muskets firing from somewhere. The wolf stalked through the frantic city until the tears in the sky caught his attention. He gave one last look at the city, and I thought he locked eyes on me for a second. I was terrified he would come for me next. Then he jumped into the sizzling sky and rushed after the axe marks. Some of them faded and others appeared. The wolf bit at the marks before it rushed off into the distance. The sky was still rippling before my view went hazy and finally snapped black.

"I had passed out. Who knows how much later I came to, feeling a bit better. I finally had strength. But something had happened. Or the hallucination wasn't over, still isn't. I was covered in dirt and ash. I found the energy to claw my way out of the cellar. The house was gone, as was the entire neighborhood. I walked a little and that's when I saw you. Have I been unconscious for days? What could have really happened?"

Hantle took in her information and thought for a moment. "Not all of what you saw was hallucination. That wolf is real. I have been chasing it for days. It destroyed my village first, and then Harsenth, and now it's moved through Bansuth."

Dalence shook her head and tried to stand. "I may still be sick, but I'm no fool." Her legs gave out and she fell against the rubble.

"No, you're not. If anything, I am the fool for chasing the damn thing. Some parts you did imagine though. It doesn't breathe fire, and there were no axe marks in the sky. It was a meteor shower. But the creature is huge. It grows each night after eating the town it attacks. Then it moves on to the next, larger settlement." He told her of Founsel, how he lost his family, and his ride from Harsenth. Pulling back his sleeve, he revealed the bite wounds, which were scabbed over and showed much less inflammation than before.

Confusion crossed Dalence's face. "You escaped your death, only to chase after it. Why?"

Hantle pulled the ring from his shirt pocket and turned it over between his fingers. "If I can kill the wolf, I won't have failed my family completely. There's nothing left for me but to kill it. I have to kill it."

A bit of strength returned to Dalence and she motioned for Hantle to help her up. "So I haven't gone mad, but the world has."

Hantle placed his arm around her shoulders for support. She was nearly as tall as he. He indicated their surroundings and asked, "Did you see anyone else as you walked?"

"No. Only you."

"You were with your parents, but where is your home? In Bansuth?"

Together they took a few steps forward, to test Dalence's balance.

"I was visiting for my mother's birthday," she said, "since I had not seen them in some time. I live in Suu-manth, on the other side of the Knuckles."

"The trees we felled in Founsel were shipped to Suu-manth. I have not been there, but I know of it." He looked to the mountains that blotted out a large portion of the orange sunrise. "What other towns are nearby?"

He drew his arm away from Dalence's shoulder and she took a few, soft steps on her own. A grimace passed over her face and she put a hand to her stomach. "Guess this illness still has me a little. Suu-manth is the next closest city. A few homesteads between here and there, but they're far flung."

"Where would you like to go?" Hantle tilted his head to the direction he had come. "I can gather my horse for you."

"No, I am fine for now." She waved an arm to dismiss the idea. "I want to return to my parents' house."

"Okay. Just let me know if you need my arm."

She walked slowly, easing her way around and over the rubble strewn about. "What's next for you? Where will the wolf go from here?"

"I want to see you safely back to Suu-manth. And the wolf will be there next, seeing as it's the nearest city. Do you have a family there?"

"I live with my brother." She paused with a faraway look in her eyes. "He is now the only family I have."

Hantle laid a hand on her arm. "That is why I want to help you return."

They walked the rest of the way to the ruins of her parents' home. A field of coals gave a faint light to outline the cellar pit. Tears fell from her face to mix with the ash at her feet. Hantle pushed the torch ahead and looked for anything recognizable but noticed nothing at first.

"Here, Dalence. You'll need some light."

She sniffled, took the torch, and stepped into the rubble. "Thank you."

---

Dalence turned over pieces of wood, stone, cloth, and shattered plates. The torch allowed her to see, but made sifting more difficult. Slowly, she searched. Few things survived intact, but she gathered a few armfuls and looked through them. With only a fraction of her normal strength, and not wanting to burden Hantle with her trinkets, she could take very little. What of these surviving items best reminded her of her mother and father? She mulled it over as Hantle sat above, along a few remaining pieces of foundation.

For her father, she decided on his favorite lorebook. Its edges were darkened with soot but it had escaped the flames. Seeing it made her feel like a young girl again, sitting in her father's lap as he read her a tale before bed. She clasped it to her chest and closed her eyes to see his face, smiling as he turned a page.

As she opened her eyes, something glimmered in the corner of her vision. She turned in its direction but the glint disappeared. She crawled to the general area, char staining her knees and hands. Beneath a pile of fractured crates, she found a necklace just peeking out. The silver setting of a long lilac crystal caught the light another time. It was a piece her mother had owned as long as Dalence could recall. This, she would prize the most. Setting aside the torch, she fastened the chain around her neck. The crystal was warm, as if from her mother's chest.

With the book secured in a small bag, she found her way back to the street where she rejoined Hantle and handed him the torch. She fastened the bag around her waist.

Hantle said, "When you are ready to move on, I can gather my horse. It's just outside the city walls."

"May I wait here?" Dalence said. "To spend a few more minutes with my childhood home before we leave it behind?"

"Of course." Hantle stepped into a small clearing in the rubble. "I will be quick."

Dalence took in the scene. The sun was nearly above the mountaintops. She pictured her parents before her, standing just outside their home. The inviting scent of pies wafted from the kitchen, through the front door, and greeted her on the street. At least she had the fortune of spending the last few days with her parents. Maybe those memories would stay fresh in her mind for a while yet. Another wave of nausea passed over her. When Hantle and she arrived in Suumanth, she would have to break the news to her brother, Brust. It still did not feel real. Each time she considered never seeing her mother or father again, she wanted to retch out her entire gut. Instead, she thought of the trip to Suu-manth and rejoining Brust. Deciding what to tell him was something she could worry about later. She still wanted to see him. Hantle had the goal of stopping the creature she had assumed was a hallucination. Was he brave or insane? Either way, he was her partner for a time.

---

"I collected a few provisions," Hantle said as he returned to Dalence on the horse. He dismounted and offered her a hand up. "How about you ride until you're feeling better?"

After she was seated, Hantle adjusted the musket sling so it would not rub against her leg. He then led the horse by the bridle, walking alongside it. They picked their way through the remains of a bustling city of thousands. The two approached Bansuth's eastern gate. Just inside the walls was a courtyard. Clothes and other items were scattered around, most of them charred. A flock of crows occupied the cobblestone yard and Hantle thought they fed in the debris. As the horse approached, the birds cawed and flapped into the sky. From their mouths fell small, grey, waxy things. He walked over one of the pieces to realize they were parts of the dead. Toes and fingertips. Teeth and tufts of hair lay nearby. The crows circled, as if to land once they had passed. He shouted at the birds, "Go, get out, you damn scavengers. Go!" which forced them to wheel away over the city walls. Their awful racket faded as the flock receded.

He noticed Dalence's look and said, "They were desecrating the dead. Give them at least a day."

Hantle turned his eyes from the human remains to the gate. The doors were broken and fallen from their hinges. The archway was cast down and its stones choked the opening. Two stone bowls flanked this gate, like those he had seen at the other, but these were overturned and their coals spread wide.

Dalence must have noticed his gaze because she said, "Those fires once welcomed all to the city and wished well those who left it."

"Maybe those braziers will burn again one day," he said. A building shifted behind them and the noise of its collapse spooked another flock of crows to flight. Although no day soon, he thought.

---

Morning spread as the sun climbed into the air. The road ran flat for a while. Once the wind faded, sunlight warmed their bodies. Hantle could see the road snaking its way up the mountainside.

"How long," he said, "does it take to reach the top of the pass?"

"About five hours to the Splitskin. Give or take a little."

When the cobblestone paving ended, the slope started. Upward they went. Long grasses spread out next to them and ran along until small, gnarled bushes sprang up. The road led through the dense scrub. Hantle's body felt heavy as he changed his gait to match the incline. Shortly, the path began a series of switchbacks through deep forest. He pulled out the pack of jursant and placed a pinch under his tongue. Dalence leaned forward against the horse and rested.

"How many people live in Suu-manth?" he asked.

"Somewhere between ten and fifteen thousand." Dalence kept her eyes closed.

"Wow. Far more than the number living on the entire Far Finger." Yes, he was pushing his limits again, but ten thousand lives was good reason.

## CHAPTER TWENTY-ONE

HANTLE WALKED JUST AHEAD of the horse with its reins in his hand. He looked back to Dalence, whose head rested on the horse's neck. Her hair was slick with sweat and fell over her face. Not wanting to disturb her, he watched the road for a time.

When Dalence shifted, she spoke so softly Hantle had to lean closer to hear her.

"I can't rest with my eyes open," she said. "But the horse sways too much to keep my eyes closed."

"Are you going to be sick?"

"No," she said. "I just can't stay still for more than a minute."

Hantle gave her an understanding nod.

———

Ground cover grew so thick, Hantle was unable to see beyond the road's edge. He brought out his waterskin, drank from it, then offered it to Dalence. She took it but refused any food. Hantle ate half an apple and gave the other half to the horse.

He said, "Let me know when you get hungry. My odd sleep schedule has me eating at all hours of the day."

She nodded and they continued in quiet for a ways.

---

When the road wound along the top of a steep ravine, Hantle broke the silence. "Is your strength any better? Does your stomach still pain you?"

Dalence sat up and replied, "Yes, I do feel stronger now. The stomach doesn't hurt as much, but I feel nauseous thinking about my parents."

"Ah," Hantle said. "Grief and sickness do feel the same."

Dalence shrugged and said nothing further.

Hantle thought aloud. "Loss is a part of every person's life, but that makes it no easier to accept or bear. If I think of Lorenca or my sons for more than a moment, I—" His voice broke and they both left the conversation at that.

---

Hantle sat on a fallen log and gave a long sigh. "I'll just take a minute or two to rest."

"You look like you're going to fall asleep." Dalence dismounted and sat beside him.

"Me? I'm doing fine." He yawned. "Got two hours yesterday." A wry smile passed over his face. "A person can't need much more than that, right? Anyway, you mentioned living in Suu-manth with your brother."

"Yes." She nodded. "Brust and I have a small place we share to help make ends meet."

"What took you to Suu-manth?"

"Better job prospects. Work pays better and is more abundant in

Suu-manth. He moved there a month before I did. Got his job and living quarters sorted out before I came over."

Hantle straightened his legs and bent forward to stretch his muscles. "And what do you each do?"

"He's a fisher and I work in a textile shop. That sort of job would never have existed for me in Bansuth because of how much larger the Fist's population is."

Hantle stood and moved his arms in large circles. When Dalence gave him a strange look, he said, "Helps get the blood moving. Don't mind the windmilling."

Dalence stood and imitated him. She said, "Now you're rested enough for another day, huh?"

"Or at least another twenty minutes," he replied. "You ready to press on?"

Dalence had a foot in one stirrup, but before she threw her other leg over, she pointed to the horse. "You should ride for a while."

"Eh." Hantle shook his head. "My legs still feel raw from riding for so long yesterday. I'll walk for now."

———

After rounding a few more switchbacks, a clearing in the forest allowed them to look westward. A layer of fog lay over the ground below that made it impossible to make out any features. Hantle wondered if the wolf lay enshrouded in the mists. Toward the horizon, a few stray peaks broke through the fog and jutted skyward. The tree cover remained sparse for a while as they traveled. He took frequent glances down the mountainside, half expecting the wolf to dash out of the fog and take them. Over the next few minutes, he noticed the Knuckles seemed to erode the fog. All the better, since his nerves would settle when it was gone.

Hantle noticed Dalence sitting up for longer periods of time and took this to mean she was feeling better. "How did you spend your time with your parents?"

"It was my mother's birthday and we spent most of a day making pies." Dalence looked down to the fog that covered Bansuth. "Every birthday, she makes more than enough for our family, as well my aunts and uncles, to enjoy. Always the giver."

Hantle smiled at her. "That sounds like a lovely time together."

"It is a memory to cherish. Though I keep coming back to the question of how long it had been since I last saw them." She paused and Hantle let the silence sit until she continued.

"I have always felt guilty for moving away from my family. At first, I visited often. But it's quite a distance to cover and that regularity is difficult to maintain over time." She took the reins in her hand and mindlessly fumbled with the straps. "The time apart also gave me opportunity to think. Could I have made a life for myself there, near Mom and Dad? If so, what would it have been like? I felt this guilt, yet it didn't bring me to move back. So what was its purpose? To just gnaw away? Other times I wonder whether I missed them or simply felt like I should miss them."

He hoped these were rhetorical questions since he felt unable to comment. Before his parents had died, he had lived just a few houses away.

After a moment, she said, "Tell me of your family."

---

She listened to stories of Hantle's boys, their love of playing in the meadow and getting muddy in the creek. His wife was a loving mother as well as a painter of local renown. They had both lost family, Dalence realized, but different kinds of family. What type of pain did he hold within his heart?

The pair passed over a shallow creek lined with thin trees. Feeling well enough now to recognize a bit of hunger, she asked Hantle for a handful of fruit. She ate the dried dates as they traveled through a corridor where sun dappled the road around them. The food gave her mood an immediate lift.

A mile later, they rounded a bend where the trees gave way to a steep cliff and they got their first good look at the Far Finger cleared of fog.

As she bounced with the horse, she saw the darkened patches of far-off Bansuth, which stood in odd relief to the surrounding forest greenery.

Hantle spoke and drew her from thoughts of her parents. "I wondered whether we would see the wolf after the fog had passed. Yet I see no trace of it. Would it still be capable of hiding somewhere during the day?"

"If I didn't hallucinate the size," Dalence said, "it was truly gigantic. Perhaps it already passed over the Knuckles?"

Hantle's eyes grew wide. "I had not considered that. The thought alone creates a pit in my stomach."

———

They had climbed a long way and the trees dwindled to bushes. The slope of the mountain steepened and scree dominated the landscape. A massive clearing spread before them. Dalence thought the depression looked out of place and, a moment later, the shape registered with her. "Hantle, do you see that crater?"

"The one straight ahead? Yes."

"Do you recognize its shape?"

Hantle stopped walking, which brought the horse to a standstill. "A . . . wolf print."

Dalence swallowed hard. "That's what I thought. As if it were going over the mountains." The print cleared a huge swath of land of the typical boulders. She noticed Hantle's long look over the range, from north to south. "What is it?" she said.

"When I found my boys, all that was left was their heads and spines." His voice became thick. "Just now, I feel as if we are walking over a great spine protruding out of the world. Crossing this backbone will take me farther away from their graves, but no further from the memory of what happened to them."

Dalence was glad to have momentarily paused. Pain sat heavy in her gut, and she couldn't bear any movement.

Hantle started the horse forward again, now at a quicker pace. "If the beast did cross the Knuckles, Suu-manth might have already been attacked."

Not Brust too. Her mind raced at the thought. "When we reach the Splitskin," Dalence said, "we will have a view of the city." She looked up the mountainside. "Not much farther to go." Brust, stay safe, she thought, at least until I return.

Hantle looked over his shoulder at her. "What can you tell me of Suu-manth? All I know is that they take their lumber fast. What is its history? Who is in charge?"

"The people of Suu-manth are proud of their heritage and are eager to share it. Such is how I came to learn it." The horse stepped up a natural staircase and Dalence jerked with each step. "The countless lakes of the area supported many people. Fishing tribes originally competed and grew in size. Several generations ago, the tribes pooled together their resources and opened a central marketplace. It brought consistency, fair prices, and allowed fish to be transported to a wider area, because it handled distribution.

"A governor was introduced some years back, and the position serves as head of the fishing industry and settler of disputes. The role is currently filled by a woman nearing the end of her term. She has an adviser that rotates each year."

"How is the adviser chosen?"

"The title of Chancellor of the Catch is, I guess you can say, earned. Each spring, on First Fish, a race is had to catch a fish and behead it on the Bleedstone, a special spot at the Marketplace. The winner is the Chancellor of the Catch until the next First Fish. They say that fisher has luck in the catch and will impart their luck on the governor."

"I imagine the entire city gets excited by that competition."

"Oh, yes." Dalence nodded in agreement. "All the shops close for the day and the streets are packed. It's entertaining."

"What is the governor like?"

"I have seen her a handful of times at events, like First Fish, but never met her personally, so I am not sure what she's like."

Hantle held up his hand and crossed his fingers. "I hope she is at least a person of reason."

---

Dalence watched Hantle walk and wondered what drove him. She had lost family, as he had, but her first reaction was to collapse. His seemed to be to press on. Hantle had helped her up and was leading her back to her brother. She admired his persistence, his focus, and that he did not give in to paralyzing pain as would be so easy to do. Were it not for his singular purpose, she would still be in Bansuth, wandering through the ruins. As she had seen briefly, he felt a deep pain, though it did not overwhelm him. His quest for revenge lent urgency to his actions. Might she be able to ease her guilt for surviving when her parents did not if she espoused even a modicum of that revenge?

---

Near the top of the pass, a channel of water runoff cut down the center of the road. Patches of snow and ice sheltered in north-facing pockets had so far withstood summer's temperatures. But they still fed the stream, little by little. Hantle's shoes had muddied from the path and he stopped to clop them along a rock.

From horseback, Dalence called to him. "Hantle, look."

Ahead of them was a sight he did not expect: a makeshift stable that held several horses.

# CHAPTER TWENTY-TWO

HANTLE LET the horse's bridle go and stepped closer to the stable to investigate. Behind, he heard Dalence dismount and follow him on foot. A breeze came toward him through the pass and he noticed it carried a sound. As Hantle walked, a man initially hidden behind a boulder became visible. He was chopping firewood, facing away from them, and did not notice their approach.

The man's strokes stopped as he reached for another log to split. His head was shaved and he had a form that spoke to familiarity with his weighty maul. Hantle took advantage of the break in the man's chopping and coughed, then cleared his throat. He hoped to get his attention without scaring him. The sound drew the man's gaze and he turned, setting the maul down beside him. Dark eyes hid beneath thick eyebrows. A look of confusion crossed his face and he said, "Dalence?"

"Darbor?" She looked to Hantle. "We work together at the textile shop." She walked past Hantle and shook the man's gloved hand. "What are you doing here? I mean, what are you doing here in the Splitskin, and why are there horses tied up?"

Darbor removed his gloves and tucked them into his waistline.

"Chopping some firewood for tonight. I dabble in astronomy and am up here with a group on Mount Vulteeb to study the meteor shower that began yesterday." He grew more animated and spoke more quickly. "But the most exciting thing last night wasn't the meteors." He turned to Hantle and vigorously shook his hand. "Hi, I'm Darbor. What's your name?"

"Hantle. Pleasure to meet—"

Dalence cut in and asked, "What else did you see?"

"Oh," Darbor said, "I wasn't up here last night, though I wish I was. I came up this morning."

"Fine," Dalence said, and Hantle noticed her impatience. "What happened last night?"

"They saw Bansuth destroyed."

"Did they say how?"

"Bellice said it was a monstrous wolf that did it. Can you believe it?"

Hantle spoke up. "Who is Bellice?"

"She's the head of Suu-manth's Association of Astronomic Exploration."

"And where is she now? On top of Mount Vulteeb?"

"Yes," Darbor said. "She's always the first one up and the last one down. Why—" Hantle saw his eyes go wide. "Wait." Darbor shook his head in disbelief. "Did you just come from Bansuth? How in the hell did you survive the night?"

Hantle ignored his question. "Can you lead us to her?"

"Sure"—Darbor picked up his maul—"I'm sure she'd love to hear what you have to say." He swung the bit into a log and left it there.

Hantle turned to Dalence. "If you're not feeling well, you could stay with the horse and I'll go up alone."

She shook her head. "No, I'm coming with you. I want to hear what this Bellice has to say just as much as you do."

Hantle smiled at her determination. He took the horse to the stable and tied it there. "Lead on, Darbor."

The three of them started up a steep slope of scree that led from the Splitskin to Vulteeb's peak. Few people ventured higher than the pass itself so there was no clear trail. Over the next thirty minutes, they stopped a few times to catch their breath and wipe the sweat from their brows.

During one stop, Darbor, between deep huffs, said, "Mount Vulteeb becomes a semi-permanent settlement during meteor showers. Five or so people stay around the clock. Hence the stable below. The vantage from the mountain top is incredibly clear."

Hantle's pack slapped his back with each step as he climbed the last stretch of boulders. He followed just behind Dalence, in case she lost her balance, but she scrambled better than he did. On the summit, several canvas tents filled an area cleared of stones. Below him and to the west lay Bansuth's charred splotch.

Darbor called ahead. "Bellice, guess where these two came from?"

# CHAPTER TWENTY-THREE

BELLICE SAT BEFORE A TENT, writing in a journal. She heard Darbor's question, stood, and walked to the three of them. A swirl of wind blew her long silver hair over her face. She drew the hair back and pinned it behind an ear. Her green eyes took in Hantle and Dalence.

Darbor waited for Bellice to answer his question, but when none was forthcoming he continued. "Bansuth! They came from Bansuth."

Hantle preempted any questions from Bellice by asking one of his own. "But found it already destroyed. Would you be able to share what you saw happen?"

"It was unbelievable," Bellice said as she drew her jacket closed against the stiff wind and placed her pencil in a chest pocket. "First, we felt trembling in the mountain. Our first thought was a quake, but the trembling was too abrupt and not a single, long tremor. We looked down on Suu-manth to find nothing. A howl came faint from behind us, from the Far Finger."

The hairs on Hantle's neck stood. He knew exactly what the howl sounded like.

"We walked over and saw Bansuth dotted with fires. That's when we realized it was in the throes of destruction. A creature moved through the city. A second later, we knew it was a wolf." She stretched her arms as wide as she could. "Mammoth thing, it was. Probably the size of a small mountain. How's a creature even grow that large?

"When it moved, it lunged. And flames grew up after it passed by. We guessed it was feeding on the people there, which was an awful thought, except we couldn't help but watch it for some time. Then something else caught its attention. The wolf looked to the sky, where the meteor shower was at full force. It jumped into the air and bit at the meteors but, after falling back to the ground, drove into the city. Once it had moved through all of Bansuth, the wolf turned to the sky again. With a running start it leapt, pushing off from the Knuckles—knocking us to the ground in the process—and landed in the welkin."

Bellice paused as she took a breath and wet her lips. Then she continued. "It was like a phantasm before us, and we all stared skyward. The wolf darted after a few meteors—snapping its jaws at them—but it was too slow and small to catch one. Who knows how long after, it gave up, looking exhausted, and disappeared behind the moon."

Hantle was captivated. He and Dalence stood speechless. The warmth that fell on him from the sun was quickly drawn away by the breeze. Several seconds passed before he found his voice. "The wolf jumped off Iomesel?" he said, incredulous. "How could anything leap off the planet without crashing back down again?"

"That's the part you can't believe?" Bellice replied. "What about a wolf the size of a mountain?"

Dalence whispered, "So I didn't hallucinate it?"

Bellice turned to her. "Didn't hallucinate what? Did you feel the tremors too?"

"While Hantle only arrived in the city after the wolf had gone, I was in Bansuth when the wolf attacked, although feverish with sickness and unsure of what was reality and what was dreamt." She relayed her experience in the cellar, how she awoke later to a ruined city, and when she found Hantle walking alone through the wreckage. Bellice and Darbor had their chance to listen, equally speechless. Hantle followed to recount details of the wolf's destruction in Founsel, his chasing it through Harsenth, and his ride that led to meeting Dalence in Bansuth.

Hantle's eyes widened with realization. "Dalence," he said, "this means that the print we saw on the mountainside was made as the wolf took its leap into the sky." The idea still went against everything he knew. How could anything go into the heavens?

Dalence's face showed relief. "And Suu-manth is still safe."

The discussion had drawn the attention of the remaining astronomers on Mount Vulteeb, and four others stood nearby, listening.

Bellice considered the new information for a moment. "It is awful to hear of the damage this creature wrought even before Bansuth. My heart is with—"

A portly man with wild, curly hair could no longer contain himself and burst out, "But do you know where the wolf came from? How it has this ability to grow so large? Scientifically, it's quite curious."

Hantle ignored the man and responded to Bellice. "I appreciate that, ma'am." Then he turned to the group at large. "Beyond a creature of this size being a curiosity, it is a danger we must deal with." His gaze fell to Bellice once more. "After the wolf initially disappeared, did you see it again?"

"No," she said. "For a time, we trained our telescope on the area near the moon where we last saw it. But when nothing followed, we resumed our watch of the meteors."

Dalence stepped a foot forward and asked, "A telescope? Can you explain what that is?"

Darbor motioned for them to follow him to the middle of the camp. "We have it right over here." He gently peeled back a tarp to reveal a long tube sitting atop three legs. "With it, we can see four other planets in the firmament." He set the cover aside and stood with his hands on his hips. "It's nice, isn't it?"

Hantle said, "I thought there were only three others."

Bellice pointed the telescope toward them. "Those three are visible with the naked eye. *This* does better. Astronomers elsewhere on the Fist have found one planet, called Coubae, that we cannot see unaided."

Dalence ran a hand along the frame. "How does it work?" The sun glinted off a curving design etched into the metal.

Bellice indicated the front of the tube. "A large crystal lens focuses the light to a smaller one at the rear through which we look. This iteration has a better viewing angle and clarity, thanks to the crystals used, although the image one sees is upside down."

Hantle found the artifact interesting but steered the conversation to what he felt most pressing. "There is still the matter of what we do with our knowledge of the wolf."

The group quieted and Hantle gave them a moment before continuing. "I found Dalence ill in Bansuth. There, I told her my first priority is to reunite her with her brother. And once they are back together, I plan to seek out the governor of Suu-manth. With a force more formidable than what we had in Harsenth, we may stand a chance."

Bellice's silver hair caught the sun as she shook her head. "A force to do what?"

"To be prepared for the wolf's attack."

"Maybe the wolf will never return," Bellice said. "Perhaps the prey he now seeks is among the planets."

"That could be," Hantle conceded. "But every night, the wolf has murdered people. And each night it attacks a city larger than the last. This makes Suu-manth the next target. The wolf may prove me wrong tonight, but I would not risk being unprepared."

The stocky man again interrupted. "Shouldn't we tell the entire city, at the Marketplace, instead of just the governor?"

This time, Hantle did not ignore him. "With this kind of news, I'm surprised none of you have already done that."

The man looked to the notebook in his hand. "I . . . Uh, we have all been focused on writing down our experiences and poring over the information we collected during the night."

"Regardless," Hantle continued, "I *would* tell them. Though after speaking with the governor. To have a plan to share, instead of only fear and speculation."

A quizzical look crossed Bellice's face. "Why bother scaring them with conjecture?"

"Wouldn't you want to know if your life could end?" asked the portly man. "I know I would."

Bellice replied, "So you could waste the time with worry? Give me death unknown and swift."

"As if our lives are certain at any other point," Darbor quipped. He gave a resigned laugh.

Another woman, with red hair tied into a bun, said, "We have to at least tell the governor. The people elected her, so we should let her decide."

Bellice said, "We seem to be split. Shall we hold a vote?"

Hantle turned and walked away. "Seems it's always up to a committee."

Bellice took a few steps after him. "Where are you going, Hantle?"

He glanced over his shoulder then back to the boulders ahead of him, before he turned around to look each in the group in the eyes. "This handwringing is tangential to the real point of what Suu-manth will do as a city. I agree that telling the wider population is important, but the governor has the best odds of coordinating resistance to the wolf. Bringing that fiend down is why I'm here. It's easy to debate the correct course of action until the danger's come and we're all dead. But my mind is decided on what I will do."

Dalence walked to his side and adjusted the pack on her back. "I lost my parents in Bansuth. That's hell enough, so there's no way I'm going to let the creature take my brother and me without putting everything I can into a fight. The governor will be able to do more toward that end than any lone individual can."

Hantle put a hand on her shoulder and smiled at her. Then he passed his eyes over the group. "Does anyone have a horse I can borrow for the ride into Suu-manth?"

"You can borrow mine," Darbor said. "Let me come down with you."

———

They descended the boulder field more quickly than they had come up it. It was rougher on Hantle's knees, but the muscles in his legs were thankful for the break. He shivered when they passed through the shade of a small prominence. He had not before realized how much a role elevation played in the temperature.

His mind moved on to how he had seen the shooting stars but not the wolf chasing them down. That should have been impossible to miss. Yet, he realized, for hours he rode in the slot canyon that reduced his view of the sky to a sliver. Other times, the trees atop it crowded together to completely obscure the night sky. Hantle had trailed the wolf by more than he originally thought. He would beat it to Suu-manth, at least. For the rest of the hike, he focused on his foot placement. The rhythm was hypnotic.

When they reached the Splitskin, Darbor untied his horse and handed the reins to Hantle. "If you leave her at the Marketplace, I can get her there tomorrow."

Hantle nodded and stepped into the saddle. "Thank you, Darbor. She'll be there when you get down."

Dalence mounted her horse and joined Hantle. "Now that we both have mounts, we'll make much better time down. Two or so hours." She directed the horse down the trail.

Hantle gave a look up Mount Vulteeb and saw two figures scrambling down the boulders. Maybe they would flee the area. Maybe they would tell their friends and watch for the wolf during the night's meteor shower. Maybe they would pick up arms and be ready to fight. It was not for him to decide or pass judgment. Just now, it *was* up to him to get word to the governor of Suu-manth.

# CHAPTER TWENTY-FOUR

DALENCE'S HORSE walked out of a narrowing in the Splitskin and followed the road along a cliff top. She was happy to be on the horse again. The hike to Mount Vulteeb's summit had been worthwhile but exhausting. Over the last half of the return hike to the stable, her stomach pain increased and made the trek difficult, but the churning settled once she was in the saddle.

She glanced over the drop-off's edge and, down a fall of a thousand feet, saw boulders ringed about a granite spire. That was enough for her. She turned to speak to Hantle, riding behind her. "This side of the Knuckles is steeper and harsher than the one we came up." She pulled on the reins to put more distance between her steed and the edge. The road before them continued south for some miles, occasionally snaking north via switchbacks. Ahead, she recognized the first turns they would encounter. A few trees clung to shelves and cracks in the mountainside, but no forests grew above the foothills far below.

The precarious position gave a view unrivaled by anyplace else on the road. Midday breezes turned the lakes dotting the land below into an undulating spread of glimmers. Countless villages bordered the waters and extended far out onto the plain, until a distant haze obscured any details.

Behind her, Hantle muttered, "Wow." He cleared his throat and said, "It's like hundreds of gems tumbled out of the mountains."

She laughed. "Yes, you're right. But, if you can imagine, it is even more colorful in the morning."

"Since I left Founsel," he added, "I've traveled alone. It is a relief to have a companion again. Particularly one who knows the burden of loss."

"I can understand that. The grief is ever-present but moving forward keeps it at bay. Having something to work toward focuses your thoughts, for the most part." She looked over her shoulder to Hantle.

"That is, if the lack of sleep doesn't scatter them." He smiled and slapped a hand to his cheek in a mock attempt to wake himself up.

The wind that had chilled Dalence on the summit and in the pass lessened during their descent. Goosebumps on her arms disappeared as the warmth from the sun finally stuck to her body. A yawn escaped her lips. "You can't talk about being tired," she said. "That makes *me* tired."

"Then we'll talk of what's ahead. What do you know of Suumanth's army?"

Dalence had a thousand-yard stare and her eyes darted from side to side as she considered the question. "'Army' is a bit of a stretch. They are more of a guard for the city. The Marketplace, especially, has a large presence to help encourage orderliness. Taxes from the fish trade pays for the personnel, so they also protect caravans and storage buildings."

"They'd have to be well-outfitted for those roles. That's a start. We'll have to ask the governor how many strong they are."

"What are your plans?" Dalence asked. She readjusted her position to be able to look at Hantle without awkwardly twisting her neck.

"To be honest, I am not sure. In Harsenth, they had two cannons that I hoped to use to kill the thing. But I botched it and took the artillery and a couple squads too far away from the city to be useful.

Cannons had a chance of working when the wolf was smaller." Hantle opened the pack he had lashed to the saddle strings and pulled out the waterskin. "Now, though?" He took a drink and wiped a stray drop from his lips. "Is there even a cannon large enough to try that again?"

Dalence went quiet and imagined what a cannon of that size would look like. Would it have to be as long as one of the lakes below? The cannonball so large it must be moved by teams of oxen? Would any forge be able to cast that caliber? She turned forward on the horse and it turned down the first of many switchbacks. For quite some time they rode in silence. Dalence was pensive. Her mind drifted to other means of stopping the wolf: catapults, nets, leg-hold traps, crossbows. Their options might not be as bleak as it had first appeared.

Eventually, her mind's eye turned back to her parents and anguish gripped her mind. She lay forward on the horse and stared at the ground. Nausea swirled in her stomach when she imagined seeing Brust. She might rather speak with the governor before going home. Having a plan to relate to him would make the conversation easier. "Yes, Brust," she pictured herself to say, "I lay there while they died and could do nothing. But now I can do something and here's what."

---

Hantle removed his jacket as the horses carried them into the foothills of the Knuckles. He knew he would not find the wolf out on the Fist, but he looked anyway. The forests stretched to the horizon and he imagined the wolf lying down, looking like a set of mountains breaking the flatness.

The road wove east through barrows and cut north to avoid a ravine. As they rounded a bend, the mountains towered to their left. A large clearing left by a landslide ended in a talus littered with dead tree trunks jutting out in myriad ways.

He noticed Dalence sitting upright, focused on the mountains, and said, "You look much better than you did this morning."

Her horse followed a curve and Hantle saw the determination in her face. Dalence said, "I am picturing the best location to place a grand weapon like you mentioned."

He had dismissed that idea as too outlandish and had spent much of the ride dwelling on his record of failure. But here was Dalence, plotting out action instead of ruminating on defeat. The wolf's growing size did not limit her imagination.

"Good. Ideas to propose to the governor will be necessary when we speak to her. After getting you back to Brust, of course."

The hills shrank as they neared Suu-manth. Tendrils of smoke rose from chimneys that spread out before them. No walls demarcated the city's boundary, but they closed in on the outer reaches.

Dalence shook her head and said, "Enlisting the governor's forces will help put Brust out of harm's way. I need to do that first. I owe that much to my parents."

He watched her sling her pack to her lap and feel around its interior. She drew out the crystal necklace and latched it around her neck. The clasp caught the sunlight and Hantle was encouraged to see the motivation she embodied.

"Anyway," she added, "we have to pass the Marketplace to reach my house."

# CHAPTER TWENTY-FIVE

HANTLE DREW his horse even with Dalence's and rode past a cluster of squat, fieldstone homes that seemed to lean against one another for support. How did the walls manage to stay upright? They passed several other homesteads standing in the same slouching fashion and he concluded it was a regional style.

Shortly, they came by a small wooden guard hut sitting alongside the road. Dalence gave a brief wave to the guards who stayed seated and hardly seemed to notice the passersby. A fieldstone wall, only a foot tall, followed the road for a few hundred feet before grasses took its place. Their horses' shoes sounded on a bridge, laden with mosses, that led them over a stream. Farther south, the stream fed into another before emptying into a lake.

Hantle absorbed the city's layout and hum of activity. "From here, you'd think the city never ends."

Dalence glanced at him from the corner of her eye. "Some reckon there are ten times more fish than people. There's certainly enough water for them all."

Lakes occupied most of the city's area. Stone homes sat in the strips of land between adjacent bodies of water, which were filled with docks, piers, pylons, and boats. Many other homes were built over the water and stood on stilts. Due to the unfamiliar style, Hantle could not tell whether they looked to be of newer or older construction. He saw people scattered everywhere across the landscape: fishing from piers or boats, walking over bridges, tending to chores outside the home, or chatting with friends across the channels that connected most of the lakes.

Hantle followed Dalence's lead and soon lost track of where they were. He asked her, "How do you keep your bearings?"

"When I first moved here, I got lost more times than I can count. Still happens on occasion. But you learn the main roads soon enough. While circuitous, the largest ones, like the one we're on, run in to the Marketplace."

Hantle thanked her for the tip. "I'll commit that to memory."

A group of clouds moved in from the north and broke the heat with their raindrops. Hantle offered his jacket to Dalence but she declined, so he draped it over his back and lowered his head to the drizzle. The many roads curved around lake edges and split into or joined with others at intersections seemingly every few feet. Standing puddles pocked the dirt roads and their horses splashed through as they continued.

A stone slab rose ten feet into the air and had the word "Loamshoal" chiseled near the top, the letters painted white for visibility. "What does the stone mean?" Hantle said.

"Those indicate districts," Dalence replied. She pointed to a few vague places. "Other ones are scattered around different areas of the city. Loamshoal has many open-air food markets and pubs."

They passed a pub that blended in with its neighboring buildings. The only things to set it apart were the faded signage hanging from a metal rod that dripped rust down the sign, and two hitching rails in the street. Nearby was an alley where vendors occupied stalls, and individuals impervious to the rain browsed the selections of fruits and vegetables.

Before long, they arrived in a sizable clearing that lay between lakes. The ground was mostly occupied by one sprawling building. Dalence pointed to a sign half-hidden under nets and oars that read "Marketplace." She dismounted and Hantle followed her. A stone slab to the far left indicated "Mainlake." Hantle removed his musket from its sling and hung its strap over his shoulder. She turned their horses in at a corral and they walked into the Marketplace.

A door in the wall's rough-hewn timbers led into stifling air and a cacophony of shouts, music, and sounds. The main passage splintered off into a labyrinthine bazaar that resembled the drunken layout of the streets they had just traveled. Hantle again followed Dalence as she wove her way through the passages. A low-hung roof covered large portions of the market, but breaks here and there allowed in light sufficient to navigate and transact business.

An opening appeared among the stalls and the roof stood three times taller. He was thankful for the cooler air in this area. To his sides, the rain splattered on the lower, shingled, moss-patched roof. Dalence entered a line of people and, after catching Hantle's eye, nodded her head to the wide stone nearby. "That's the Bleedstone, and the governor's seat on top."

Wooden stairs from either side led to the Bleedstone's flat top. The frame of the governor's seat was built from oars and the arms were draped with netting. Half a fishing boat stood upright as the seat's back; its bow, a dozen feet up, curved over as an ornamental hood.

"Does she actually use it?" Hantle asked.

"Yes, when she holds daily audience."

When they reached the front of the line, Dalence gave her name to a man who added it to a list that already stretched to a second column on the paper. The man said, "Audience will begin shortly. Listen for your name to be called," and simultaneously waved her to the side and the next person forward.

The two of them walked under a break in the roof that dripped onto their shoulders, and they moved on into a thin passage. "Might as well eat as we wait," Dalence said. She folded over the waistband on her pants and, with some effort, removed a few notes that were rolled up and pressed flat.

"Never would have thought of that," Hantle acknowledged.

Dalence held up the stick of bills and smiled. "You never know when you'll lose everything but your pants."

The funds were enough for them to procure soup, bread, and two pints of ale from a few vendors. They stood nearby, ate, and discussed what they would say to the governor. Dalence proposed that Hantle lead since he had the most experience with the creature. The more times Hantle repeated the story, the stranger it felt. With each recital, it felt less real than the last. It was now more like a fable that hoped to draw veracity from being spoken. He set those thoughts aside and focused on the meal. The food was an improvement over what he had found during his travel and it left him filled. Hantle became distracted watching the goings-on, enjoying the bustle after so much time spent in relative quiet.

As he finished the last pull of ale, he gave a contented sigh. Suddenly, Hantle realized this was his first taste of life after grief. His stomach twisted into a knot for so easily forgetting Lorenca and his boys. Yet he hoped they would not resent him. He took the ring out of his breast pocket and rolled its warped shape between his fingers. The reason he was in Suu-manth was to honor and avenge them. Eventually, he might forge a new life from the fragments he had left from Founsel. Once he laid the wolf to waste, he might find some semblance of a home here. He would make the ring round again, even if he could not give it back to Lorenca. With a simple chain, he could wear her memory around his neck.

Hantle's attention jerked back to the Marketplace as Dalence tapped his arm. "Governor's called us." She stood and walked to the Bleedstone. Hantle took a deep, tired breath and followed her. His musket was taken by one of the guards next to the Bleedstone. As he climbed the stairs, he felt how heavy his legs had become. Would he have enough stamina tonight to do what replayed in his mind again and again?

# CHAPTER TWENTY-SIX

THE WOOD of the stairs groaned as Hantle stepped up them and onto the Bleedstone. The stone was wide enough to be a platform for the governor's seat and those seeking audience. Ahead of Hantle, Dalence stopped and pivoted to stand at an angle that included both Hantle and the governor. With her stance and look, she deferred the introduction to Hantle. Hantle took a few steps past Dalence and was caught by surprise when the governor raised her hand. "Stop. That is close enough."

Hantle stopped and rotated to include Dalence in his view as well, to show they were united. The leader's face was round but her expression was flat. She wore her hair pulled tight and fastened behind her head. Her eyes absorbed the dark of her wardrobe and surroundings such that Hantle could not be sure of their color. Freckles gathered around her eyes and hinted at her time spent in the sun.

The governor spoke again. "What brings you here today?" To her right stood a woman with a fishing hook pinned to her shirt. Hantle took this to be the governor's adviser, the Chancellor of the Catch. She had short-cropped, unkempt hair that fell across her face in several strands. Flushed cheeks called out her sharp cheekbones and small nose. A broad frame was enhanced by the way she stood with legs and elbows planted wide.

Hantle said, "We bring news of a grave danger to Suu-manth. May we convene in private to discuss this delicate matter?"

The chancellor replied. "It is customary for the governor to perform all her transactions in public." With an outstretched arm, she indicated a position closer to the governor. "But you may step forward to be more discreet."

Hantle approached until within arm's reach. Dalence drew up as well, to stand flush with him. Feeling the eyes in the Marketplace on him, Hantle stood straighter. "My entire family and village, Founsel, were destroyed before me. I raced to Harsenth and, while it survived, the city and inhabitants suffered great damage. From there, I came to Bansuth and found it decimated. Except for my companion, Dalence, none survived. All the cities on the Far Finger were brought low, and we fear the same will happen to Suu-manth next."

The governor's brow furrowed and she leaned forward to clasp her hands. Beside her, the chancellor tilted her head back and raised an eyebrow. "What danger," the governor asked, "do you speak of?"

Hantle wanted to add additional context before he mentioned the wolf. "We spent the entire day making our way here from Bansuth." He remembered the difficulty of talking to Harsenth's mayor and wanted to show the reality of the danger prior to introducing the hard-to-believe cause. "Dalence is still getting over an illness. She has pushed herself to stand before you. I suffered injury in Founsel"—Hantle rolled up his sleeve and exposed the network of scabs, still pink and prominent—"but have ridden nonstop for several days in the hopes of heading it off."

"You beat around the bush," the governor said. "Come to the point." She leaned back a bit, and Hantle worried he would lose her interest.

"The danger is a wolf that has killed thousands and eaten them all. With every soul it takes, it grows larger, then moves on to larger cities for more prey. The next city, we expect, is Suu-manth." He temporarily omitted the aspect of the creature leaving the planet. "As far as was last known, it was the size of a mountain, although it will have grown since then from the people it consumed in Bansuth. Its size makes it capable of destroying Suu-manth in a single night."

The governor let out a laugh, for which Hantle was unprepared. She threw her arms and hands out wide and addressed the chancellor. "Did you put them up to this?"

"Absolutely not," the chancellor said. "Someone here must have though." She cast a glance around the Marketplace. "Do you see anyone snickering?"

The governor turned her eyes to Hantle. "Shall I run home and pull the blankets over my head. Is that what you'd like me to do?"

"No." Hantle had not considered being laughed at. What approach could he take next? "We hoped you would set the city's army against the creature and use all your might to kill it."

The governor addressed the chancellor again but spoke just as much to Hantle and Dalence. "The problem with their 'warning' is that it's too fantastical. Over the top."

The chancellor nodded and locked eyes with Hantle. "Agreed, Governor. An advancing military would be much more believable. Or a robbery in planning, some spreading sickness, even economic saboteurs."

The governor turned to Dalence and said, "Are you just his body guard? What would you add?"

Dalence's face hardened and her voice carried weight. "Do not mock us. Our families have died, and we are here to prevent you from such a death, if you'll put back your small mind and step forward with a hint of courage."

The governor took an offensive tone to counter her. "Come from out of town, have you? Might have plied yourself with drugs that cause hallucinations and paranoid thoughts. There are enough concerns for me without listening to the nightmares of addled minds."

The chancellor stepped around the governor's chair and motioned for Hantle and Dalence to move to the stairs they had walked up. "That's enough. Let's move along now."

Hantle leaned around the chancellor to see the governor. "Yes, it's unbelievable, but Harsenth is still standing because they took swift action. Wouldn't it be prudent to take precautions instead of ignoring a threat?"

"Remove yourselves or you will be removed." The chancellor snapped her fingers to beckon forward her guards.

"We have proof!" Dalence shouted.

The governor's face scrunched with skepticism but she lifted a hand to pause the guards. "What proof?"

"A group of astronomers saw the wolf last night," Dalence said. Hantle saw the plea written on her face. "They can verify our claims."

"Bring them here," the governor said, "and let them speak for themselves."

"They are still on Mount Vulteeb," Hantle said. "But we could send word."

"How convenient," the governor mocked, "that your only witnesses are hours away. This is a plot to waste my time." She motioned again for the guards to move in. "A wolf has no more destroyed a city than an ant has built a mountain."

The guards gripped Hantle's arms and dragged Dalence along with him. "You don't understand how *this* wolf operates," Hantle said, struggling to keep his footing.

"Oh I understand enough. Goodbye." The governor waved a condescending farewell. "And if I come to hear that you're spouting this off to anyone else, you will be jailed."

The guards tossed them both out of the Marketplace. Hantle stumbled and fell to the ground as the rain pelted his back. His musket clattered down behind him. Their escorts disappeared once more into the building's dim interior. Dalence had kept her balance; she gathered Hantle's weapon and helped him to his feet. A group of people stood in the Marketplace's entrance, murmuring and looking at the two.

This was worse than he feared. "How did it go so wrong?"

Dalence kept his arm in hers and brought them to the corral where she spoke to the attendant. "Just my horse, please. The other belongs to a man named Darbor who will claim it tomorrow." The attendant gathered and returned the horse before retreating wordlessly, as if afraid to get too near. Dalence mounted the steed and pulled Hantle up to sit behind her. "We can discuss it at my house," she said.

"Yes," Hantle mumbled. "Okay. You're right." He gripped her shoulder as they rode away from the Marketplace and threaded their way between lakes.

The interaction with the governor squelched his ability to think. He had expected the leader to set him to some task and to spend the rest of the day preparing the city. He had expected a repeat of Harsenth: having a difficult time convincing them of the danger but ultimately succeeding. Instead, he faced jailing for breaching the governor's forbiddance.

Hantle looked to the boats on the water and imagined the wolf impacting them like a meteorite. He saw it dredge the lakes to feed on a hundred thousand fish. Then it licked its lips and its eyes burned fear into his chest.

The meaning sank in: The wolf was outside his reach. There were no soldiers to unite. The beast would come, unopposed, and find more than ten thousand people averting their eyes from the omen above. Would they believe only after its jaws clamped around them?

Hantle's remaining goal was to get Dalence back to her brother. At least he could accomplish that. She could get some rest, giving him time to figure out what the hell to do next.

# CHAPTER TWENTY-SEVEN

DALENCE TIGHTENED the reins on one side and directed her horse over a bridge. Hantle sat quietly behind her. The stonework included a high arch and wide-set pier columns. On the river, several people stood on a barge that drew closer to the bridge. They used long poles to maneuver the vessel under the arch. Stacked high on it were fish on their way to the Marketplace. Their oily scent was accentuated by the rain, which slowed to a drizzle. Because Brust came home each day redolent of the day's variety of catch, Dalence now associated the smell with home.

After the bridge, she continued along a strip of land that curved between several lakes. With each step, she drew nearer to the conversation with Brust. One she knew she must have, but she felt clueless as to how to begin it. All that came to mind were the terrible lines that might feature in a short story. "Hi, Brust. Yes, our parents have died and I was wondering what we might want for dinner."

She took a different branch at each of the next several intersections and knew Hantle would be turned around again. Two hunting dogs barked through a window in a home whose facade was completely covered in half-dead vines. The affordable residences were never easy to navigate to, especially in Suu-manth. The variations in the homes, landscape, and area grew on you though. She might never love the barking dogs, but they signaled she had nearly arrived. They were as predictable as the rising of the sun.

The horse carried them between two boulders and through the small basin between that always contained some amount of standing water. Her home then appeared from behind another it neighbored. Sheer curtains drawn across the windows highlighted the candles perched atop their stands. The slight lean of the front door was probably only noticeable to her. Patches of flowers stuck out of clay planters, which hung under the windowsills. The lavender of the irises was her favorite because it reminded her of her mother's necklace. The very same that she now wore.

Dalence stopped the horse just before the path that led from the road to their door. She looked back and smiled to Hantle. "Welcome to my home."

Hantle stepped to the ground and looked it over. "It's a lovely place," he said. "Your brother, er, Brust, will he be home?"

Dalence dismounted and looked to the curtains. "I am not certain, but it's likely he is."

She faced Hantle only to find his gaze had moved to the ground. He seemed fascinated with a particular rock as he went on. "Maybe you, uh, would like some privacy when you speak with him?"

Until Hantle mentioned it, she had not even thought about Hantle's presence as she broke the news to Brust. "That is a good idea. If you don't mind waiting. Much less awkward for you."

"Please, take all the time you need." Hantle brought his eyes to hers with a sheepish look. "Family is important. I'm fine to wait here." He adjusted the musket strap on his shoulder.

Dalence reached for the reins and started toward the house. "I will just take the horse around back and put him up. The back is more likely to be open, anyway." Without a backward glance, she said, "Thank you, Hantle."

Tending to the horse was her way of delaying the inevitable. She hoped the few extra moments would give her some idea of what to say. Behind the house was a small yard that contained Brust's mount. Hers had been lost in Bansuth. The gate squeaked open and Dalence threw the reins over the horse's neck then let him loose. She turned and grabbed an armful of hay before she closed the gate with her foot. Brust's stood under a small shelter and ate from its hay net. Dalence gathered an empty one, added the hay in her arms, and tied it to a post for the new steed to eat from.

Finally, she felt as ready as possible. Delaying would not do a thing for her except let her build the moment into a more impossible task. With a heavy exhalation, she opened the rear door and stepped inside.

Brust sat in his chair near the unlit fireplace. "Hey, hey. She's back!" He looked up from the net he was repairing and gave her a large smile. His auburn hair was a mess and fell past his ears. The thick beard was the same color and was even longer than when Dalence had left last week. A woad shirt clung to his large frame.

She walked straight to him, leaned over, and gave him a hug. "I love you, Brust."

Brust dropped the netting from one hand to reach up and return part of her hug. "You too, short stack." His hand felt like a stone on her back.

Dalence let him go and moved so she did not have to look at him. Instead, she drew the curtain back from the rear window, removed her backpack, and sat it under the windowsill.

"How was your trip?" Brust asked. "How did Mom and Dad look?"

Dalence, still facing the window, placed her hands over her face and broke into a sob.

"Whoa," Brust said. He put the net down and stood. "What did I say?"

She turned, tears running down her cheeks as she finally faced her brother. "Brust . . . They died."

Brust's face screwed up and he staggered back two steps, as if Dalence had punched him in the chest. "What? I . . . How?"

She wiped a hand across her nose and sniffled. "You're going to think I'm mad. But something awful happened in Bansuth. Mom and Dad were killed. The entire city was destroyed."

"So you found the city in ruins and Mom and Dad weren't there? Maybe they escaped before it happened."

"No, Brust. They had no chance to escape."

The chair broke Brust's fall and tears welled in his eyes. Dalence sat beside him and gathered her composure enough to relate the story. She spoke first of what time she spent with them, celebrating their mother's birthday. Then of her sweats and illness and how they moved her to the cellar to keep her cool. How their childhood home was knocked from its foundation and she saw a creature she thought was a hallucination. How it destroyed the city around them, eating all it found. How she passed out only to come to and find a silent wasteland surrounding her. The eerie walk through the rubble where she found a stranger, Hantle. How he chased the beast. That this man gave her aid and led her over the Knuckles. How they met Darbor in the Splitskin and learned the creature had grown so large it leapt off the planet and disappeared into the night sky. The ride to Suu-manth so she could get back to her brother. Dalence paused and both she and Brust cried together.

When he could speak without his voice breaking, Brust said, "All this since yesterday? They were there two days ago and now we will never see them again?" He shook his head and stared through the ground.

Dalence cleared the phlegm from her throat with a cough. "I felt so guilty that I survived when Mom and Dad did not. When we came into the city, Hantle and I went to speak to the governor. I couldn't see you until after I made it up to them. Made it up to you. For getting sick and not standing right there with our parents. Or keeping them down in the cellar with me. We told the governor of the wolf and how Hantle thinks it will come to Suu-manth next. But she laughed us out of the Marketplace and I couldn't even do that right. So I had to come back to you empty-handed, to say it was my fault. They went and I didn't do anything."

Brust dried his eyes with a sleeve. "Dalence, look at me." He took her arms in his hands and found her eyes. "You should *not* feel you did that to them. This . . . That thing, if it's a wolf or a monster or a demon, I don't know. But *it* killed them. Not you. Do you understand how fortunate I am that you escaped and made it back here?" He pulled her into a hug. The netting was still draped across his feet, and, when Brust let go of her, he bent over to gather it and throw it in a corner to be out of the way.

Dalence stood, sniffled, and walked to the rear window. "I managed to get a couple things of theirs before we left." She picked up the pack and opened its drawstrings.

Brust moved to the edge of his chair and looked expectantly. "What do you mean? From the house?"

Instead of answering, she handed him their father's lorebook. "Remember when you and I would sit outside at night and Dad would read us the same story as many times as we wanted to hear it?" Brust took the book with a delicate touch and his fingers immediately darkened with soot. He flipped open the cover and thumbed through several of the pages. As he did, Dalence removed the necklace and laid it across an open page.

Brust picked up the necklace and held the jewel to the light from the window. "I remember," he said, "when Dad came home with this. He made Mom close her eyes and he set a box on the table in front of her. On each side he laid a few irises, like the ones you planted outside. The look on Mom's face when she saw it. You'd never seen a more surprised woman. He saved up money for a year to be able to get that."

Brust choked up once more and set the book, still opened, on a table beside him. He handed her the necklace and walked to the kitchen, his steps heavy on the floor. Glasses clinked as he pulled a tumbler from a cabinet, along with a dark brown bottle. The cork squeaked out of the bottle's mouth. "Do you want one?" he said.

"No. Not right now," Dalence replied. She fixed the necklace around her neck.

He filled the glass completely and spilled a few drops lifting it from the table to his lips. The grimace on his face made her wonder how he could drink liquor like that. But he took several deep gulps before returning to the chair.

"This Hantle," he said. "Where did he go after you spoke to the governor?"

"Came here with me." Dalence pointed out the front door. "He's just outside. I didn't figure it'd be right to tell you with a stranger here."

"Well, hell, bring him in. Is it still raining?"

"It was barely spitting by the time we got here." Dalence unlocked the front door and motioned for Hantle to come in. Brust left his chair and joined Dalence at the door. She felt comforted by his size and the six inches he stood over her.

Hantle stepped inside and took Brust's hand in a firm shake. "Hello, I'm Hantle." He then covered the shake with his other hand and said, "I am sorry for your loss."

"Brust," her brother said. "And I can't thank you enough for helping Dalence get back on her feet." He stepped back into the room as Hantle leaned his musket against the wall. "Take a seat too. Dalence didn't mention she left you in the rain." He pulled a chair from the kitchen into the sitting room. Hantle accepted it with a nod and ran a hand through his wet hair, which made it stand out at odd angles.

Dalence and Brust resumed their seats and Brust took another pull from his glass. "Dalence told me you found her in Bansuth and that you were chasing the wolf. But she didn't say how you also survived the night."

Hantle shared his story with Brust, nearly the same one he gave to the governor. Brust asked a few questions of clarification, eager to hear the details.

After Hantle finished, Brust sat quietly for a moment before speaking up. "In a way, I can't imagine how this is true," he said. "But I'm not calling you a liar. Boggles the mind, is all."

Hantle nodded. "Understood. I was floored when some of what Dalence saw was backed up by the astronomers on Mount Vulteeb."

Brust finished the liquor in his glass and stood. Dalence couldn't tell whether he was feeling the alcohol yet or not. The mood on his face had darkened, though. He returned to the kitchen, poured himself another full glass from the open bottle, and capped it. "You'll have to excuse me." He walked through the sitting room, toward the small hall that led to their bedrooms. "I gotta be by myself for a while."

A pensive silence fell across the house and Dalence relaxed her body now that the dreaded revelation was complete. Hantle stuck his legs out, settled deeper into the chair, and leaned his head back on the padded top rail. She saw him close his eyes and did the same. How he had lasted this long was a mystery to her. A yawn escaped her. They would only relax for a few minutes. The governor had forbidden them from talking to other denizens about the wolf, but that would not stop her.

# CHAPTER TWENTY-EIGHT

A NOISE STARTLED Hantle awake and he looked to the kitchen. Brust rummaged through cabinets, slamming them shut again.

"I don't see a damn thing to eat," Brust said.

Dalence's eyes crept open and she looked behind her, toward her brother. Brust opened one more cabinet. From within, he drew a different liquor bottle, set it on the table, and picked up his empty glass. "Guess another drink will do." The pour sloshed over the side of the tumbler and Brust ran a finger through it. He licked the liquid from his finger and used his other hand to fit the cork back in, nearly spilling the bottle in the process.

Brust shakily walked from the kitchen to his room. The door slammed shut and Hantle heard something topple over. He pushed himself up straight in the chair and rubbed his eyes. He asked, "Feeling better after some rest?"

Dalence yawned and stood. "Let's see if this grogginess wears off first."

He leaned forward, elbows on knees, and felt his stomach rumble. It was yet another reminder that he could not press himself indefinitely and ignore basic needs. It seemed his entire journey was one of discovering unavoidable limitations.

Dalence said, "Your stomach's grumbling too? Guess I ought to make something then." She walked to the kitchen.

"Can I help?" Hantle offered. He started toward the kitchen.

She waved him off. "No, thanks. You helped enough on the way back here. Just rest."

"Okay." Hantle smiled and walked to the window. The sun was at an angle now for its light to spill into the house. He closed his eyes and felt the warmth crawl over him.

Metal scraped against metal as Dalence searched her cooking wares. She said, "Brust seemed a bit unsteady on his feet, didn't he?"

"That he did," Hantle replied. Through the window, he saw a large lake with boats pulling in nets full of fish.

"How about something hearty, then?" A thud came from the counter as Dalence set down an enamel pan. "A good casserole will help Brust soak up the liquor." She pulled a sack of potatoes from a corner and reached for a knife to slice them.

"Brust," she yelled to be heard through the door. A grunt answered. "Go grab us some fish."

Brust burst out of the bedroom, flung open the front door, and, still barefoot, headed out.

"Actually"—Dalence caught Hantle's attention and jerked her head to the fireplace—"you can get that fire going. And put some water on."

Hantle gathered the flint, steel, and kindling from the mantle and crouched down. He arranged kindling in a small pyramid in the existing ashes. He could hear Dalence's knife slicing through the potatoes behind him.

She asked, "Do you know what the most terrifying thing I've realized so far is?" Hantle shook his head as he set steel to flint. She went on. "That all the opportunities to spend time with my parents are passed. I always considered time to be in endless supply. There was always a chance to get to it later on. But I come to find that time is scarce and unpredictable."

A spark caught and the kindling smoked. Hantle blew gently on the flame and it leapt up. He said, "It's cruel that the promises of the future don't come to be."

Dalence's knife kept slicing. "Now that I've realized it," she said, "I want to be with my brother. But he seems intent on drinking himself to death."

Hantle added a few smaller logs to the kindling. He sat back and spun to face Dalence. "Everyone copes. How does he normally handle grief?"

"Like he is." Dalence picked up the bottle and mimed taking a swig from it. "At least the errand got him away from the booze." She set the bottle down and placed pieces of potato in the pan. To it she added other vegetables, cheese, and a creamy stock.

Hantle looked back to the fire and found it well established. To the growing blaze, he added larger logs. Dalence handed him a kettle to hang from a bar stretching across the fireplace, and then the dish with the casserole. The food, he sat on a grate that folded down from the side.

"Once the water's warm," Dalence said, "I planned to wash up. You're welcome to it first."

Hantle gave a small laugh. "I'll take the hint. Thank you."

"There's a wash basin right behind that screen." On the other side of the room, next to Brust's bedroom door, was a folding screen decorated with a variety of stylized fish.

He splashed a handful of warm water over his neck. "You know," he said, "I did not expect to be drug out of the Marketplace. Completely changes what we can accomplish tonight." Soot and dirt clouded the basin. He dunked his scalp into the water and scrubbed.

He heard Dalence fill the kettle with more water and place it back over the fire. She said, "But now we understand that fighting this wolf is up to us alone. No aid will come unless we bring it."

Hantle washed his face and used a damp cloth to wipe down his chest and arms before he grabbed a towel to dry his head. Cleaning up lifted his mood, like he had washed off a layer of mental crust too. He tossed his shirt back on and walked out from behind the screen to take his seat. Brust opened the front door and carried in three fish fillets. Dalence set them on a wooden plank, coated them with herbs, and placed the plank on the fire grate. Brust sat at the kitchen table and picked at some bread and oil Dalence had set out. With the food cooking, Dalence took the kettle and disappeared behind the screen to wash. The house filled with the delightful scent of the food.

Brust spoke to Hantle through a mouthful. "I am sorry you lost your family but glad you can be here with us."

Hantle said, "I'm fortunate you and your sister are so kind as to invite me in."

Dalence returned from behind the screen, drying hair that, now untangled, fell straight and well below her shoulders. She smiled to Hantle. "You have to work for it though. Go ahead and take the food off the fire."

Hantle complied and Brust spread the wood around to break the fire into smoldering coals. Each served themselves a plate of the fish, casserole, and bread. Hantle took a chair at the kitchen table and tucked into his food with his companions. The fish melted on his tongue and the potatoes hit the spot.

Hantle tipped his head toward Dalence. "Fantastic meal here."

She accepted the compliment with a nod but kept her head down in her food.

After a moment, Brust said, "Hantle, how have you coped with it?" The slur in his voice was unmistakable. "With your . . . loss. And, I'm sorry to say it, the future looking bleak?" Hantle could feel the pain that creased his face.

"I'm not coping. Everything I've done feels like flailing at the future. Trying to do something—anything—to help make sense of it." He chewed on a mouthful of casserole. "But I always come away thwarted."

Brust looked back to his plate, took a bite, and mulled on his thoughts.

Hantle looked out the window and found the sun. It was edging lower in the sky. He imagined being back on the Splitskin as the sun set and the wolf returned from the depths of the sky. Imagined watching the entirety of Suu-manth being taken into the wolf's maw at once. Thousands dying without a moment's notice.

Hantle swallowed and pushed the potatoes around on his plate. "The night's coming and I feel powerless," he said. "Much more so than previous nights. Other nights there was a goal to work toward: readying the city, preparing the defenses, traveling to the next town." He looked to Dalence and Brust, though he did not expect an answer from either. "Tonight, can we only watch defeat descend unopposed?"

Brust kept chewing.

Dalence filled her glass from a jug of water. "You had no army in Founsel, but that did not stop you." She drank. "You decided what was within your power, and you accomplished it. What is within your power tonight?"

Hantle shrugged. "Telling others of the creature . . . even though the governor forbade us to speak of it."

"See," Dalence said, "now that's something. I'm more afraid of the people not knowing what threatens them than I am of the governor."

"Yes. Keeping quiet would be the greater crime. If even a single family were to escape, it will have been worth it." Encouraged, Hantle turned to his food again.

"If we are lucky, we will set the city to panic and empty it." Dalence brought another piece of fish to her mouth.

"The governor be damned," Hantle said.

Dalence nodded. "The governor be damned."

Hantle had no thoughts on how to stop the wolf, but he felt sure that warning the city was one step closer to that end. Additionally, it was a way to honor his family and make amends. Uncertainty left his mind as he pictured the city in exodus. He poured himself a glass of water and drank deeply. Tonight, the wilderness would be safer than civilization.

Dalence finished the food on her plate and scooped another helping of casserole. "We also have a chance to be proactive."

"What do you mean?" Hantle asked. "How can we be proactive?"

She spoke between bites of food. "If the wolf comes to Suu-manth tonight, we can't control that. Which is why we ought to warn people. To give them a chance to get out. But before we crossed the Knuckles, it was just Suu-manth in danger. When we found out the beast left Iomesel, that changed. Now, when it returns, it could settle on scores of other cities as large as Suu-manth. If the wolf chooses another city, we may have time to figure out a plan."

This idea had not occurred to Hantle before: that the wolf might not return to Suu-manth. He had been so bent on getting to Harsenth, then Bansuth, then Suu-manth that the scope of the danger had never seemed to extend beyond it. Yet she was right. He said, "If the creature attacks another town, it'll be back the following night, and the one after. To consume more and grow further. If we use the intervening days to prepare, we can be ready to strike. No, we do not have an army tonight, but we can begin recruiting one tonight."

"I remember what you said of Founsel," Dalence said. "How people reacted differently to the danger. Some fled. Others stayed to hide. Others, like you, stayed and fought. It's those in Suu-manth who want to fight that we need to organize."

Hantle said, "Those disinclined to believe us will have a chance to see the proof overhead tonight." Finished eating, he set his fork on the plate. "Perhaps the governor is not the only one with power. Individuals can do things she has no power to. An army of volunteers is the fiercest kind." He pushed away his plate. "Though, while we may raise guns, we do not have weaponry heavy enough to properly resist the wolf."

Dalence scooted her seat back and stood, now excited. "On the way down the Knuckles, you asked whether there was now a weapon large enough to kill the wolf. I cannot say if one exists. But the thought has stuck in my head ever since and it won't let my mind go. If we do not have what we need, we can build it!" She walked to the front windows, threw back the curtains, and pointed out. "Set them right up there, on the mountainside. *That's* how we can harness the city's energy. Build the weapons to bring the damn beast down."

Hantle smiled at her ferocity and stood too. "Then we best set to it."

"The Marketplace draws crowds during the evening as well."

Brust stabbed one last piece of potato and raised the fork to his mouth. "If the wolf does make for Suu-manth tonight, I'd rather die with a beer in my belly."

"You do have the right idea," Dalence said. Brust stood and listed into the table. "Something lighter will do you good, anyways."

Brust walked to the back door and bent to slip on a pair of boots. Dalence reached out to steady him while he worked. Hantle followed them into the backyard. The sky glowed bright pink before them.

## CHAPTER TWENTY-NINE

DALENCE ENTERED the open doorway of the Marketplace, and Brust and Hantle trailed her through the passageways where vendors of food, drink, and treats still conducted business. She knew the largest congregation would be in the spacious common area near the Bleedstone, and she worked her way there.

Sounds of talking and laughter grew louder as they approached. She ignored a man's catcall and drew her group deeper into the crowd. At the center was a stand where people milled about. Two bartenders worked madly to serve pints of the brews on tap. Dalence wedged her way in. With a look over her shoulder, she motioned for Brust and Hantle to follow. The three squeezed up to the stand and a bartender —a grizzled, thin man—shouted over the nearby conversation. "What'll it be?"

"What do you have?" Brust asked.

The bartender looked back at the logos on the casks, as if uncertain. "Eh, summer ale from Flathold. A red from Three Casks."

Brust answered immediately. "Three Casks."

The bartender looked to Dalence next.

"I'll have the summer ale, please."

Hantle said, "The summer ale, same as her."

The man nodded, grabbed three empty mugs, and turned to the casks. Brust fished through his pockets for coin to pay the tab. The discussions around them ranged from fish reports to recent events to beer. Beyond the throng, long wooden tables stretched out, nearly full of occupants.

Their bartender returned, passed them the mugs, and took Brust's coin. The three of them moved out of the crowd and took up seats that came free at the end of a nearby table. Dalence raised her mug and said, "To unexpected friends." Hantle and Brust raised their mugs and joined her in drinking. She gave a look to the beer and took another sip. "The Flathold is a city far out on the plains. I don't know much more than they make good beer."

Brust smiled and said, "Trust me, that's the most important fact there is to know about it."

The three enjoyed their drinks amid the sounds of the crowd. Soon, though, Dalence was eager to turn to discussion, even if it made her nervous. She looked to her brother and Hantle and leaned closer. "How do we go about telling them?"

Brust shook his head and took a gulp, as if to excuse himself from answering. Hantle caught her eye and said, "I have been thinking it over. Mind if I start?"

Dalence leaned back, feeling relieved. "By all means."

Hantle shut his eyes for a moment of preparation. Then he stood and walked away from the table, holding his beer mug high. "I am not here," he said, his voice growing in volume, pressing over those nearby, "to tell you what to do." Those closest began to quiet. "Only to tell you"—the quiet spread farther afield—"what you should know." Within two sentences most of the discussion had died down and Hantle kept his speech loud. "Something the governor would prefer to keep secret." The stragglers acquiesced to the shouting man and all the court's faces pointed to him. "We all may be dead by night's end." Hantle paused and took a drink but launched ahead before the side chatter could pick back up. "Did you see the sky last night and the portents it held?"

Dalence read a mixture of emotions on the crowd: frustration, interest, impatience, confusion. A handful of replies came back. "Cheers to the sky!" "Will someone shut him up?" "Meteors. A meteor shower." "What's he saying?"

Hantle took another sip and wiped foam from his lips. "A demon has prowled the lands and killed thousands. Last night, it leapt into the sky to grow beyond measure." He pointed to Dalence. "She's seen the beast. Told me it jumped from the planet to the firmament. I didn't believe her at first and I've been chasing it for days. But it's true. It killed my family and I want to claim its soul. To keep it from claiming yours."

Hantle set his mug down and stood on the bench to gain visibility. A few people in the crowd lobbed comments but he had the crowd's attention. Even Dalence was eager to hear what he said next. "You are welcome to laugh me away, to attribute what I say to drink or to madness. But you will see, after dusk has come, that the sky reveals a wolf. Bloodied teeth and gargantuan claws. And you will hope it does not come for Suumanth. Then, I hope you will be eager to join us"—he motioned to Dalence and Brust—"to bring its end before it can bring ours."

Hantle stepped off the bench, and silence hung over the crowd for a few heartbeats. Then the chatter started, quietly at first, but it built into an uproar. Individuals pushed through the group and approached Hantle. Dalence soon lost sight of him in a sea of hands and faces. Several others approached her and asked her to explain what he had meant. Out of the corner of her eye, she saw handfuls of people leaving the court and Brust shrugging off questions as he reached to finish off Hantle's mug.

She told her story of seeing the wolf in Bansuth, meeting Hantle, and the astronomers on Mount Vulteeb who witnessed the creature leaving Iomesel. Accusations and inquiries followed. The naysayers, she petitioned, should join them outside once darkness had come.

Through breaks in the ceiling, the purple and deep-red sky signaled that it was not far off. Her details spurred others to back off, consider the implications, and rush away through dim-lit passageways.

Hantle emerged from the roiling crowd and drew close to Dalence. Behind, someone called out, "You failed before, why wouldn't you fail again?"

"Because"—Hantle turned to face the accuser—"Dalence has designs for weaponry to challenge him. Once we gather a force to build them, these killworks, we will stand the best chance of any on the planet to bring the wolf down." Hantle picked up his mug only to find it emptied. Brust belched and looked away. Hantle abandoned the mug, straightened up, and continued. "Success is by no means guaranteed, but when is it ever?"

Brust stood, steadied himself for a few seconds, and moved toward the bartender's stand. Dalence felt compelled to follow him, to watch over him. She spoke to the group to take her leave. "Join us in the clearing before the Marketplace. We will be there shortly to watch for the wolf." She disengaged and Hantle followed her cue.

The bartender refilled their mugs and Brust passed him more coin. The three made for the Marketplace's main entrance, to exit into the cooling night. Black and purple mingled overhead as the sun dipped farther below the horizon.

Dalence drank and craned her neck to the sky. How large would it be tonight? Some time passed as the night deepened and the stars shone brightly. People filtered out of the Marketplace and others walked in from nearby neighborhoods. The bartenders rolled out a cask in an attempt to follow the crowd. The number gathered there soon surprised Dalence.

An occasional streak flashed in the sky. The meteor shower had come. At first, the crowd looked to each meteor trail with expectation. But the wolf did not yet make an appearance.

Someone called out, "I bet they've taken bets on how long they can keep us out here waiting."

A young girl gasped and pointed. "Is that it? Is that the wolf?"

A man waved her off without looking. "That's what they'll have us do all night. Hang on every blip we see."

Commotion spread from the girl to her family and others besides. Dalence located the light source in question. A pinprick grew in size and brightness as she watched. It persisted much longer than a meteor and did not move quite so quickly. The spot grew a long silver tail, much like a comet. In time, the shape was recognizable. The wolf. It zigzagged through the sky, the burning slash looking bizarre as it faded.

The meteor shower's intensity had increased, one following right after the other. Farther out, the creature passed by the moon and his shadow raced across its face. The beast grew in size as he darted closer. Dalence could now make out individual teeth. A scream went up from the girl and she clutched her mother's leg.

Hantle leaned over and said, "It could be more colossal than the entire range of the Knuckles."

The wolf came to a stop and surveyed his surroundings. Its fur was much darker than before, though Dalence was not sure if it had actually changed color or was just singed from racing through the sky. Her heart clenched as she waited for it to lock eyes with her and bear down on Suu-manth. Instead, it moved through the sky and chased a meteor's flare. He caught nothing and raced in pursuit of a few others before he succeeded in capturing one in his jaws. As he swallowed, the ball glowed down the length of his throat. It went dark when it hit his stomach and a concussion reached Dalence's ears.

A collective gasp went up and mutterings spread through the crowd. Fragments of a discussion made their way to her. "The governor didn't take *that* seriously?" "Wouldn't even give us a chance to say goodbye to our loved ones?" "If you don't say you love them each night already, what difference will a few hours make?" People ran off, promising to bring back others to see for themselves. Behind, she heard a different group. "Every person thinks they'd like to know the day they'll die. But who sits staring into death's face and doesn't wish it'd come quickly already?" "That sounds exactly like giving up."

The next meteors were taken more swiftly, and Dalence felt the concussions rock the onlookers. She was certain the wolf had grown as much in size as it had in intensity. From somewhere else came, "If we left now, could we escape? Or hide? Something?" "If you're going to die, face it head on." The wolf's throat now had a persistent glow. Occasionally, it disappeared over the horizon in pursuit. Dalence was relieved to see the creature as it returned, because that meant it had not descended to the surface.

A question went up, targeting Hantle or Dalence. "You believe we can kill that?" The tone indicated skepticism. Above, the wolf came to a stop and let up a howl that reverberated off the mountains. The hair on Dalence's neck stood on end. Sparks from the eaten meteors escaped the wolf's throat and trailed off until their embers darkened. His belly glowed a molten red through the thick fur.

Dalence stood transfixed until the beast moved again. She swallowed a lump in her throat and replied, "What option do we have other than to try?" Recklessness flared in a corner of her mind and spread. "I can picture a crossbow bolt piercing its side, and a trebuchet launching shot that explodes upon impact. Pierced and burning, it would crash to the ground."

She could not tell who spoke next. "Can you imagine the value of its pelt?"

"More than all the relics in the world, I'd wager."

"Or the glory of felling that bastard?"

Hantle nudged her elbow and whispered, "Good. We have some interest."

Dalence spoke up. "We will have to build the killworks. Fortunately for us, Suu-manth is filled with people of ingenuity."

Brust raised his mug and beer sloshed over the side to run down his arm. "This creature took our parents. I want to make things right. Help balance the world. You others have a chance yet to prevent it from taking your loved ones."

Over the course of several hours, the creature grew many times in size. The wolf darted after one meteor only to get distracted by another. He chased one, then a second, then many others without eating any at all. Dalence thought it seemed to enjoy the sport of it. Once more, it halted and let up an enormous howl. Its stomach had faded to a barely detectable luminescence. Slowly, it rotated to face the moon.

With a snarl, he raced to the orb, where his landing threw up a large cloud of silvery dust. The wolf reared back and slashed with claws that left deep gouges. The moon did not yield like the meteors it devoured. He left scars along the surface but was too small yet to do more damage. Frustrated, the wolf jumped from the moon and disappeared into the far depths of the night. His trace faded quickly after him.

The crowd observed the final moments in silence before stirring again. Dalence spoke to Hantle. "Those claw marks will be additional proof."

She found Brust seated near the corral fence, slumped and asleep. She shook his arm to rouse him and helped him up. His head oscillated from side to side, and he did not seem to know where he was. Instead, he asked, "Did us leaving Mom and Dad mean we thought we were better than them?"

"No, Brust, it means that times change and we can't all live similar lives."

The corral's attendant had either left for the evening or was amid the animated group. She passed the leaning Brust to Hantle so she could round up their steeds. Brust muttered unintelligibly. Once she had the animals, they helped him splay across the saddle of his horse.

Hantle looked around them, the clearing dimly lit by a few burning lamps. Dalence saw a thin smile. He said, "Looks like we might have the help we need to build your weapons." She nodded and patted Brust's horse.

Turning to the crowd, she shouted, "Return here at seven tomorrow morning and we can begin building the means to kill the wolf. There is no way to know when it may next visit us, so we must work swiftly. With our efforts and some luck, we will stand a chance."

She took the horse's reins in hand and started toward home, with Hantle following on his horse. The task ahead was monumental, but she felt ready to attempt it.

## CHAPTER THIRTY

THE NEXT MORNING, Hantle rode with Dalence and crossed the bridge to enter the Marketplace's front yard. Brust followed several horse-lengths back. The grassy clearing was full of activity. A clear sky ran to the horizon and the temperature steadily climbed. People left their horses at the corral, dragged watercraft onto the lakeshore, or walked into the Marketplace. A handful of people stood off to a side and looked about expectantly. Hantle presumed that was their group. Dalence dismounted and greeted the individuals. Hantle turned the horse in at the corral. Brust's horse had come to a stop and Brust slumped forward on its neck. Hantle did not envy the man's hangover.

Turning back to Dalence, he saw her gathering information on each person's skills. Hantle followed her lead and introduced himself. By the time they finished the rounds, several others had trickled in to join them.

Dalence spoke to the group. "We have a nice turnout. More are welcome to join as they get here. Most of you, I expect, are returning after seeing the wolf last night. I'm encouraged to see your interest in doing something about it. I spoke of my ambition to build weapons that we may use to kill the wolf, but I must admit I do not have the experience. Every hand here will be useful in our task. Any others we can later bring to our cause will greatly help."

She looked across the faces that surrounded them. "Just from the introductions, I know this group possesses knowledge we will need. There is much to consider. Drafting designs, enlisting merchants for materials, engaging engineers for the construction, selecting a site for the placement, arranging transportation, providing meals and supplies for laborers. And, above all, coordinating these activities in the short timeframe we have."

Hantle nodded and said, "That may be the most uncertain aspect: the timeline. We expected the wolf to return to Iomesel last night, but instead it feasted on meteors. Tonight or the next, we may not be as fortunate. However, even if the wolf does return, it is uncertain whether it will attack Suu-manth or another city." A new thought came to him as he spoke. "Not to mention its increasing size. If we wait too long to strike, our window of opportunity will close. It may grow to such a scale as to make our weapons look like matchsticks." He finished the sentence and went quiet considering the possibility.

Dalence picked up. "So we have two or maybe three nights. Next, shall we get the ideas for the crossbow, trebuchet, and their ammunition onto paper? Much else can only follow on that preliminary work."

The next several hours passed in a flurry of activity. Dalence sketched her initial designs, and many questions and ideas followed. More specialized groups splintered off and drove out details. The relative of an architect brought in the woman to iterate on and finalize the structural diagrams. A blacksmith pledged his forge to the creation of crossbow arrows. A crew offered its muscle to the construction. Three cartwrights would construct several vehicles to move the parts of the killworks to the location of assemblage. Dalence and Hantle moved between groups to answer questions and plan what was needed next.

Hantle noticed that Brust stayed quiet and kept to the fringe. He was not taken up with the bottle, which was an improvement over yesterday. Hantle's gaze then traveled over the area to take in the bustle. His eyes drifted past the Marketplace itself, but then he did a double take. Just outside the entrance, a woman stood in a spot of shade, her legs planted wide and her arms akimbo. Dalence joined Hantle's side, facing away from the Marketplace. "Have you spotted the Chancellor of the Catch?"

Hantle nodded and moved his gaze away from the governor's assistant. "Has she been there long?"

Dalence shrugged. "I only just noticed her."

Hantle replied, "Our presence here does ring of flaunting disregard."

"I'll keep an eye on her if you will."

"Okay," Hantle said. "We will see if things escalate."

Around noon, a brother and sister joined the group. Last night, they had witnessed the wolf scarring the moon from their estate on the edge of Suu-manth. The siblings had inherited the city's largest lumberyard and heard of the effort here to build weaponry. Hantle recognized their name but took a moment to place it. The lumberyard was the largest consumer of timber from Founsel. The two declared the company's stores available for any amount of wood needed. Hantle thanked them profusely and Dalence asked for more details on the wood products available.

Hantle's eyes darted back to the Marketplace to where the Chancellor of the Catch had stood, only to find her spot empty. He scanned the area but she was nowhere to be found. Would they see her again before the day was done?

Brust broke his silence. "Dalence, Hantle," he said. "What if the wolf does not return?"

# CHAPTER THIRTY-ONE

HANTLE BECKONED the two to step a few yards away from the main groups for privacy. Brust ran a hand through his hair and Hantle noticed the uncertainty on his face.

"We can build these weapons," Brust said, "but they won't do any good unless the wolf is close enough to hit. It did not come back last night, and you've said it might attack some other city besides Suumanth. Might it also just stay in the sky?"

He had a point, but something told Hantle that was not the case. While Hantle thought, Dalence said, "If the wolf did stay away, no more families would be taken. Though the prospect of it changing its mind would still loom over us."

Hantle said, "Who of us could sleep soundly night after night knowing what was overhead? We will only be safe, and certain of it, with it dead."

Brust shrugged. "Bringing it back is inherently risky. If the goal is to save lives, doesn't drawing it here fly in the face of that?"

"In the short term," Hantle said, "yes. The long-term threat, however, extends to all people on Iomesel, which makes the risk to

Suu-manth a more reasonable one to accept. Although not a trivial one, by any means."

"Hmm, yes, I can see that," Brust said.

"And to bring it back on our own terms gives us more control than simply reacting to its sudden appearance."

Brust asked, "How do we lure it here though?"

"Could we use something as bait?" Dalence wondered.

Hantle looked to the sky. "The meteor shower worked like a bait. Does it continue for a few nights more?"

"Yes, from what I recall Darbor telling me." Dalence pointed to Mount Vulteeb. "We could ask one of the astronomers. That would get the wolf into the sky. But what of bringing it to the ground?"

"What was it about the meteors that attracted it?" Brust said.

"It has a reaction to the light," Hantle said. "Dalence, when you described the beast in Bansuth, you made it sound like it got distracted by the meteors. It leapt into the sky after them. And last night, we saw it flit from one meteor to another, changing its mind as soon as it saw a new one."

"Okay," Dalence said. "Can we mimic that light in some fashion? To get its attention. In order to distract it from the meteors and draw it to us."

Hantle shook his head. "A large fire? What other means of light do we have?"

Neither Brust nor Dalence could identify one. Hantle racked his brain, but nothing came to mind. He thought of the absurdity in building weapons they could not guarantee to use.

Dalence said, "Could we . . . If the weapons were large enough, could we hit it in the sky?"

"The distance and its speed would make that challenging," Hantle said, shaking his head. "We will only have a few pieces of ammunition. If we missed, or didn't mortally wound it—"

"I just remembered," Brust interrupted. "On the coast, in Dusath, they recently finished a lighthouse, meant to guide shipping vessels around the deadly rock outcroppings off the shore. It's said to be the brightest in the world. If we could redirect the beam into the sky, it would be much more visible than a fire."

"Yes," Dalence said. "And interrupting the beam would cause it to strobe and grab the wolf's attention. Brust, that's fantastic."

Hantle patted Brust's shoulder. "Strong work. Not even a hangover holds you back."

"The next concern is enlisting that lighthouse's aid," Dalence said.

"And hoping the keeper of the lighthouse is more agreeable than the governor here."

"What if they are not?" Brust said. "Our plan depends upon that light. Are we prepared to use force?"

"Yes," Hantle said after several seconds. "If it comes to that. But let's not rush to that end so quickly."

"Of course not," Dalence said. "After they agree to help, they will need time to perform the work, same as us. Whoever of us rides there will need to arrange a time to put the light and the weapons into action. The two must be coordinated."

"Dalence," Hantle said, "you have the vision for the killworks. You should stay here to lead their construction. And Brust with you. I will ride to Dusath and seek out the lighthouse."

Brust nodded. "That's fine with me. There is more to do here than one of us could manage."

"Three nights?" Dalence questioned. "Will that be enough?"

"Three nights," Hantle repeated. "To ride and enlist their help. To complete their and our work. To act together despite the intervening miles. Any less time is a fool's errand. Any more time is sloth."

## CHAPTER THIRTY-TWO

THE HORSE that carried Dalence to Suu-manth now carried Hantle toward the Fist's northern coastline. He set out in the afternoon and passed over plains that stretched until they met hills, river valleys, and coastal forests. The road was well kept and he made good time. The air in Suu-manth during the afternoon was stifling, but the temperature cooled significantly as he approached the forests. The trees had huge trunks and towered a hundred feet above him. Hantle wondered whether any company had rights to log these parts. A single tree here would contain many times the lumber of one near Founsel. It might be an opportunity for him to capitalize on. A grimace passed over his face as he caught himself in the daydream. This was no time for a luxury like planning for a day beyond the wolf. They had come up with a plan, and much to accomplish still lay ahead of them.

Low-hanging clouds moved over the treetops and obscured the sun. Noises in the distance told him Dusath neared. He smelled the salt in the air, the scent bringing to mind Founsel's Trasach Cove. At the city's edge, the trees thinned. Terraces stepped down to the coastline, each level packed with brick row houses for homes and businesses. He looked along the oceanfront and caught a glimpse of white stone partly obscured by a stand of trees. Hantle urged his horse onward. It plodded down the wide, steep stairs between terrace levels and he realized the white stone belonged to the lighthouse. Unlit but lustrous, it dominated the view of the eastern portion of the city.

The prominence of the lighthouse and the grid-like streets made navigation easy. People filled the streets with an air of activity. He maneuvered through the roads, followed a main artery beyond the terraces, meandered through a scrubby patch of vegetation, and climbed a rocky prominence toward the foot of the tower. The sun was lowering in the sky and he felt as if the warmth on his back pushed him up the final pitch to the lighthouse's foundation.

But for the wind, the area was silent. Hantle dismounted, tied the horse off to a railing, and hung his pack alongside his musket. He took a deep breath and approached the lighthouse's entrance. The wooden door was painted white and otherwise unadorned. He swung a knocker, the sound carrying through the vicinity. Moments later, the door moaned on salted hinges and revealed a small, thin man.

"What?" he said. His voice rasped as if not used in some time.

"I'm sorry to bother you," Hantle replied. "Are you the keeper?"

The man responded with a nod. His eyes were sunken and beckoned Hantle to come to the point. His clothes were worn threadbare, and large patches kept the fabric from falling to pieces. In the humidity, curly brown hair swam around his head in chaotic strands.

Hantle asked, "Did you watch the sky last night?"

"Aye," the man said. "Each night I do."

"Notice anything different last night?"

"Indeed." The man smiled and stepped to the side. "I've never seen a wolf in the sky before." The sunset illuminated the man's features as he motioned Hantle inside. "Nor've I seen the moon scarred."

Hantle stepped over the threshold and the keeper closed the door behind him. "The beast is what brings me here," he said. The wind outside whistled, but inside, the air calmed and quieted. "Just two nights ago it was on Iomesel, destroying Bansuth."

The man's eyes widened and he moved to bring a lantern to life.

The light showed Hantle the provisions that occupied most of this room. Barrels of fuel and foodstuffs stacked several people high. A staircase on the edge of the light wrapped around with the wall and disappeared into the gloom above.

"I'm Hantle." He stretched out his hand.

"Good to meet you, Hantle." The keeper accepted the handshake. "Name's Goseth. Care for a seat?" Goseth pulled a chair out from a table and sat down.

Hantle tipped his head in gratitude. "Thank you, but I'll stand. Just rode from Suu-manth and it's nice to stretch."

Goseth put an elbow on the table and placed his chin in his hand. "Well," he said. "Go on."

Hantle worked from the beginning in Founsel to his arrival in Suu-manth. He focused on how near they had come to felling the beast. How each move seemed to bring them closer to its demise. In reality, it seemed the opposite, but Hantle figured reframing the events to hint at the surety of the wolf's death was more likely to gain him an ally. He had not seen any portion of the killworks, but he painted a picture of their grand and imposing sight. "I've ridden to Dusath," he said, "to ask for your help. To help us bring the wolf within range of our munitions so that we may end its threat, once and for all."

"And how," Goseth said, "will a solitary lighthouse keeper do that?"

"It was distracted by the meteors," Hantle said. "Distracted by their flashes in the sky. Last night was evidence of that. It raced after the meteors, their trails' flare and intensity. Your lighthouse is the brightest in the world. If we can direct its beam to the sky, we will have its attention. Once lured to the ground, we in Suu-manth will launch our assault, killing it before it has the chance to harm any more people."

"Are you aware," Goseth asked, "that the beam projects out toward the ocean, not toward the sky?"

"Yes, but it can be modified, can it not?"

"I suppose." Goseth shrugged. "But not without permission from the Merchant Shipping Consortium. They own this lighthouse, not I."

Hantle took a moment to formulate his thoughts. "Preparations are underway in Suu-manth, and the lighthouse is crucial to the success of our plan. Does the thought of saving so many lives not sway you?"

"What of the mariners who, without the guidance of the light, would run aground and drown in the surf? This lighthouse serves a purpose, Hantle."

"Can you take me to this consortium? I could speak to them and explain the situation."

"No." Goseth slowly shook his head. "The decision making is communal and they only gather every few months. The next gathering isn't for some time." He adjusted in his seat. "Why risk bringing it back? Why not leave it to the stars?"

"Unchecked, it is a specter that will haunt us each night. Not just us in Suu-manth or Dusath, but those on all of Iomesel. Its nature is one of aggression, hatred, and rage. Such is why I appeal for your help to bring its haunting to an end."

"I am sorry," Goseth said. "Without their leave, my hands are tied."

"Damn." Hantle sat down and slapped a hand on the table. "We are in quite the bind now, but I understand your obligations. I would leave immediately, except that, over the past several days, I have ridden hundreds of miles and feel past exhaustion. May I stay the night, at least?"

The keeper stood and searched through nearby crates. "I cannot promise comfort, but I have a spare blanket or two."

"That will be enough," Hantle said.

# CHAPTER THIRTY-THREE

DALENCE LIFTED the last piece of lumber from the cart and set it on the ground. Beside her, others drove nails into the scaffolding they were building around the crossbow's base. Once the scaffolding was in place, they could add more to the weapon's frame. She wiped an arm across her forehead and her sleeve came away darkened with perspiration.

The sound of raised voices to her side drew her attention. Brust walked backward, engaged in a heated discussion with the governor. When the governor noticed Dalence, she stopped and snapped her fingers. The Chancellor of the Catch moved to her side, placed a hand on Brust's shoulder, and moved him back several steps.

He shouted, "Get your damn hands off me!"

Workers nearby laid down their tools and closed in on the commotion. The governor made eye contact with Dalence while speaking to Brust. "We are here to speak to your sister. Not you. Now settle down before you land yourself in trouble."

She had no right to treat him like that. Dalence took a step forward. "He's no child."

The governor cocked her head and raised an eyebrow. "His petulance fooled me."

Dalence shot Brust a look to keep him from doing something foolish. Don't prove her right, she thought. He let out a deep, irritated breath but stood his ground under the chancellor's grasp.

"Come now, Dalence," the governor said. "Would you care to explain what you're doing here?"

"Something you were not willing to do: working to save this city."

The governor looked to the chancellor. "The last time we saw her, did I imagine it, or did I forbid her from speaking to anyone else of her outlandish claims?"

The chancellor replied, "You did forbid her, Governor."

Brust broke away from the chancellor and said, "She did nothing wrong." He strode to Dalence and stood at her side, much larger than either the governor or chancellor.

Dalence looked beyond the governor and, amid the crowd, caught glimpses of uniforms and weapons. So the governor's guards were present. She spoke next. "May I ask you what you are doing here?"

The governor slowly pivoted her head to take in the scene surrounding her. "This morning, my sources brought word of a small group that spoke of a wolf in the sky and gathered people to build weaponry. This sounded similar to what I had dismissed yesterday. But who, after being told to keep silent, would be so foolish as to press the issue? Particularly right here in the city. I had to come see it for myself. And here you are, defying me.

"The city is distracted by your fairytale blathering, which is bad for commerce as well as irritating. I promised you punishment for disobedience. And you disobeyed. There are consequences, and they are here." The governor gave Dalence a wicked smile then looked over her shoulder. "Guards, apprehend her."

The crowd split apart and the guards marched forward.

Dalence grasped Brust's arm and felt his body become taut. "Brust," she said as she pulled him down so she could whisper to him. "We don't stand a chance right now. We can't both end up in jail.

Gather some people and come for me later. Once you've gotten me out, we will continue building the killworks."

One guard grabbed Dalence's arms and pulled her away from Brust. Another locked manacles on her wrists and spun her around. The first presented Dalence to the governor and said, "As ordered, Governor."

"Take her away." The governor then addressed the rest of the crowd. "Disband, or I will have no choice but to arrest others of you for disorderly conduct." She turned and followed the guard procession to the jailhouse.

The chancellor, the veins in her neck standing out, looked to Brust and said, "I suggest you listen," before hurrying after the governor. The procession was lost around a bend in the road and a heavy silence fell over Brust and the remaining crowd.

After a time, Brust spoke up. "These weapons are still our first priority, but we will need their designer to complete them. Anyone have experience with that kind of delicate retrieval?"

# CHAPTER THIRTY-FOUR

THEY FINISHED EATING a small meal of bread, cheese, and a few strips of jerky. Hantle sat back in his chair and nodded at Goseth. "I appreciate you sharing your provisions with me."

Goseth smiled. "If you ever decide to become a lighthouse keeper, you'll know it's not for the food."

Hantle nodded again and grinned before changing the subject. "You mentioned earlier that you take in the sky each night. Might I join you tonight?"

"Yes, of course. I have a few chores before I can do so. You are welcome to head up now or wait until later." Goseth cleared their two plates from the table and put them away.

"Thank you," Hantle said.

The keeper opened the door to the howling dusk and disappeared into darkness. Earlier, Hantle had watched Goseth ascend the stairs to light the torch. He was curious as to its design and took this opportunity to investigate. He lit a lantern and climbed the stairway that spiraled up the column of the tower, making sure to hug close to the outer wall as there was no railing to steady oneself or prevent a fall. The stairs deposited him in a room under the torch. The walls had many windows for observation of the ocean and coastline.

He climbed a ladder through a hole in the ceiling and came into the torch room. An incredible brightness filled the space and Hantle stood in awe of the lenses. A metal lattice suspended an array of precisely ground crystals. The crystal-work reached twice his height. Light poured from three sides of the apparatus, while the back was an odd fusion of three bowl-like mirrors. He guessed they collected and reflected light through each of the lenses. The fire inside sounded like a long, continuous exhalation. He respected the detail and care put into making a device such as this. Yes, they needed this lighthouse and he knew it was capable of performing the task they had in mind.

A bead of sweat ran into his face as he descended the ladder. The room beneath the torch was much better suited to sitting. The temperature was considerably cooler and two chairs could be moved freely about. One of these Hantle took to the western windows and sat upon. He turned down the flame on his lantern to dim the room. A dark purple outlined the Knuckles in the distance, and he wondered what the astronomers had recorded last night in their journals.

Goseth twice made an appearance, but was either on his way to the torch room or to the tower's base. Alone, Hantle watched night fall completely, the meteor shower begin, and, much later, the moon rise. He walked the perimeter of the observation space and anxiously awaited the creature. Shortly, as if provoked by Hantle's pacing, the persistence of a thread on the horizon caught his eye and he called down the staircase for Goseth to join him. By the time the keeper walked into the watch room, Hantle could see the wolf's shape in the sky. He pointed through the glass pane at the figure. "The beast has returned."

Goseth's jaw dropped and he pulled a chair forward so he could sit right against the window. The wolf wasted no time in chasing after meteors. It had grown even more and now filled a larger amount of the sky than the previous night. Its fur had gone darker still, taking on a heathered texture when it caught the moon's light. Goseth watched, completely silent, as the creature took every meteor it chased, each followed by a concussion. Soon its stomach glowed brighter than the moon.

The canine disappeared beyond the Knuckles for a time and Goseth turned to Hantle with horror in his eyes. "Was it so large last night?"

"No. It devours all it can and grows with each bite. I've seen it a new and terrifying size each evening." Apprehension gripped him and he wondered if the wolf would crash to the ground before them. A moment later, he swallowed and stilled his mind. The fear drew further off as he thought instead of the weapons under construction in Suumanth. And the purpose that brought him to this lighthouse. He turned once more to watch the sky.

The wolf reappeared, his form lashing through the sky. He came to a stop and his chest heaved with a burp. Flaring particles escaped through his teeth. He licked his lips. Meteors rocketed past the creature and the flashes glinted in his eyes. Hantle was certain his size had grown from even just a few minutes ago.

With a new ferocity, the wolf darted out of view beyond the horizon. Seconds later, the wolf-streak reappeared on the opposite side of the world and plunged toward the moon, whose size his now rivaled. He snarled and swiped his claws across its surface. Dust spread and shimmered around the canine. These gouges covered more than half of the visible surface and Hantle could only guess at their depth. Hantle cast a glance at Goseth and saw him transfixed.

The creature whipped his tail against the moon, ejecting boulders and other components of its regolith in an arc away from the point of impact, glinting as they tumbled off. The force of the collision sent the satellite careening out of its orbit. The wolf twisted around, jolted forward, and its teeth flashed as they sank into the crust. A powder of debris on the far side of the orb kept its motion and floated on, after the main body jerked to a stop. The wolf's jaws clenched tight on the moon itself. A webwork of fractures crawled over the landscape. With a yank of the beast's head, the moon splintered around his teeth. A solid piece of crust peeled away like an onion layer, only to disintegrate when the wolf chomped down.

Another heartbeat, another bite (this one wider yet), and the moon ruptured into several large hunks and uncountable smaller bits. The wolf tossed his head from side to side and the fragments scattered. The portion in his mouth, he greedily gulped down. Moondust covered his face and his stomach gave up its glow.

Lumps of the moon twisted and spun and tumbled, turning the sky into a kaleidoscope of light. Its molten interior shone in places as the exposed core deformed in sluggish bulges. The canine chased after the largest pieces of bedrock first. These crumbled in his bite and the sky roiled with glimmers. Flashes peppered Hantle's view as moon rocks became burning meteors.

The wolf steadily chipped away at the mantle and Hantle lost track of how long they watched it feed. As the creature delved further, the rock became darker until he reached a point at which it started to glow—faintly at first, a barely perceptible red. The beast clawed at the core and slush splashed out to reveal a white-hot center, which he dwarfed. His muzzle snapped, slicing the glob in twain. His skull took on an inner radiance that trailed down his throat as he swallowed. A sound, like that of a titanic eruption, shook Hantle to the bone.

As the tremor passed and the world stilled, he watched the remaining core-half mutate from a solid to a near liquid that distorted and approached a spherical shape. The demon made a final lurch and consumed the nucleus's scraps. This time, the wolf let up a howl to accompany the death-sound of the moon. Hantle leaned forward against the glass and saw rays of heat surge from its gullet. The creature's eyes beamed a dazzling white, which brought to Hantle's mind the lighthouse torch combusting above him. Down in its stomach, the moon particles continued to throw off heat, lending his gut a luminescence.

After the howl quieted, the wolf appeared sated. Nothing larger than crumbs existed to entertain him. Where the moon had been, there dispersed a faint, dusty haze. Little else hinted at its obliteration.

As he fled into the depths of the cosmos, the wolf's path blazed upon the pitch-dark. The mark slowly faded above them and Hantle made eye contact with Goseth.

Goseth pointed to the sky. "You mean to kill that?"

Hantle nodded. "But it will only be possible with your help."

Goseth exhaled through his nose. "I said, earlier, that I could not help for fear of causing the deaths of sailors." His eyes wavered from Hantle's and sank to the floor. "Truthfully, I was more afraid of being tossed from my position here. I have no family left." He shook his head and glanced back to Hantle for a moment. "Without the lighthouse, I would be living in squalor. Yet, after what I just witnessed"—he nodded and straightened up—"I will risk that to help kill the creature before it takes us all." Goseth's brows furrowed with resolve. "Tell me what I can do—" The keeper paused as he fought to swallow through a parched throat. He eventually managed, "And I will do it."

# CHAPTER THIRTY-FIVE

A TORCH in the hallway guttered from a draft. Dalence sat crosslegged on the dirt floor in the middle of her cell. Two others bordered hers, separated by bars, and faced others across the hall. Dalence was the lone occupant in the jailhouse, the flame her only company. Night crept in through the window behind her and spread through the cells, kept at bay by the flickering torch.

She heard a faint noise. It came from the front of the building, toward the guardroom, and grew louder over the course of a minute. Dalence stood and leaned against the iron bars but could see nothing beyond the hallway. She could, however, hear the guards stand up and open the door. A wave of yelling, whooping, and jeering flowed down the hall and Dalence took a step back. She jumped at a "psst" behind her and spun to face it. Her brother's face smiled at her through the window bars. She let out a sigh of relief. "Brust!"

He motioned her to the window and stuck in an arm to proffer a length of rope. "Tie your best knot," he said.

With a tug, Dalence pulled in additional rope, wrapped a loop around a bar, and set to work. Brust revealed another length of rope and affixed it to a different bar. When she finished, she stood on her tiptoes and looked past her brother. Three people stood there beside two yoked oxen.

A shout carried from the guardroom. "Hey!" Dalence looked back. The woman who had locked Dalence in the cell rushed down the hallway. "Don't you even think about it." She unclipped a key ring from her waistband and flipped through the keys.

Dalence turned to Brust. "Come on!"

Brust rolled his eyes, finished the knot, and nodded to the people behind him. One of them slapped the oxen on their hindquarters. The animals snorted and stepped forward. Each rope pulled taut and the window frame groaned.

Keys rattled against the cell-door lock and the guard shouted to her peers. "She is making to escape. It's all a distraction!" The guard shook her head with frustration and pulled up another key to try.

Mortar crumbled and spilled from the joints. A second later, one bar buckled and the other followed. Rocks in the wall shifted. The guard slammed a hand against the cell and shouted at Dalence, "You go out that window, you're going to end up here a lot longer." A second guard appeared in the hallway just as the window bars pulled free of the building and clattered to the ground. Several large stones tumbled out into the yard and Dalence scrambled through the resulting hole.

Brust and another person helped extract her and place her on her feet. The oxen kept walking, dragging the barred frame behind them. Dalence peeked back through the hole and saw the guards run toward the front of the building. Brust gripped Dalence in a hug that turned into a shove. "Move!"

Dalence and the group hurried past the oxen. Commotion around the front of the jailhouse grew more boisterous. The building was constructed on an island in Mainlake, which bordered the Marketplace. Ahead of her, Dalence saw torches mounted on boats. The five of them reached a boat, scrambled in, and pushed off the sandy shore. Dalence saw several barges tethered nearby, which must have been used to ferry the crowds and oxen. Oars drove into the water and carried them away from the island. The chants and shouts of the crowd faded as they drew away. Dalence looked up and a meteor blazed across the sky.

---

As the five reached the site of the weaponry, sounds indicated ongoing construction. Dalence looked to Brust. "You were able to break me out and keep work going here?"

"Word of what we're doing has spread. You'd be surprised at how many people volunteered their help. They feel the governor's leaving them for dead."

The crossbow's frame was a recognizable shape now. Hammers thudded and saws buzzed. Brust said, "We got a start on the trebuchet framing before the group left for the distraction at the jailhouse. They ought to be back before long."

Dalence nodded. "I expect the governor will be too."

---

Groups of laborers filtered back in from the mock protest at the jailhouse. Lanterns burned brightly and momentum picked up on the work. For a time, at least. Progress came to a halt when the wolf was spotted in the sky. The streak gained the shape of the canine as it grew in brightness. It was with her neck craned to the firmament that Dalence heard her name called out. "Dalence Hetross."

The governor strode into the construction site, backed by two dozen guards. "You escaped the jail just to stand out in the open? Is the view worth the extra time you'll face?"

Brust stepped to Dalence's side and made visible a pistol hanging from his waist. "No," Dalence whispered to him, "don't do anything stupid." She spoke to the leader next. "I'm glad you're here, Governor."

"Glad for what reason?"

"Because we have the chance to show you the truth of our warning. If you only look skyward, you will see the wolf."

The chancellor laughed. "Even still she thinks us gullible?"

Something caught Dalence's attention and her eyes drifted up. The wolf chased and consumed a meteor. It appeared to be no more than a stone's throw above them. She heard a sharp intake of breath and looked back to the governor whose upturned eyes were wide.

"That is what we work against," Dalence said. "It's why we build these weapons." Commotion spread through the guards behind the governor. "The danger, though, has grown beyond Suu-manth." She pointed to the north. "My companion, Hantle, has ridden to Dusath to seek aid."

The governor regained her composure. "The fact remains," she said, "that you cannot flaunt the law and remain a free woman."

"Before, you made a mistake in arresting me for fear-mongering. You see above us that it was nothing of the sort. Yet still you double down on your initial mistaken behavior. Why?"

Both the chancellor and the governor stared to the sky for several seconds. Only after the wolf disappeared beyond the horizon did the governor look back to Dalence. The leader's face flushed and her voice carried vitriol. "You are not this city's protector! That role falls to one person: me." She motioned to her guards and pointed to Dalence before making eye contact with her once more. "Will you come peacefully? Or must you always be difficult?"

Dalence looked to the ground and smiled. The volunteers spread around her stepped forward and held their weapons against their chests. She nodded her gratitude to every one of them. "I don't believe the denizenry share your views."

The wolf appeared in the sky again and belched its sparks. The governor looked to the crowd, which outnumbered her force by more than two to one. She spoke to them all. "If lawfulness must be forced upon you, so be it. I will convene the bodies and take your precious weapons and guerrilla leader from you." Her guards made room as the governor turned and walked through them. They followed her lead and marched toward the Marketplace. Dalence felt the tension abate and let out a slow breath. Above, the wolf dove toward the moon.

---

It was only after the creature disappeared into the starry depths that attention returned to construction. Dalence was happy to put her hands to use. Her time in the jail had wasted precious time. In two nights, the piles of materials standing about them had to be transformed into the killworks.

# CHAPTER THIRTY-SIX

HANTLE WOKE before dawn and enjoyed the warmth of his blanket for a final moment. Outside, the sky began to lighten. He rose to shake out and fold the blanket, which caused Goseth to stir. Hantle said, "I best head out early, sir, since it's a decent ride."

The two shared a quick breakfast during which neither spoke. As Hantle unlocked the lighthouse door, Goseth handed him a pouch and said, "Jursant—for the ride."

Hantle shook his hand with a solemnity that gave way to a smile. "Have any for yourself?"

"Aye, I do. Plenty." Goseth's face remained stern. "The lighthouse will shine to the stars in two nights. You have my word, Hantle."

"Two nights." Hantle nodded. Then he was out the door.

The horse carried Hantle away from the lighthouse, through the city, and up the terrace steps. He shivered in the chill air. In the east, the sun crested the plains and lit the top of Dusath's forest-edge. His gambit to make Goseth reconsider his initial declination had paid off. Finally, something had gone the right way. He placed a pinch of jursant under his tongue. Although, considering the wolf ate the goddamn moon, could he actually say that? Through the tree trunks to the west, the Knuckles glowed red.

---

Hantle knocked on Dalence's door. When no one answered, he tried again. Louder, this time. The door opened to reveal Dalence wiping sleep from her eyes.

"Sorry to wake you," he said.

Dalence opened the door wider. "Come in."

Hantle entered, unable to tell if her eyes were open. "I looked at the site first, but they said you'd gone home."

"Yes." Dalence nodded. "We worked through the night and early morning. Had to get some sleep though."

He sat down at the kitchen table and Dalence joined him. Light filtered in through the sheer curtains and threw a dim light about the house. He saw Brust's door was shut. Either he had not woken up or he had dismissed the door knocking.

"The progress on the weaponry is fantastic," Hantle said.

Dalence rubbed her eyes. "It's encouraging to see the result before your very eyes. Each day we get more people to help. The energy in the city is palpable. How was Dusath?"

"Took some doing. The lighthouse keeper was reluctant to help but I stayed with him over the night and showed him the wolf. We watched it . . . devour the moon."

Dalence shook her head. "The entire damn moon."

"That's what changed his mind. He's promised to look into the details and modify the lighthouse to be ready in two nights."

"That's a relief." Dalence moved to the fireplace and started a fire. "Would you like tea? It'll be the strongest we have." Hantle accepted. Next she added water to the kettle and set it over the growing flames. "We had a complication yesterday with the governor."

"What was that?"

"First, she arrested me," Dalence said. "Held me in the jail near the

Marketplace. Brust gathered people to break me out last night. Then she showed up again at the killworks. We outnumbered her, so she left promising to return with a larger group." She shrugged. "We have that to look forward to."

The kettle whistled and Dalence poured the steaming water into mugs. She tied three bags of loose leaves and placed them in the water. Hantle got up to take his mug while Dalence walked to Brust's door and knocked.

"Afternoon, Brust. Let's get back out there."

———

As the three of them rode back to the site of the weaponry, Hantle noticed the frenzy of the city. It paired well with the day's heat. Wagons loaded with provisions rumbled through the streets and joined streams of people fleeing the city. In the lakes, others pushed boats that contained provisions to sell or hoard. The differing reactions reminded Hantle of Founsel.

The construction site was relatively quiet, yet bustling. Hantle smiled. The project was a good way to contain anxiety and direct focus. There were more than twice as many volunteers as when he left the day prior.

"Suu-manth is riled up," Brust said, "and these people are eager to do something productive."

"It appears so," Hantle said. "Care to show me the progress?"

Dalence led them through a clearing where workers rested and ate. The nearest structure was the crossbow. "This is the closest to completion. They're working on the ratchet and winch system to cock the bow."

"What about ammunition?"

"The blacksmith shall soon have a bolt for us to test. A portion of the metal has come from a meteorite."

Hantle laughed. "Apropos."

Dalence continued through a path that cut between stacks of

materials. "The trebuchet is still getting going. Design issues set us back a bit. But we think those are fleshed out."

"Design issues?"

"The initial framing was not rigid enough. Its tendency to twist would only have been amplified when counterweights and a projectile were used." Dalence showed a clearing where a group was working to assemble multiple pieces of timber into a single leg for the frame. "Speaking of the projectile. Do you remember the landslide we passed on our way down from the Splitskin?"

"Yes," Hantle said.

"Stone workers from a quarry on the Knuckles have offered their expertise to refine boulders from that landslide. They are devising a way to make them function as grenades and explode into fragments on impact."

"Incredible work, Dalence. I am impressed." Hantle patted her on the back. "These are the kinds of artillery I wished we'd had every other night."

"These skilled individuals are the heroes. Without them, none of this would be possible."

"Indeed. Brust, I hear you rescued Dalence from the jail. Equally impressive."

Brust winked to Dalence. "What choice does a brother have when his sister goes and gets herself locked up?"

Hantle held up his hands to encompass their surroundings. "Now, where can I make best use of myself?"

Hantle helped Dalence and Brust distribute additional weapons, ammunition, and gunpowder to new builders. The arms were precautions against the governor's potential return. Dalence was unsure of the size and training of her force but felt the hundred or so volunteers they now had would be as good a deterrent as any. They would hand out the remaining weapons to those who joined the crew throughout the day. With the group outfitted, the three turned their focus to the trebuchet. Each leg piece took more than a dozen people to lift and maneuver into place. Several hours passed and the trebuchet's frame stood solid.

Efforts had turned toward the leveraging arm's construction when Hantle recognized Darbor riding through the work site. Dalence called out, "What brings you through, Darbor?"

He looked over to Dalence and waved. A woman wearing a porter's garb followed behind him. From a seat, she drove a mule that pulled the cart and wooden box with which it was laden.

"On my way down the Knuckles this morning," Darbor said, "I saw this large gathering and wondered what it was. Decided to pass through on my way back up." He gave a short laugh. "Figures that you're involved though."

Dalence replied, "The governor would do nothing about the wolf, so we took matters into our own hands. How go your observations?"

"Very well. The nights have been clear and there's no shortage of events to chronicle." He held up a leather notebook and tapped the cover. "And tonight we shall have some additional help." He indicated the box on the cart behind him. "We just received a telescope even more powerful than the one on Mount Vulteeb. We were fortunate enough to obtain its exclusive use for the next week."

"With such an historic event," Hantle said, "it's no wonder. Mount Vulteeb is a prime location." He walked over to the crate. Its side was branded with an insignia foreign to him. He rapped the crate. "How much difference does the elevation make in viewing?"

Darbor thought for a moment. "The higher you go, the less atmosphere there is to distort the image. And you can avoid low cloud cover."

"Is the difference like night and day?"

"Nothing that drastic. But it is noticeable."

Hantle walked closer to Darbor's steed. "The reason I ask is, I hoped you would consider keeping the telescope here tonight."

Darbor's face scrunched up. "For what purpose?"

"We aim to complete these weapons in two nights. That goal is in no way guaranteed, but the wolf is the real wild card. The telescope would help us better track what the wolf does."

"I see," Darbor said. "I can understand the usefulness of that, but Bellice is the one to approve such a decision."

Hantle nodded and thought.

Dalence spoke up in his stead. "Your research would come first, of course. And, here, *you* would have sole use of the telescope to study to your heart's content."

A smile spread across Darbor's face. Hantle gave Dalence an approving glance. She was quick on her feet.

She went on. "Every piece of information you can glean would help us be better prepared. Yes, the mountain might provide better clarity, but on the ground we would have immediacy to act on your observations."

Hantle followed her logic. "Knowledge for its own sake is a worthwhile ambition, but would you agree that knowledge put to action is even more powerful? You can be the one to effect that change."

Darbor mulled it over, eventually nodding. "Okay, I will stay. As long as we can send a message to Bellice. If she disagrees, however, I must leave."

"That's no problem," Dalence said. "Let's find a messenger."

Soon, a messenger was off and Darbor, with the porter's help, unloaded the crate in an opening located some distance from the main construction activity. He would not risk damaging the equipment by placing it near the crowds. He flipped the crate's latches and opened the lid. The metallic tube sat in a straw bed. A cloth-wrapped bundle contained a tripod, and at its top was a mount to which he affixed the telescope itself. The eyepiece was the last component to be added before he calibrated its focus.

---

Evening neared and lanterns shone throughout the worksite. In the darkening east, Hantle saw the pinpoint light of a planet. He turned back to the trebuchet's arm and ran a length of rope through a pulley. They would raise the arm and attach it to the pivot. A noise caught his attention. He set down the rope and turned. A line of people moved backward and spread out so an opening formed in the middle, through which the governor walked. She carried a torch and marched to within a dozen feet of Dalence. Behind her came the Chancellor of the Catch. As she came to a stop, the governor's trailing soldiers deployed in a line and awaited orders. The volunteers nearby rearranged themselves in a circle that included the governor and her troopers.

"Cute," the governor began. "Formed your own militia now, have you?"

Footsteps sounded and the circle temporarily broke as two more columns of soldiers marched in from either side of the governor. They stopped a handful of yards away and spread out in lines perpendicular to that behind the governor. Hantle, Dalence, and Brust were surrounded on three sides by these forces.

The governor wore a smirk. "You've been able to recruit people for your cause, but so have I. Each of my troopers feels that the weapons you're building would best be controlled by the city. I am elected by the residents of Suu-manth to represent their interests. That does not include abdicating our defenses to a ragamuffin outfit fueled by delusions. The time of your defiance has come to an end."

She motioned to the captain behind her. He called out, "At arms."

The soldiers raised their weapons to their shoulders and aimed at the builders.

"Can we talk in private?" Dalence asked. She turned her palms up to show she was unarmed.

"There is nothing to discuss," the governor sneered. "You are not in a position to negotiate."

Hantle raised his musket to the governor. It was bullshit. She was more likely afraid to admit how much power they really had. The volunteers followed his lead and took up their arms to hold the soldiers and the governor in the crosshairs.

The governor's face blushed. She lowered her voice and addressed

Dalence. "Are you prepared to be responsible for the death of these people?"

"It seems you are," Dalence said.

The governor let out an angry breath and walked forward. She tossed the torch in her hands onto a stack of beams meant for use in the trebuchet then gripped Dalence's neck with both hands. Dalence grimaced and struggled to breathe.

Hantle moved his sight to follow the governor but did not have the clearance for a shot. The governor growled, "Give up, little girl. You do not have the power here!" Spittle hit Dalence's face.

Dalence staggered to her knees as the governor forced her down. Brust leapt in and pried her from the governor's grasp. "Get your damn hands off her." Dalence collapsed to the ground, coughing. A shot roared and Hantle braced but felt nothing hit him. The governor staggered back, though, lifting a hand to a spot on her chest that bloomed red. Brust held the smoking pistol and aimed another at the chancellor. The governor tried to speak, but blood leaked from her mouth instead to run down her jaw. She slumped to the ground and let out a sickening gurgle.

"Call them off," Brust ordered the chancellor. Hantle would never have guessed from the tone of his voice that the man had just shot someone. "I am not afraid to die here, but you'll die first." Brust looked to the captain. "We are working to save this city." He nodded with a certain finality.

Silence hovered over the scene as soldiers and volunteers held each other at gunpoint. Flames jumped into the air as the lumber caught. The stalemate was broken when the captain called for his soldiers to fire. Brust forgot his threat and dove to cover Dalence with his body. Hantle aimed at the captain and fired. Other shots rang out from civilian weapons as Hantle crouched and reached for his powder horn. His aim had been true and the captain toppled backward, grasping his stomach.

People fell on both sides, screaming or dead. Individuals moved to reload their weapons. The chancellor, during this brief lull, shouted above the screams. "Stand down, soldiers! Stand down." She rushed to the governor's side and cradled her in her lap. Hantle finished reloading and cautiously placed the chancellor under aim, in case she reversed her order. Builders nearby pulled materials away from the spreading blaze. Brust sat on the ground next to Dalence and held his bicep. He looked to have been struck by a musket ball. Dalence's mouth gaped in shock.

The chancellor shook her head and gently let the governor's head lower to the ground. She stood and spoke to all. "The governor is dead. I will not watch the groups here trade shots until everyone has joined her." The captain squirmed on the ground and placed pressure on his gut wound. He offered no disagreement. The troopers lowered their weapons. She pointed to a handful of soldiers and motioned them to her. They carried away the injured captain and the deceased governor. To the rest, she shouted, "About, face. Route step, march."

Dalence tore a strip from her shirt and bound Brust's arm. The chancellor walked to Dalence's side. "I do not support you, but neither did I support the governor's plans to take your weapons by force. Do for this city what she could not. Protect us." She spun and left the volunteers to nurse their wounded and tend to their dead.

# CHAPTER THIRTY-SEVEN

THE DEPARTURE of the soldiers gave the volunteer crew a chance to recover. Dalence crouched beside her brother. She untied the wrap she had placed around Brust's bicep and looked at the damage.

"There are two holes," she said, "so the musket ball looks to have exited."

Brust gulped down the pain and spoke through gritted teeth. "Won't need a surgeon to remove it, at least."

She retied the bandage. "Keep pressure on both sides until I can get gauze. Can you move the arm?"

"No, it just flops there."

"Must have shredded the muscle. We can rig up a sling." Beside, Hantle stood, watching them. Dalence reached out and stuck a finger into a hole in Hantle's shirt. "You were nearly hit as well."

Hantle looked down and pinched fabric to align the entry and exit marks. "Others weren't so lucky."

No, they weren't, but Dalence had Brust to focus on first. She reached for her pack and emptied it of contents. The fabric would be ideal for a sling. Cries, screams, and shouts overwhelmed her senses. Turning her focus to the sling helped stay the anxiety that clenched her stomach. She folded the pack's fabric to contain Brust's arm. Its straps she ran over his head to cradle and support. She fiddled with adjustments until Brust leaned away.

"That's fine there," he said. "Thank you."

With her brother tended to, Dalence looked at the chaos about them. Nearest was a sobbing teen crouched over his father. The man's neck was pure gore and blood soaked through the boy's shirt. A single volley had done this. Lumber set aflame by the governor's torch burned itself out. They were lucky to have kept the fire from consuming more.

The unscathed moved the injured to a central location for treatment. A few physicians and surgeons soon appeared to address those worst hurt. A handful of nurses tended to those with less threatening wounds. The dead were laid together in a clearing. Dalence knew it would take some time to identify them and notify the next of kin. The soldiers left behind by the rapid dismissal of the force were the last gathered.

Dalence sat on the ground and stared into the indigo sky. What would they do now? Her gaze fell on Hantle. He had moved off and carried a woman on a sling to an operating table of sorts. Next to it, a surgeon scrubbed his hands of the blood left by his last patient. Thanks to Brust's bravery, she had gone unscathed and would be able to direct her energy toward their plans. Although, how would this impact the construction's progress? She felt a pang of guilt that her main concern was what this setback meant for the weapons instead of for those hurt. But time was short.

She stood and walked through the site. The air and sky were calm in Suu-manth. Barely visible on its fringe, she spotted Darbor by the telescope. His idea of keeping the device a distance off had proven wise. Both he and the equipment had escaped trauma. A group peppered him with questions. As Dalence neared, she heard a few making predictions about what the night held in store. Darbor spotted her. "Dalence, join us, please."

A young boy drew back from the telescope's eyepiece. The look of joy on his face struck Dalence as grotesque, considering the pile of dead nearby. She curbed the instinct to judge the boy. It was strange how quickly normality resumed after major upheaval, but wasn't the ability to move past events that bogged down adults what gave children the future?

She looked to Darbor; lantern light danced across his face. She would focus on something else as well. "What knowledge are you sharing?"

"What observations we recorded while watching the wolf last night. We were stunned when it attacked the moon."

"With the telescope, could you see it up close?"

"A bit." He shrugged. "It's made for stationary observation, not for panning around, which makes it difficult to follow the canine as it moves."

She turned her face to the sky, located a bright dot, and said, "That is Romd, correct?" Darbor nodded. "What does it look like through there?"

"It is much more than a point of light. The best way to experience it is first hand. Let me train it on Romd and then you can see for yourself." He swiveled the tube and squinted into the eyepiece to make adjustments. "Yes, there it is." He beckoned Dalence forward.

She stepped to the telescope with a tinge of hesitation. "I'm afraid this is a foolish question. What do I do?"

"It's a natural question, not a foolish one. Close one eye and look into that viewfinder. That's all there is to it."

She did as he said and a large disc occupied most of the view. "Wow, it looks like a blob of mustard." The tone varied from a faint yellow near the poles to patches of olive here and there. Dark lines veined haphazardly across the surface.

"Yes, we think Romd has a large concentration of sulfur. Other planets have different compositions that give them their own distinctive palette."

"What are the black lines?" she asked.

"We do not know for certain, but they may indicate valleys or ravines."

Dalence held her breath for a moment to steady her body as she took in the planet. She hoped the memory of the other world now so easy to see would be stamped into her mind. Eventually, she stepped back and offered others in the group a chance to look. It wasn't right to hoard such a sight.

"What did you think?" Darbor said.

"All that is visible through a tube? It's incredible."

Darbor smiled wide. "It uses Liamathen crystals to focus and amplify the light. They are found in a cave system across the Fist. Each shard has properties some liken to magic." He laughed. "I get a tingle in my hands whenever I come near it, but that could very well be a figment of my imagination."

She could not help but smile back. "That sounds like sheer excitement to me."

Darbor leaned in. "Can you imagine what Iomesel would look like through a telescope on one of those planets?"

What a curious thought. In fact, she could not. The very idea was difficult to comprehend. The view of Romd was not one she could have imagined. That planet was a place fully formed, like Iomesel under her feet.

"Later," Darbor said, "I may be able to show you the other planets."

"I hope you can."

"Ah"—Darbor raised a hand to the sky—"the meteors have begun."

The young boy in the group tallied them on his hands but soon forgot his task as he was overcome with awe. Dalence keenly watched the sky alongside the observers. Others, including Brust and Hantle, trickled into the area.

Darbor gave his journal to a woman who must have offered to be his scribe for the night. By the dim light, she jotted notes as Darbor narrated. "There seems to be an uptick in the number of meteors.

Strange. I thought the peak was two nights ago." He turned to the west and stared for a time. "That haze, just above the Knuckles. I think it is all that remains of the moon. Excuse me." He resumed control of the telescope and brought it around. "Yes, I can see chunks spinning and casting light as they tumble." Pulling away from the eyepiece, he indicated the sky at large. "Perhaps some of those flashes above are made by pieces of our former satellite."

Someone indicated a trail that was more than ephemeral. A hush stole through the crowd and Darbor spoke. "Yes, I believe it's the wolf." The streak began first a zig and then a zag, which confirmed it. "Heading toward . . ." A squeak sounded as Darbor rotated the tube yet again and lowered his head to the ocular lens. "Mmhmm, that is Seligar. Without the telescope it is difficult to discern from a star." He gasped and Dalence stared at his face, scrunched up to look through the telescope. "It passed so close to Seligar that part of the atmosphere dragged along behind him in an eddy! Then it fell back to the surface in wisps. He's kept moving and . . . My word." He scoffed and went quiet. Dalence looked skyward but saw nothing more than a band of light. She jumped at Darbor's next shout. "All four moons. It just swallowed all four of Seligar's moons like they were candy! And now I can't track it." He gave a frustrated sigh and craned his head up.

The line grew brighter and traversed the cosmos. Shortly, the observers needed no telescope. His goliath form was in the sky above them, jaws gaping. The beast dove at an angle through the sky and flames wreathed him. Meteors now appeared small and slow in comparison. Its mouth was so large, it gulped down dozens of meteors each second. Some hit his teeth and shattered like flint striking steel. Each fang was so long that, when he did close his mouth, they stuck beyond the snout. He disappeared beyond the horizon and surfaced seconds later, the flames streaming even farther behind him as he picked up speed and launched away from Iomesel.

Darbor was back at the telescope and moving the sight after the canine. He adjusted the focus on the fly and told them what he saw. The wolf's form receded for a time, coming nearer to their horizon each moment, before it lunged toward the innermost planet, Lii-meth. Lii-meth gave under the beast's momentum, broke its orbit, and wheeled toward the nearby Vouyesh. The two celestial bodies collided and ruptured into countless fragments of molten rock. Dalence saw a twinkle that hinted at the calamity above. The creature drank the magma down and his stomach shone. And he grew. What he did not devour cooled and formed glassy lumps. Debris circled in eccentric orbits. Pieces smashed into one another, splintering apart to become smaller yet. Hair on the wolf's back, for some reason, smoldered. He thrashed and clawed and bared his fangs. With a portion of the planet carrion in his fangs, the creature moved to the darker reaches of the sky and faded completely from view.

With the sight fixed on the planetary wreckage, Darbor turned the telescope over to the crowd. He conferred with his assistant, who had kept voracious logs and still scribbled feverishly. Dalence leaned against her brother, on his good arm, but said nothing. How could she follow that up?

Half an hour later, the wolf returned from the vast interplanetary twilight and dragged off another helping of the carnage. For hours, he repeated this sequence of pillaging the spoils of Lii-meth and Vouyesh then vanishing farther out. Dawn came upon Iomesel and the wolf was lost to their sight.

Hantle turned his eyes to his companions and wondered aloud, "Does it even stop to rest anymore? Or does it only work to fuel its growth?" He shook his head and let out a sigh. "A pit in my stomach opens knowing that it continues its destruction, hovering just beyond view."

# CHAPTER THIRTY-EIGHT

DALENCE SHIVERED in the early morning cool. Nearby, Darbor sat beside his assistant. Before each a journal splayed open, in which they wrote. It occurred to Dalence that she did not recall the messenger returning last night; likewise, Darbor had not seemed to notice. He was lost in his work. Work . . . Hers had not ended either. They lost precious people, time, and materials to the governor. Would the skirmish hinder what the group could accomplish? She would do her damndest to offset its impact on the night's readiness.

She spoke to Hantle, who lay on the ground resting his eyes. "What time did you settle on with the lighthouse keeper?"

"Eleven tonight." He pushed up on one arm. "Time to get sufficiently dark and allow the light to be plainly visible to the wolf."

"Okay," she said. "That gives us the entire day to complete construction and test the armaments. Shall we pull together as many as possible to continue our work?"

The three of them set to the task and soon the area bustled. The temperature climbed and the day became the warmest of the summer. Clouds dotted the sky and moved swiftly westward over the plains to disappear beyond the Knuckles.

Trees captured in the landslide talus served as the first pieces of ammunition to test the crossbow. Woodworkers split the trunks and worked the resulting pieces into darts. Artillery operators fired these into the mountainside where the impact disintegrated each dart. Between shots, they performed calibration of the firing mechanism and sight, honing its accuracy.

After midday, the blacksmith, bleary-eyed, returned to the site at Hantle's request. His oxen drew a crude bolt, which weighed several hundred pounds and used horsehair fletching. Dalence was eager to see the bolt put to use. This would be the true test of whether the contraption was suited to the distance required. Before the blacksmith drove off, he reassured Hantle that he and his team were in the midst of forging three more arrows that would be ready before nightfall.

The crew practiced loading the arrow until all felt comfortable with the act. Next up was testing the range. Draft horses dug huge hooves into the ground and rotated the crossbow to point to the northwest—a direction, they agreed, devoid of any settlements to endanger. Winches strained rope and metallic parts clanked as the operators fine-tuned the aim. Brust took the honors of pulling the firing pin, but they all watched the bolt sail high into the distance, skim the Knuckles, and vanish from view where they expected it plunged below the ocean's waves. A cheer went up from the crowd. Dalence's heart pounded with excitement: their work had not been in vain.

---

Lunch was taken in shifts and when their turn came, Dalence, Brust, and Hantle grabbed plates of food and relaxed on the grass for the few minutes afforded to them. Clouds above thickened as a new wind pushed them in, but the cover did little to reduce the temperature. Hantle devoured the victuals and returned for a second helping before he felt sated. Dalence also had a second plate, while Brust managed a third.

When finished, Hantle set aside his plate, stood on a crate, and called for the company's attention. "We have just performed a successful firing of the crossbow. We owe a debt to those who stood at our side yesterday and gave their lives so that we might continue this effort today. Tonight, we face the true test of the beast. Tomorrow, we will honor the fallen with a ceremony that befits them. There is no better group of people with which to face the unknown." He paused for a moment and smiled; his gaze panned across the gathered workers, sprawled over the construction area. "I thank you all." He raised a hand in gratitude and stepped down from the chair.

Hantle resumed his spot next to his two companions. He first considered Dalence. "You and your brother have been a powerful sight for me. Seeing you together has reminded me what family looks like from the outside." His gaze turned to Brust. "It looks like never giving up on one another. I saw that when I was close to giving up myself. Your welcoming attitude and unfailing determination, from you both, have spurred me on. Tonight we will attempt what no one else could dream of. That is a worthy revenge."

Dalence reached over and patted Hantle's shoulder. "It was you that sparked that determination. The loved ones taken from us deserve nothing less. Let us seek their revenge to whatever end."

"Aye"—Brust pounded the ground with his good arm—"our kin shall not be disappointed." He pushed himself to his feet. "The trebuchet awaits."

---

The three of them found the trebuchet still some time away from a test. Quarry workers shaped granite blocks they intended to join together, which would serve as the device's counterweight. The sounds of chisels and hammers permeated the worksite. Others put finishing touches on a model of the fragmentation shot that would prove the design they had begun implementing on a larger scale. The amount of help present left little for the three to tackle without getting in the way.

Instead, Dalence tied her hair back as she surveyed the distance. Thunderheads towered over the plains and threatened rain. The front seemed to extend over the entire Fist. She tilted her head to the east and spoke to Brust and Hantle. "Looks like that front will be on us before long."

Hantle asked, "What are the storms like here?"

"That," she said, eyebrow raised in disapproval, "will likely be severe."

Brust took stock of the surroundings. "We will need to cover the telescope, trebuchet ammunition, and weapons if we can. Couldn't hurt to make shelters for the rest of us."

Dalence did a rough estimate of the number of people. "Yes, I imagine our volunteers would appreciate staying a bit dry. We'll need another trip to the lumber yard."

"It'll be a good task," Hantle said, "for people with a bit of slack as the killworks move toward testing."

The group split up. Dalence and Brust headed the effort to create shelters in various spots, while Hantle set out to find tarp in quantity and size enough to cover the critical equipment.

---

The day grew muggier as the afternoon wore on. Dalence nailed into place one of the last boards for a shelter's roof when she heard an explosion. She looked to the Knuckles and saw a black plume rising. Pieces of stone ricocheted off the mountainside and the trebuchet arm swung to and fro. "And to think," she said to Brust, "that was a small one."

Further tests drew significant attention. The following two projectiles landed nowhere near the first, but the operators persevered. They launched a collection of boulders, which allowed them to tweak and tune. Within an hour, a cluster of closely placed impacts lent them confidence in the trebuchet's precision. A final stone, cast the same direction as the crossbow arrow, arced beyond sight, soliciting applause and congratulations.

---

Twilight brought the arrival of the first delivery by the blacksmith and his apprentice. Clouds crowded most of the sky when Hantle met the craftsman at the crossbow. This missile was more streamlined than the original bolt, which granted it greater speed and range. Offset fletching provided better stabilization over the increased distance. Hantle and his team loaded and cocked the bow as the blacksmith left to complete the final two arrows. Brust spotted a wall of rain pressing toward them, and Hantle motioned for others to help him cover the readied crossbow.

---

Activity in the area slowed and volunteers sought protection under the shelters. Dalence moved toward Darbor and ran through a mental checklist: crossbow, arrows, trebuchet, projectiles, shelter, telescope, food, and provisions. Each item was addressed. The day had proceeded smoothly and, thankfully, neither the Chancellor of the Catch nor the captain made an appearance to upset that. Darbor peered through the telescope, and Dalence, wishing to avoid startling him, made extra noise to announce her approach.

"Are you prepared for the storm?" she asked.

Darbor pulled his head from the eyepiece. "Yes. Observing what I can, though, before we need to cover it." The crate and tarp lay beside the tripod. He leaned back in. "The remains of Lii-meth and Vouyesh are gone. All that's left is a patch of soot in a slow spiral."

"Here he is," someone called from behind them. A group of horses rattled into the clearing. Bellice held a torch aloft that danced in the wind. "Decided you prefer their company to ours, eh, Darbor?" She laughed.

"They weren't fighting me for a view all night," Darbor quipped. "It's nothing personal."

The rider behind Bellice drew a cart. Dalence eyed it and said, "I see the telescope made it down safely."

"Aye." Bellice looked to the mountains. "I don't fancy being atop Mount Vulteeb when that storm hits. The boulder field is difficult enough without it being slippery." A flash preceded a loud peal of thunder by a few seconds. "And that lightning would be death."

Dalence motioned to the nearest shelter. "You are more than welcome to join us. I'm eager to have your telescope here when the clouds part."

Bellice dismounted and moved to the cart. Three astronomers joined her in taking leather straps to move the cargo to the ground. Dalence felt a stray raindrop or two as they assembled the second telescope, but Bellice was too eager to resume their observation to mind. Meteor streaks again carved through the sky, though they were no longer the main attraction.

Darbor peered into the welkin and clapped his knee with joy. "Found 'em."

Bellice tightened the screws that fixed the tripod to the tube and pointed it up. "Lead me to it."

"Romd," Darbor said. "Bottom left quadrant. Just appearing from the planet's shadow."

"Adjusting focus." Bellice dialed in the eyepiece. "Clear . . . and sighted."

# CHAPTER THIRTY-NINE

DARBOR AND BELLICE narrated to the crowd what they saw through the telescopes. The wolf ran past Romd and struck one of its moons at full speed. The orb exploded outward, throwing pieces in every direction. Fragments expanded in a ring that grew every second, like some sort of firework. The canine lunged after the largest pieces and Bellice turned her sights to Romd's second satellite. It was no longer in orbit around the planet. Instead, a misshapen ball of rock tumbled away. The wolf had already struck the moon, taken out a sizeable chunk, and left it to aimlessly tumble through the void.

The wolf soon grew weary of chasing bits of debris and circled his way to Romd's surface. Yellow air rushed away in what must have been a hellacious storm as the beast's bulk hit the ground. He gave a few curious sniffs, then reared up on his hind legs and bore down on his front paws. Cracks radiated from the impact and dust swirled into the sky. Several more times the wolf did this, the rifts spreading farther and deeper each time. A carpet of splinters lay beneath him as he jumped from the ground and dove at the weakened planet. His head disappeared underneath the crust, leaving his tail to wag in the air and stir up yellow tornadoes. The canine's body went rigid as he braced and extracted his head. His fur was covered in molten rock that glowed a cherry red. Blobs of the planet-blood dripped onto the surface and turned jet-black.

In again dove the wolf, and splinters shifted to jut chaotically from the crust. The beast shook his head and chasms spread throughout the rest of the world. Neither Darbor nor Bellice could see the wolf feed, but they saw the effects. Dust billowed out of geysers and sinkholes opened up as the planetary core disappeared within the canine's belly. Eruptions from new volcanoes coughed boulders into the sky that arced down to the shattered surface, punching holes in the eggshell crust.

Drops pelted the back of Hantle's head and he turned to see an opaque wall of rain some ways off. Clouds thickened overhead but Romd was still visible for the moment. He moved to place a tarp over a majority of the telescope, including Darbor, but left the stargazing side exposed. Under the sheet, Darbor continued to call out his observations. Hantle then covered Bellice and her telescope in a similar fashion. Bellice asked for someone to wipe the lens of water droplets and Dalence obliged her.

The canine withdrew his head from the globe and licked at the magma on his snout. He had grown in size yet again. Romd looked more like a mound of scree than a planet. He scooped scraps into his maw and swallowed them whole. To the astronomers, the wolf and Romd were equal in size. Rocks tumbled into sinkholes and the holes grew in diameter as the edges eroded and slipped down. Powerful ejections launched pieces of the bedrock away to chase the stray moon. The wolf stalked and batted these emissions with his claws before devouring them.

When the largest chunks were gone, the wolf returned to the skeleton of Romd. In the brief time he had left it, the oddments had melded together under their own weight to form a lumpy concretion. In three sharp pounces, the mass buckled further and fractured permanently. A shockwave rippled through the stones and they burst into myriad particles. The beast snapped his jaws shut over a few nuggets that skimmed past and leapt to toy with and feast on the rest. Romd's residue glimmered like a handful of crystal flecks scattered by the wind.

On Iomesel, the clouds merged together to obscure the last pieces of sky. Both Darbor and Bellice emerged from the tarps and drew the protection over the rest of the telescopes. Wind buffeted Hantle as he moved to a shelter. The storm overhead let loose the rain it bore and inundated the city in a deluge. Gusts carried ribbons of water under the shelter and drenched those crouching there. For some time, the storm raged and none in Suu-manth followed the wolf's actions above.

---

A gargantuan forepaw descended through the clouds and its claws raked through the Knuckles like they were little more than clay. Hantle's head nodded and he jerked to wakefulness. The dream ran off his back and into the ground with the rain. Dalence knocked his shoulder and he rubbed weariness away before making eye contact. She placed a pinch of jursant under her tongue and handed him the pouch. Hantle followed suit and the urge to close his eyes dissipated.

The tarps nearby were held down by stones, but the fabric's loose edges whipped in the wind. Farther off, a few torches continued to burn, silhouetting the covered weaponry. Unbroken cloud cover above meant Hantle and his group had to bide time. He turned to thoughts of his family. He pictured a day, thousands of years ago, when Lorenca, Dolcium, and Hultier had rowed into the Trasach Cove. A gentle breeze brought small swells, which moved the boat in a rhythm. Each of them attached bait to a hook and cast out line. Hantle looked to each member of his family. For a brief few seconds, he could picture everything about them, except their faces. These remained blank. A spark of worry caught in his stomach, when at last his mind painted the eyes, noses, and mouths of his loved ones. How long would it be until the memory faded and he could no longer recall any portion of their persons? Even now, the memory grew fuzzy at the edges and the clear day blurred into the current night.

Reluctantly, the clouds separated and the rain slowed. A tear of sky grew into an opening through which they could train their telescopes. The observers followed a vein in the sky, the wolf. He rushed along, toward Seligar, picking up speed as he closed in. The creature plunged like a dart into the planet. Through the blue orb he pierced, emerging from the other side, where the gases spread out like blood trailing a bullet from an exit wound. The fiend looped around and inhaled strands of vapor. Patches reminiscent of fog floated away, and what had been Seligar lost coherence. The canine ignored its remnants and moved away so erratically that Darbor and Bellice both lost view of him.

Darbor's assistant remarked that Coubae and Iomesel were the only planets that remained. The comment brought Hantle's focus to their imminent plan. Eleven o'clock was minutes away, but the opening in the clouds sealed itself shut and thickened. From north to south, the cloud layer ran unbroken. Drizzle resumed and, with a knot of anxiety in his throat, Hantle covered the telescopes once again. He called to Dalence, Brust, and all the rest to move with him to the kill-works. They tore off the covers, exposing the devices to the elements. A faint strobing to the north indicated the keeper's success in modifying his lighthouse. Yet Hantle guessed its visibility in Suu-manth meant clouds obscured the sky over the coast and reflected the beam back to the ground. He instructed the volunteers to aim the weapons at Dusath, and, presently, heard horses straining at the load. Several minutes passed and Hantle wondered if the storm would render all their efforts irrelevant. Then the light in Dusath went out.

# CHAPTER FORTY

A DULL ROAR reached Dalence's ears and she stared toward the darkened sky above Dusath. Over several seconds, the sound grew in intensity. In a blink, something impacted her chest, ripped her from her feet, and carried her yards from where she stood. Her breath left her when she landed on her back, but it took a moment for her body to realize this and struggle for a gasp.

The roar receded and, as she pushed herself to her elbows, she saw everyone had been thrown. Her gaze sped to the killworks. Fear abated when she noted that they stood solid. The clouds were gone from the sky and the entire star field lay above her, expansive. On the northern horizon, she saw the wolf illuminated by the lighthouse. A tsunami wave rushed away from the beast and temporarily blotted out the lighthouse as it drowned the coastline. When the shockwave cleared the Suu-manth, dust, vapor, and flecks of cloud swept in to fill the void it left.

Dalence clambered to her feet and helped Brust to his. "The wolf is come!" she cried. "To your positions."

The gale had extinguished all the lanterns, but the wolf caught and reflected enough of the lighthouse beams to be seen. Brust looked through the sight and instructed his sister as she cranked a lever to fine-tune the trebuchet's aim. Others beside her yanked the leveraging arm farther down and stood by to light the projectile's fuse. Just yards away, Hantle and his crew readied the crossbow.

The wolf towered above the horizon and the world shook with each step it took. A scar marred the charcoal-colored pelt on its left shoulder. Its eyes glowed with madness. One ear pivoted to sounds while the other hung a ragged mess. It peeled its lips back and bared white, glistening teeth. Patches of obsidian, left from his feasting on Romd, clung to the creature's throat, and imperfections in the glass scattered light.

Dalence made eye contact with Hantle as the crossbow's aiming gears ceased their clinking. She nodded and Hantle squinted into his sight. He must have been satisfied, because he brought the lever down. The crossbow jerked and the arrow sped away. Beside her, Brust clasped his bad arm with the good and held his breath.

The wolf slumped forward as the bolt drove deep into his right shoulder. A bark escaped its throat that Dalence felt in her chest. The arrow had pierced all the way to the fletching at its end. The wolf staggered as it took weight off the injured limb. Blood poured from the wound around the arrow shaft and ran down his leg. Brust laughed and Hantle called for his crew to reload.

Dalence drew a mallet from her belt. She eyed Brust. "Sighted?" The few pieces of ammunition gave them no spares. Every shot must strike.

"Aye," Brust said.

A hiss told her the fuse was lit. Dalence swung the mallet, knocked away the firing latch, and watched the trebuchet weight drop. The arm spun in a blur and the sling loosed its shot. A trail of sparks arced toward Dusath. She lost the projectile to the darkness but caught a brief glimpse as it passed through a beam of the lighthouse. The wolf snapped his head and clenched his jaws around the shot as if it were a meteorite from the sky. The burning ballistic concussed when it hit the stomach, and the fiend grew larger. Grew enough in fact that the arrow fell in pieces from its thickening hide and blood coagulated in the laceration.

The demon looked toward Suu-manth and Dalence felt the stare bore into her core. She shivered and heard the winch pull the crossbow drawstrings taut. As the wolf reared up, Hantle fired the second arrow. It had made the same movement on Romd, in order to shatter the surface. Dalence braced for the coming tremor but the arrow impaled the canine's gut. The beast shriveled up and collapsed on the ground. She watched the wolf scramble to its feet, lean over to the Knuckles, and sink its fangs into the mountains.

In the time it took Dalence's group to haul the trebuchet arm back to receive the next projectile, the fiend had swallowed Mount Vulteeb. Brust checked the weapon's sight once more and gave Dalence the okay. The wolf sat on his haunches, bayed into the sky, and revealed how blood from the second arrow coated its belly. Dalence feared the howl would split her head in half as she hit the firing latch. Away sailed the shot and its ignition cord left behind burning breadcrumbs.

The shot missed the creature and flew over its left shoulder. A split second later, though, it detonated and the wolf's call ceased as fragments of stone pierced his back. The impact spurred the creature forward and he scooped up the lighthouse with his lower jaw. Dusath snapped black as his saliva doused the lighthouse torch. The canine's form was yet partially visible—ghost-like and illuminated from within.

She heard Hantle shout for the third bolt and Dalence felt a surge of excitement. Three of the four shots had landed and the beast was shaken. They had one more apiece. Enough, she thought, to bring the bastard down. In the welkin, two meteors left their own ephemeral trails. The canine stepped toward Suu-manth and blood dripped from his gut. Hantle adjusted the aim to follow the creature and cranked the crossbow down. The last arrow flew with a twang. Lightning branched over the mountains and, in the brief light, Dalence saw the bolt meet a piece of solidified magma on the wolf's throat. Instead of passing through and puncturing its jugular, the arrow reflected off the obsidian face and spun erratically to the ground. Their aim was perfect but that had not been enough. Dalence urged her compatriots to move swiftly.

The ground heaved up as the canine buried his head under the surface and swallowed. Boulders thrown up by the move traveled with enough speed to leave the planet, glowing bright red as they soared into orbit. The trebuchet lobbed its final grenade and Dalence let up a yell to accompany it. The wolf lunged into the hole before him with a greedy desire. Their explosive shot burst high above him and the beast chomped at the world, unfazed. His attention turned next to the rocks he had launched skyward. He moved to the Knuckles and jumped after the burning rubble. Iomesel lurched as the demon pushed off the mountain range and the night in Suu-manth instantly turned to day.

# CHAPTER FORTY-ONE

THE PLANET MOVED like a cosmic rug being pulled from under his feet and Hantle pitched backward to the ground. From the depths of night, the beast had forced the day upon them and the sun sat directly overhead. Hantle stood and watched the wolf disappear, beyond the eastern horizon, into Iomesel's penumbra. A wave of air buffeted him, seeking the emptiness left behind by the wolf. Hantle shivered, as it was yet as cold as midnight.

Unsure of what to do, Hantle moved to Brust and helped him stand. The fall had reinjured Brust's wound and blood soaked through the bandaging. Dalence pushed herself up and clutched her necklace. A moment later, the wolf emerged into sunlight from the west. It kept moving through the sky at breakneck speed and disappeared once more.

Flocks of birds took to the air and animals wailed as a tremor passed through the ground. A building on the periphery of the city saw its roof collapse, and a nearby bridge toppled into the water rushing beneath it. The wolf cruised across the sky and another spasm surged under the city. Rocks broke free of their hold on the Knuckles and tumbled in an avalanche. An incredible clamor washed over

Hantle and he extended an arm to Dalence and Brust to stabilize them all. The weaponry heaved and failed and crashed, along with other structures, and the air resonated with cacophonous ruin.

Miles to the east, within Suu-manth itself, a great chasm yawned. Lake water drained into the gulch and steam spewed skyward. The wolf orbited past again and brought reinvigorated quaking that forced Hantle down. Dalence started to say something but her voice faltered and Brust clutched her in his good arm. The vapor and warmth of the steam from the trench drifted to them on a wind. Cliffsides slipped down the mountains and the sky was thick with vibration and fear. A scream rose from Hantle's own throat to join the shrieks of others. He covered his eyes and waited for a landslide to bury them all.

Gradually, the convulsions lessened. A crack of thunder broke around them and the ground settled to a nervous jitter. Hantle uncovered his face and saw the wolf dashing away from Iomesel. After a few final spasms, the shuddering ceased and the world lay quiet. The air settled and sunrays pricked at his skin. Relief flooded Hantle's body and he loosened his tensed muscles. "We drove it away." His voice sounded as if it originated leagues away. He spoke to both no one and everyone. The wolf's form shrank a bit as it drew off, but still appeared larger than the moon ever had.

A wild grin spread on Dalence's face and she gripped Hantle's shirt, shaking him as she laughed. She rolled to face her brother. "Your aim was perfect, Brust! Did you see how many times we hit it?"

"Yes," Brust replied. "A lot of blood poured from the arrow wounds. Wish I'd seen what we did to its back."

The crew that surrounded them cautiously took to their feet. Claps and cheers went up as they understood their frantic efforts had paid off.

Hantle rose and looked to the wolf. "The question," he remarked, "is how much damage we caused." Would it disappear into the cosmos? His relief gave way to anxious déjà vu. He recalled speaking with Rounfil after the canine escaped with wounds into the forests surrounding Founsel. Together they had pondered whether the creature was mortally injured. Only when the canine was dead before him could he consider the danger past. He turned to their decimated constructions. "Both the crossbow and trebuchet are in splinters; our ammunition is spent. If it returns, we have no recourse." He swallowed hard. "Our hope, then, lies in it bleeding out while the wounds are fresh."

A burning trail grew behind the wolf. The streak became bright and wide and long as he shot away toward the sun. Its angle changed and the canine's maw spread wide as his path eclipsed the star. For half a minute, the corona revealed itself. Searing filaments and pale loops—heretofore invisible—grasped beyond the wolf's jet-black form. The sky faded to twilight and cool air scraped Hantle's face. The enormity blotting out the day imbued him with dread and trepidation. With a flare, the eclipse ended and the gloom reverted to noontide.

Brust pointed to the sky and called out, "Is that blood it leaves behind?"

Dalence nodded furiously. "Yes, that must be blood."

Hantle squinted and saw red globules trail the creature. Hopeful expectancy crept into his mind. That lost blood was their deliverance. Farther back along the beast's trail, he made out the vague, crimson outlines of additional beads.

The wolf carved a wide arc to the left, first away from and then back toward the sun, slowing its approach as it neared. Hantle raised a hand to shield his eyes from the sun, enabling him to see the beast, whose face fluoresced brilliantly. Its movement stalled and Hantle thought its entire body to be molten now. Bared fangs shimmered and wavered in the intensity. Ripples rolled down its pelt and its visage lustered.

Minutes passed and the canine did not move. Was it apprehensive? As if cued by this thought, the wolf lurched forward but quickly pulled back, cringing and shaking its head. The creature receded and sent out a howl. The sound registered with Hantle as a tinny echo. With a kick of the legs, it rotated and presented its underbelly. The howl continued and its fur flared white beside the blistering orb. Briefly, the wolf-star outshone the other, but the incandescence lessened and Hantle watched the blaze burn each imperfection on the demon's body. Disintegrated and blown away as embers were the obsidian pocks, the arrows, the blood, and the scars. Even the marred ear appeared reformed. A despondent breath left Hantle.

The howl faded and, with its vigor renewed, the creature swiveled on an axis at its midriff to face the orb. It reared then struck, though before it could complete the bite, its muzzle sprang open again and the wolf jerked its head about, tongue lolling. Hantle thought it would retch. Instead, it recovered and decidedly snapped. Its fangs scintillated as they clenched shut.

Black.

# CHAPTER FORTY-TWO

HANTLE FROZE IN PLACE, blinded and afraid even the slightest movement would topple him over. A figmentary static writhed across his vision. He could hear sounds nearby, however: people moving, breathing, or shouting.

Brust called out, "Dalence, are you okay?"

"I am," she replied. "I am. Where are you?"

Hantle listened to the cues they gave to locate one another in the dark but maintained his own silence. When the killworks drove the wolf away from Iomesel, he had been hopeful. More so when they saw blood trailing the beast. Never had he considered the sun at risk.

Slowly, his vision adjusted and the sight of stars faded in. A faint silhouette indicated the wolf's position. The canine clenched his eyelids shut and flicked his tongue as he acclimated to the scorching star. When his jaws opened, filaments of sunlight burst from between his fangs. The world was again illuminated and Hantle peered around Suu-manth until darkness resumed, for the creature closed his mouth with a look of satisfaction. The jolting between day and night disoriented Hantle. He looked up and found two new orbs among the multitude of stars the wolf had not yet had a chance to devour: the fiend's eyes blazed a solid gold. Smoke poured out of his nostrils as his fur took on a radiance. He swallowed—brightness pulsing—and grew in size. Blue flames leaked from under his lips, roiled their way over the fur on his face, and trailed up and off his ears before subsiding. Soon, the glow of his body faded, but his eyes never lost their intensity. Hantle felt more than heard a low, long growl pervade the air and resonate over the planet.

He turned his gaze from the wolf and looked for his companions. The burning eyes gave just enough light to see by, similar to a quarter moon. Dalence hugged her brother. Brust winced, adjusted the sling, and held her with one arm. Back in Suu-manth, steam continued gushing forth from the fractured ground and billowed hundreds of feet up.

The demon had exceeded every expectation he had. They faced a new reality, one previously unforeseen, where the wolf forgot them. Would their reprieve last? Better yet, what impact would the lasting darkness have? This was not a future they had worked toward; rather one forced upon them. A glimpse of their fate raced through his mind and Hantle staggered to his knees, breathless. The wolf blinked, immersing the already-faint landscape in darkness for a moment.

Dalence approached Hantle. "We can gather people at the Marketplace and decide what to do next."

"I can't."

She extended a hand. "Here, I'll help you up."

He found it inexplicable but he could not bring himself to move. Instead, he shook his head. "That was it."

Dalence raised an eyebrow. "That was what?"

"The last chance to redeem myself. The last possibility of making amends to my family." Hantle pointed to the weapons. "We placed our hope," he spat, "in those. Look at them now. Pathetic and broken." His fists hammered into his legs. "We woke from a pointless dream to a futile end." He gave a resigned laugh and shook his head. "Fools, all of us."

"Yes, the killworks were a gamble, but would you have rather done nothing?"

"No," Hantle conceded.

"Then remember that and come with us now. We will find a plan."

Hantle slumped and a knot formed in his throat. "Here or there, it doesn't matter. There's nothing to do. But go on if you will."

Dalence stood and furrowed her eyebrows in disapproval. "Find us when your moping ends."

Hantle stared through the ground as she and her brother disappeared from his periphery.

# CHAPTER FORTY-THREE

DALENCE AND BRUST moved from the site of the killworks to the edge of Suu-manth. Rubble from ruptured streets and maimed homes cluttered their way. As she picked a path over fallen timbers, Dalence thought to the weaponry slumped behind her. The fact they did not kill the wolf did not make their plan a failure. Failure would have been resigning themselves to an end and settling for inaction. She regretted nothing. Hantle's reaction surprised her though, him kneeling there, staring blank-faced into the eyes of the beast. Was he resigned now? Dalence had adopted Hantle's revenge after they met in Bansuth, but she would not follow his lead this time. She had a brother to think of.

They were several blocks away from the Marketplace when Brust spoke up. "Let's stop by home first."

"Okay," she nodded. "We can see how it fared."

The two changed their route. A few street lamps that survived the quaking gave a faint light. Several collapsed bridges required them to wade through streams. Torches out on the lake indicated people rowing from one area to another. They passed wrecked and burning homes on either side as well as people in various states of shock or grief.

When they approached the two boulders near their house, Dalence noticed that one had shifted. It had slumped from its standing position and leaned against the other. The pathway between the two stones was blocked, forcing them around it. Their home appeared out of the haze. Its roof had partially caved and the front wall leaned inward. It took both her and Brust to wrest the door out of its cockeyed frame. Inside, water from the earlier storm dripped through the ceiling. Her feet, in her sopping shoes, hardly registered the puddles she stepped through.

At the fireplace, Brust lit two torches and handed one to Dalence.

"Let's grab warm clothing," she said. "Then we can put together some food."

The wall to their bedrooms had cracked and Dalence slid through an opening. A beam stretched from the roof down to her crushed bed. In the outer wall, a hole gaped, through which she saw a neighbor picking through the ruins of her house. Dalence rested the torch against the bed frame and knelt before the trunk at the bed's foot. Out of its interior, she pulled her warmest clothes and her father's lorebook. Deferentially, she set the book on the bed and reached up to touch the crystal hanging about her neck. Her heart hurt. How could she hold on to the memory of someone without also holding on to the grief of losing them? The grief and the memories were intertwined.

A shiver washed over her. Already, the air was noticeably cooler. She stripped off her wet garments, changed into dry ones, and laced up her heaviest boots. In the other room, something clattered to the ground and Brust cursed. She wrapped the lorebook and the remaining dry clothes in a bedsheet and carried her bundle to the living room. Brust rummaged through the pantry and Dalence saw a liquor bottle standing uncorked on the table.

"I've got some bread and jerky set out," he said. "Seeing what fruit we've got." He jerked a thumb toward a stack of small wooden crates. "Any vegetables over there?"

Soon, she had a head of lettuce, a few potatoes, and a bunch of carrots. Brust added an armful of apples, peaches, and lemons. Blood trickled to Brust's elbow and Dalence dug around for a clean bandage. She unwrapped the wound and inspected it. The lighting made it difficult to tell whether the skin around the injury was infected or simply inflamed. As she bound it anew, she made a mental note to check again when they had built a proper fire.

Dalence looked around the drafty house and then to her brother. She said, "I know things look bleak, Brust. We're lucky to have each other though. We'll find a place where we can keep out of the cold and figure something out."

"Lucky is an interesting way to put it," he said. He reached for the bottle and took a swig. "But I'm glad we'll do this together."

Dalence patted his shoulder and gathered the food into a pillowcase.

---

The Marketplace loomed ahead of them, scathed like all else. Most of the structure had buckled and its form looked tenuous. A group near the entrance pulled wood out from under the roofing and placed it on a growing fire. Enticed by the heat, she took a seat and Brust joined her. They had followed a different way here to avoid crossing deeper rivers, but her feet had still gotten damp. She placed the boots closest to the fire.

"Have you also lost your homes?" Brust said. He ran a hand over his auburn beard and mustache.

One person nodded, a few others shrugged, and the rest ignored the question.

Dalence spoke up next. "Can we count on any of you to help make a shelter? We'll need that, warmth, and food."

Off to their side, two men shouting caught Dalence's attention. She watched them trade threats until one's fist connected with the other's jaw. They grappled and fell to the ground. The first to swing gained the advantage and repeatedly beat his opponent's face until he knocked the man unconscious. Chest heaving, the victor toppled to the ground and spat a mouthful of blood.

Somewhere else nearby musket shots carried through the air. A group of screams followed it and Dalence turned to see a family running from three in pursuit who carried pistols. The chase passed bystanders who shied away from the trouble.

Dalence leaned over to Brust and said sotto voce, "Maybe we should head out of the city. Back to the weapons at least."

Brust's lips pursed before he replied. "Might hole up in the Knuckles, even. That would be better than getting jumped by someone here."

Decided, they both stood, grabbed their clothes and food, and left the fire without comment.

When they had put some distance between themselves and anyone else, Dalence spoke again. "A cave in the mountains is a good idea. That'd be shelter and warmth, away from those who are desperate and dangerous. Leaving us to focus on food." Water squished between her toes. "And drying out."

Brust retrieved the liquor bottle from his bundle and took a pull. "But then what? Are our options starving to death or freezing to death?"

"That's not the concern right now," she said. "We can't control what's happened, but we can control what we do now. We focus on staying safe. Save the worrying for later."

"Shall we check on Hantle once more?"

"Of course." After a moment's consideration, she added, "Although don't think his aimlessness is yours."

Brust shifted the bundle on his shoulder and looked to the wolf. "Without light, aren't we all aimless?"

Dalence's brow furrowed as she followed his gaze. The demon-star sank toward the horizon and its dim light grew fainter yet.

# CHAPTER FORTY-FOUR

THE SPEECH LIOVA gave at his boys' funeral replayed in his mind. He recalled her words as, "We must all remember the Mechanisms, which tell us how the world was created through the Cataclysm. The undoing of things past is not the end of all things." She had spoken truly then and the sentiment had propelled Hantle forward. Yet he could not help feeling a new understanding as he looked to the ever-night above him. The Cataclysm created them and so it undid them. That this was not the end of all things changed not the fact it was *their* end. What solace could he take in that? None, perhaps, but it eased his anger.

Hantle held the kneeling position he had taken when he dropped to the ground. His knees hurt, but he wanted to feel the pain. He pinched his eyes shut and focused on it. The ache in his arm and the grief in his chest were pains altogether different. What other distinctive sufferings would soon come? A shiver crept along his spine and he noticed goosebumps ascend his arms.

In his mind, he was the size of a world and, instead of Romd, it was him that the wolf rushed toward. It was his body that splintered and scattered as the canine reared and pounced, time and time again.

It was the powdery remains of his bones and the frozen air from his lungs that spilled outward in a cloud after the beast's jaws pried his chest open. It was his blood that coated the wolf's chest and further matted its fur as his essence scattered and shimmered until dawn came. But dawn no longer existed, except as a memory.

Footsteps approached and Hantle's dream faded. From his rear, Dalence and Brust came around each side, torches aloft. Dalence crouched before him while Brust stood. With one hand, Dalence set her bundle on the ground, reached in through a gap near the knot, and extracted an item she then proffered. "Care for a jacket?" she said.

Hantle shifted and brought his buttocks to his heels. "No," he replied. "You'll need it." His eyes flitted to hers for a second before returning to the ground; time enough to notice her look of disappointment.

Her arm dropped to the ground and she let the jacket go. "The city doesn't seem safe. We figure a cave in the mountains will be a good location for now. Easy to secure and heat. Far enough from the city to avoid thieves, but close enough to return when we need."

Torchlight cast shadows in the grass and Hantle focused on them. "I spent however many days chasing it. Had it in my crosshairs. Was moments away from firing cannons. Even landed shots from the killworks. Yet here I am, trying to account for what happened." He mindlessly pulled up blades of grass with one hand. "Yet this moment has been undoubtedly coming. Where either the action was done and the wolf dead, the revenge behind me such that the accounting was for what's next; or the action was tried and the wolf successful, the revenge behind me such that the accounting was for what's left. The latter played out, and there are no further deeds or ploys to mask that reality." He looked between Brust and Dalence, his expression flat.

Brust popped the cork from his bottle and liquor sloshed as he brought it to his lips. He swallowed and grimaced. "Poor you," he spat. "Things didn't work out." Hantle heard the slur in the words. "You're not dead though, so stop acting like you are."

"Brust!" Dalence jerked and took the bottle from her brother.

Brust shook his head; hair fell across his face. "No." He pointed a hand at Hantle that trembled with rage. "He doesn't get to go through the same shit as everyone else and come away with self-pity."

Dalence leaned toward Hantle and softened her voice. "You wonder what's left? We're left, Hantle. Did we come all this way to abandon each other now?"

"You've your brother," Hantle said, nodding. "I understand that. You both ought to go on. But I won't run a step farther." He moved from his knees to sit on the ground. "I've done that and am tired of it. So damn tired."

Brust rolled his eyes and muttered to himself as he moved some distance off.

"What of the funeral you promised?"

"Burying the dead is for the living." Hantle swept an arm over the city, scantly illuminated by fires and torches. "Do you see a single person grieving for anyone but themselves?"

Dalence shrugged. "So then what will you do?"

"The wolf is unlikely to take me, which is something." He looked to the creature near the tops of the jagged Knuckles. Glowing filaments streamed from its face, and its eyes were ablaze. "I'll accept my fate and meet the frigid end as soon as it'll have me. Then I can join my family in rest. They lie many miles away, but my blood will seep into the world just as theirs does. When Iomesel is buried in ice, when the core of the planet is the only heat to know, our blood will mingle deep underground and the world might know family and its love doesn't die with our bodies."

His gaze again fell to Dalence and her look of repulsed surprise. Dalence began, "I . . ." but she did not complete the sentence.

"We and that beast were in different leagues," Hantle said. "The fated and the fator."

Dalence gathered her belongings and stood. When she stared at him for a long while, he looked away. Finally, she whispered, "Goodbye, Hantle," joined Brust, and walked out of his view.

A hint of doubt crept sideways into his mind. From his breast pocket, he plucked Lorenca's ring and turned over the deformed band in his palm. Faint light from the stars or the wolf caught its edge and Hantle smiled; the relic reminded him of a life eons ago. He shook off the uncertainty. No. He would meet the end on his own terms.

# CHAPTER FORTY-FIVE

BRUST SNATCHED the liquor bottle from Dalence's hand as she came to a stop. He tilted his head back to drain down the remaining liquor and missed the disapproving look she gave him. He coughed at the burn in his throat and said, "I'm not sure why you want to do this sober."

Dalence handed her torch to him, set her bundle down, and pulled on the jacket she had offered Hantle. "If we were both drinking like you," she replied, "we'd pass out no farther than a few steps on." She buttoned up the front of the jacket and shivered. "Are you not even cold?"

"Nope." Brust listed and steadied himself on a boulder with his torch-bearing arm. "It's summertime, you know?"

"Not sure how much longer you'll say that." She brought her arms across her chest, hunched up, and looked back toward Suu-manth. "I'm surprised he wouldn't come with us."

"Good riddance." Brust kicked at a stone on the ground but missed and stubbed the toe of his shoe instead.

"Don't say that." She took the torch again. "Hantle is the only reason I made it back at all." Her vision caught on a pale, ghostly blotch. If she had not already known it was there, she would have overlooked it: Hantle's form on the ground, staring upward. Gunshots carried from Suu-manth to her ears. The dim figure winked out as the wolf's eyes finally dropped behind the Knuckles. She shuddered.

"Come on," she said. "We've still got a hike ahead of us."

The light of her torch weaved between hills and disappeared somewhere beyond.

# ACKNOWLEDGMENTS

This novel was made possible through the support, love, and care of many people.

Karla gave me the incredible gift of time to work on this project, as well as deep understanding and loving motivation to see my goal through to the end.

Zach Miller gave me countless hours of feedback, many motivational kicks to the ass, and much-needed direction when I felt aimless.

My parents introduced me to books, encouraged my creativity and education, sent me to writing camps, and put up with my favorite pre-dinner saying, "Just one more minute."

Caleb Jacob was extremely generous in taking on the project of cover design.

Meredith Tennant provided lots of edits and feedback and was a pleasure to work with.

I'd also like to thank friends, family, and prior teachers (like Vicki Packard-Cooper) who encouraged me. Finally, thanks to the cities where portions of this book were written: Denver, CO; Bakersfield, CA; Coos Bay, OR; Alexandria, VA; and Fort Bragg, CA.

# ABOUT THE AUTHOR

Kyle Tolle has been creating stories and worlds since he was a kid. He is a lifelong reader and writer of fantasy, sci-fi, and mythology. Kyle enjoys fictional mapmaking, being in the mountains, and traveling to new locations. In 2017, he took a sabbatical from his career as a software engineer in order to pursue writing full-time. The result of that endeavor is his first novel, *Thoughts of an Eaten Sun*. Kyle has lived many places with his wife, Karla, but they call Colorado home.

- facebook.com/kyle.tolle
- twitter.com/kyletolle
- goodreads.com/kyletolle
- amazon.com/author/kyletolle

Made in the USA
Lexington, KY
05 March 2019